HOME
IS WHERE
THE BODIES
ARE

BOOKS BY JENEVA ROSE

STANDALONE NOVELS

The Perfect Marriage

The Girl I Was

One of Us Is Dead

You Shouldn't Have Come Here

It's a Date (Again)

#CrimeTime

Home Is Where the Bodies Are

THE DETECTIVE KIMBERLEY KING BOOKS

Dead Woman Crossing

Last Day Alive

HOME
IS WHERE
THE BODIES
ARE

JENEVA ROSE

BLACK
STONE
PUBLISHING

Printed in the United States of America

First edition: 2024
ISBN 979-8-212-18284-3
Fiction / Thrillers / Suspense

Version 3

Blackstone Publishing
31 Mistletoe Rd.
Ashland, OR 97520

www.BlackstonePublishing.com

To my family.
You've never had to hide a body, but I know you would,
if needed. Dad sure had us pour a lot of concrete though,
so who knows what's under there?

PROLOGUE

Nothing brings people together better than death. It's like the sound of a high-pitched whistle for a dog that has strayed from its owner. When it happens, they always come. Death reminds us that life isn't infinite and that one day, our time will come too. We pause to listen to that reminder, to acknowledge it, to show it the respect it demands, and then we spread out into the world like pappi on a dying dandelion, waiting for it to call us again, hoping the next call will be to gather, rather than to be gathered around.

Knock, knock.

Don't worry. It's not for you . . . this time.

ONE

BETH

The rain falls differently today, not soft, not hard, not sideways, just different. As though it's preparing my mother's final resting place, saturating the ground where she will soon lie. The hospice nurse said she'll pass by the end of the day. It's odd. Some people never see it coming, others have a countdown, and I don't know which is worse.

I stare out the kitchen window, which overlooks five acres of property, a mix of trees, hills, flat grassy land, and a creek that cuts through it all. My parents purchased the land from a farmer back in the late seventies and had a home built here shortly after. It was their little slice of paradise—until it wasn't.

My phone buzzes. A text from my brother. His flight has landed, and he'll be home in under an hour. *Home?* He stopped visiting seven years ago, when our father disappeared. So, I wouldn't call our small Wisconsin town his home. Only one hundred and seventy-four people can call it that, but not him. Most people who leave the Grove don't come back. And those that do never return because they want to. It's kind of like a cemetery in that way.

I flick to the text I sent my sister hours ago. It's unread. She's probably strung out in some motel, a needle wedged between her toes because her veins collapsed long before she caught up with that high she's been chasing all her life. I let out a heavy sigh at the mere thought of my sister. Addiction is exhausting for both the users and the ones they use.

I pull a loaf of white bread from the cupboard and slather a heavy helping of mayo on two slices. A bowl of round and supple beefsteak tomatoes, plucked from the garden, sits beside the sink. I place the ripest one on the worn cutting board. Tomato water seeps from the flesh as my knife slides through it. I'm not sure why I'm even making Mom a tomato-mayo sandwich. She hasn't eaten anything in days but it's her favorite, she says. She grew up dirt-poor, so her favorites are her favorites because she hasn't experienced anything better. I always wanted to do more for her, to show her a world outside of the Grove—but I never got out either.

"Eliza . . . beth," my mother calls softly from the living room. She says my name the same way she consumes her Werther's candies: slowly, deliberately. It's like she's savoring it. My shoulders drop, sinking to a place familiar to those who have faced defeat. I know I'll never hear her say it again—my name, the one she gave me. I wish I could reach out and grab it, stow it away in a safe place, like some sort of family heirloom. But it belongs to this moment. Like her, it's not something I can keep forever. I take a deep breath and release the knife from my hand. It thuds against the cutting board. It's time to say my final goodbye.

The clock on the wall reads just after eight p.m. My siblings most likely won't make it in time. Then again, they've had all the time in the world to be here with her, and they chose not to. So, perhaps they don't deserve it. *Death waits for no one.*

"Coming, Mom." I force the corners of my lips up a few clicks before leaving the kitchen. All she ever wanted was to see her children happy—I can do that for her, even if it's not true.

The living room was converted into her bedroom three months ago. She wanted it that way, wanted to be able to look out the big bay window and watch the sun set. Mom worked second shift most of her life, so she said it was the one thing she felt she missed out on.

A television sits in the corner, muted, with a car dealership commercial playing on the screen. Most of my mom's belongings are floral print: the blanket covering her, the couch that has been pushed to the far wall, and the decorative pillows placed on either end. There are even pictures of flowers hung in frames behind her hospice bed. She told me flowers reminded her of life—beautiful, delicate, and short-lived.

Her bed sits propped up, and she's looking out the window.

"Hi, Mom," I say. My voice nearly croaks but I swallow the sadness. I'll break that dam later, but not now, not in front of her.

She lifts her hand shakily an inch above her lap and lets it fall back into place. She doesn't have the strength to say it, but I can hear her words, *Come watch the sunset, Beth.*

"Okay, Mom."

I take a seat in the chair beside her bed. It's molded to my behind, from all the hours I've sat with her over the past few months. She got real bad seven weeks ago, so I took FMLA leave from my job at the warehouse to care for her around the clock. Mom would have had more time, but she's a stubborn woman who visits the doctor about as often as one visits the DMV. By the time they caught the cancer, it was far too advanced, having spread to her liver and bloodstream.

She wiggles her thin fingers, and I reach for them, gently holding her hand. The rain has stopped temporarily. The clouds part and the sky shifts to a perfect blue, layered with hues of pink and orange from the setting sun.

"It's beautiful, Mom," I say, glancing over at her.

Her graying skin is like the bark of a tree, deep creases from a lifetime of stress and grief. She embraces them, though. She always has, proudly saying, "The wrinklier the skin, the harder the life." It's a badge of honor for her, evidence of her hardships.

Her chest barely rises and falls. I watch it closely just to be sure she's still breathing. She keeps her eyes on the setting sun, and I can hear what she said to me a week ago, before it became too difficult for her to utter more than a word or two.

There's not many things you can count on in life, but that . . . is one thing you can count on. It will rise and it will fall—no matter what. Don't matter if you're sick or sad. Don't matter if there is war or there is peace. Don't matter if you see it or you don't. That sun. You can count on it.

Even in her dying days, she's still trying to teach me, to guide me, to show her love her way—through lessons and words of wisdom. I squeeze her hand gently, so she knows I'm still here. The small pressure seems to push through her body, constricting the very air in her lungs. She begins to wheeze. I dunk a sponge into a glass of water and squeeze the liquid into her partially open mouth. Mom never takes her eyes off the sun. I dab her chapped lips with the damp sponge and sit back down while she catches what little breath she has left.

When the sun finally slips behind the horizon, she cranes her neck toward me. I smile at her, but she doesn't smile back. I know death is near because even her presence has dulled.

"Hi, Mom," I say. I'm trying to say Mom as many times as I possibly can because I know I'll never call another person that again. It's reserved only for her. There is no replacement. My throat tightens, and I feel my breath hitch like I'm going to experience one of those cries that comes from the deepest place, one that hurts, one you can't stop, one that makes every part of you quake and tremble. I reach for her hand and hold it again. It feels cold, and I know what that means.

She looks at me or maybe a little above me, I'm not sure. There's confusion in her eyes. She knew death was coming, but even so, its arrival is always puzzling. It's like we're all standing in one big queue waiting for our number to be called, thinking that day won't arrive—but it will, and it has. She tries to roll her body toward me but she's too weak, so I lean closer to her. With only a foot between us, I notice her breathing changes from slow and shallow to rapid. It's almost here, and there are so many things I want to tell her. But I know it would take a lifetime to say them all, so I try to get out what I can.

"I love you, Mom. Thank you for having me, for raising me, for loving me, for being like the sun . . . the one thing I could always count on." My voice trembles. It's not at all how I wanted to say it. My face crumples and instantly becomes wet, the dam bursting open all at once. Her eyes flicker with realization or something like it.

"Your father . . ." she gasps.

I lean a little closer. "What, Mom? What about Dad?"

"He didn't . . ." She tries to suck in more air, so she can get the words out . . . words that must have been living inside of her. Had they been tangled up with the cancer and that's why she's only able to speak them now?

"Dis . . . appear," she stammers.

I blink rapidly, like I'm trying to wake myself from a bad dream.

"Mom, what are you trying to say? If he didn't disappear, where is he?" My voice rattles. I don't understand any of it.

"Don't," she says. Her eyes close for a moment, and I think she's gone. But they reopen just as quickly as they closed. "Trust," she gasps.

"Mom! I don't understand. Where's Dad?" I cry out.

She exhales, trying to finish her final words, but nothing more comes out, save for her last breath. Her cold hand goes limp in mine. It's true what they say about the lights going out when a person passes. Her eyes sit still and dark. Her mouth hangs partially open.

She's gone.

She's gone.

I let out a painful sob while her final words string together in my mind. *Your father. He didn't disappear. Don't trust . . .*

TWO
MICHAEL

I always knew the only thing that would bring me home was death. I just didn't know whose it would be. I've been gone seven years, and today I got the call. *Mom's dying. You should come home.* So, I hopped on the first flight leaving San Jose to Wisconsin because when death calls, you answer.

The engine of my rental car purrs quietly as I speed along Highway X, one of only two roads that connect Allen's Grove to the rest of the world. A colorful rainbow appears in the sky, but judging from the dark clouds moving in from the west, it won't last long. I slow down and flick my left blinker on. There are no cars on the road to signal to, but I do it anyway, out of habit. The Grove still looks the same as I figured it would. Small towns don't evolve. They don't grow. They don't change. They are what they've always been.

I drive past the park, which sits in the center of the unincorporated community. Large walnut and box elder trees are scattered throughout it. They're the only things that grow here. The same slide, swing set, and picnic tables are there—just rusted and more worn now. Ranch-style houses with decent-sized yards surround the park, and I'm sure the same bloodlines still live in each one.

I make a right on Hustis Street. It's a dead end, but the last house on the left is where I grew up. I've thought about how our street goes nowhere, almost like foreshadowing for the people who stuck around. I didn't want to come back, but I can't trust my sisters to handle the estate properly. They have a plethora of their own unresolved problems—Nikki, an addiction to drugs, Beth, an addiction to mediocrity. How could I expect them to take care of this?

I feel no ill will toward my sisters, but I know they resent me. I outgrew them. I got out. I discovered a world outside of this terrarium, and they hate me for it. But I also don't blame them for their envy. When you shine brighter than the sun, it's hard for others to look at you, so you have two choices: look and be blinded with resentment or look away. It's obvious they chose the latter. They've had little to no contact with me for the past seven years. I guess if I were in their shoes, I'd act the same way. I'm a reminder of what life could have been like if things had happened differently for them. No one wants that kind of reminder.

I take the long concrete driveway slow. It curves at the top, cutting through a sprawling yard that used to serve as a cow pasture in another lifetime. The house sits at the end of the driveway, on top of the tallest hill in Allen's Grove. I used to think that our location was special but it's not. It's like saying I'm the most successful of anyone that's ever lived in this town. A giant to ants. I park the car in front of the three-car garage. The siding on the large ranch-style home is a light blue, but it's not as bright and clean as it used to be when my father cared for it. Every spring, he'd pressure-wash the driveway, porch, back deck, and siding. This home was his source of pride, but eventually pride destroyed him like it does most men.

I grab a duffel bag from the back seat and get out of the vehicle. I don't plan to stay very long, just long enough. A sweet, pungent scent hangs in the air, most likely from the rainfall and the impending storm. The wind whistles as it picks up speed. Birds chirp and sing from trees scattered around the land. At the front door, I notice the red paint is chipped and faded, another thing that hasn't been taken care of, and a reminder of why I'm here. I consider knocking, and maybe I should. I don't think of this place as home. But it also doesn't seem right to announce my presence, as though I'm a guest. My hand grasps the cold door handle, and I let out a deep breath, readying myself to enter a world I never wanted to return to.

THREE

BETH

I haven't moved from my chair. It's been twenty minutes since Mom passed. Maybe only two. Time stops when death makes a visit. I'm in shock, not only from losing her but also from hearing those final words. What did they mean? What was she trying to tell me, and why did she wait until the very end to say it? *Why?* My eyes flick between her and the swirl of colors on the television screen in the corner of the room. It's a rerun of *Wheel of Fortune*, the sound still muted. Three letters are displayed, and the phrase consists of two words. The category is *Thing*. Mom would have solved it already. She loved puzzles.

Your father. He didn't disappear. Don't trust . . .

Don't trust who or what? Or did she just mean "Don't trust" in general . . . like anyone? My eyes go back to her. She's staring at me or at least it seems that way. Her jaw is relaxed; mouth open as though she's about to say something. But I know she won't. Because she's gone. And I'm left with a body and a puzzle.

He didn't disappear. But he did, seven years ago, leaving behind a handwritten note addressed to my mother. They had been married thirty-seven years, and when he left, all he offered were five parting words: *Laura, I'm sorry. Love, Brian.*

His truck was caught on a gas station surveillance camera seven miles south of our home and once more at a tollway crossing the Illinois border, and then he was never seen again. He vanished into thin air, like a puddle of water evaporating on a hot day. None of us saw it coming. Well, except Mom. She said they'd been having problems and that Dad had struggled on and off with depression for many years. It was surprising to me because they never fought, and I didn't even know that Dad was unhappy. Mom told us she'd tried to get him help but he refused, telling her he was fine. The police investigated his disappearance for a short time. At first, they zeroed in on Mom, thinking she had something to do with it. It's always the spouse, at least, almost always. That theory fell to the wayside when his truck was found two weeks later, abandoned in the town of McAllen, Texas—eleven miles from the Mexico border. The authorities kept the investigation open after that, but no one was really looking for him.

"Where is he, Mom? Where's Dad?" I cry, wishing she'd wake up to answer me just one more time.

The front door creaks open, sucking the stale air out of the house. I quickly cover Mom with a blanket, wipe my eyes, and get to my feet.

"Hello," Michael calls out.

I haven't heard his voice in years, seven to be exact, but it sounds the same—deep, with an air of confidence. I turn to find him standing in the living room entryway, dressed in khakis and a gray tee. He almost looks the same too. His dark hair is cut short and speckled with gray now. His shoulders are broader, as though he's been hitting the gym regularly. His skin is tan because the sun shines a little longer and a little brighter in California. There's a thin scar a few inches in length running down his right cheek, one I don't recognize. It's new, and he probably did something stupid to get it. Although Michael is nearly thirty-six, a few years younger than me, and towers over me, I still see him as my annoying little brother.

"Hi, Beth," he says.

"Hi, Michael."

Neither of us say anything for a moment. We just stand there, worlds apart, glancing at one another. He's my family but he's also a stranger. A familiar stranger, what an odd thing to be.

"Is Mom . . . ?" He swallows hard, unable to finish his question but I know what he's asking. He looks over my shoulder, trying to get a glimpse, but she's hidden under the covers and out of sight.

I nod. "Yeah."

He rubs his brow and sharply exhales. "How long?"

"Not long." My answer is vague because I've lost all sense of time.

Michael shakes his head and glances down at his loafers. "The damn plane sat on the tarmac for a half hour after we landed. I might have made it in time."

I'm not sure if he's looking for comfort, but I don't have any to give so I say nothing. Just like Dad, he chose to stay away.

He lifts his head, his eyes meeting mine. "Did she say anything before she passed?"

I chew on my bottom lip and consider telling him Mom's final words. But that message was for me, not him. And I'm not sure what it even means . . . at least not yet.

"No, she couldn't really speak," I say.

He folds in his lips and nods, squinting as though he doesn't believe me. I don't blame him. I'm not the best liar, and he's not the most trusting person.

"Where's Nicole?"

I shrug. "Your guess is as good as mine."

"Is she using again?"

"She never stopped."

He shakes his head. "Geez, so much wasted potential."

I'm sure he's talking about me too. We all had things going for us at one point, like locomotives on a set of tracks with no end in sight. But my train stopped, Nicole's train derailed, and Michael's . . . well, his went full steam ahead. And I can't help but resent him for it. I've felt indifferent toward him for years. It was easy to feel that way when he was gone, but now that he's here, I feel otherwise. There's a rage festering inside of me, and I'm sure it's been there all along—simmering, waiting to boil over.

"When was the last time you talked to her?" I ask.

He rubs his chin as though he's pondering his answer. "I sent her a text on her birthday."

"A whole text?"

Michael furrows his brow. He's not used to being called out. And maybe this isn't the right time for it, but I don't care. This whole house could collapse into itself and get swallowed up by the earth, and I don't think I would even scream.

"I deserve that," he says with a nod.

His response disappoints me. I wanted a fight, someone to blame, someone to be mad at. But little brother has outmatured me. I guess you can only grow so much when you're stuck in the same place—like a house plant that's never been repotted.

I shuffle my feet, glancing down at the scratched and worn hardwood floor. I should apologize, but I'm not sorry.

His gaze glides around me. "Can I see Mom?" he asks.

I move to the side and pull the covers from her face so Michael can get a glimpse. It's not Mom though. It's just a body. If it were Mom, she'd be smiling, but instead her jaw is slack. Her eyes would be bright and animated, but they're clouded and still. She doesn't look peaceful in death.

My throat tightens, and I swallow hard. I'm the oldest. I'm supposed to be the strongest. "Do you want a moment?"

I see his eyes go to her but he has a blank expression. I wonder if he's trying to be strong too. Then again, he was never one to cry. None of us were. Dad raised us to be strong and stoic. I remember his words, *If you can control your emotions, you can control anything*. He made it seem like it was some sort of superpower. But really it was just a terrible coping mechanism—one that left us unprepared when he disappeared.

Michael's steps are slow and cautious as he walks toward me. I don't know what to do or how to act. When he reaches his hand out, I nearly flinch. He rests it on my shoulder and looks me in the eye. "I'm sorry I wasn't here, Beth."

I stare back at him, chewing on several sentences before I finally spit one out. "I'm sorry you weren't too," I say, stepping away from him.

His hand slides from my shoulder, returning to his side. You know how they say there are some relationships you can slip in and out of, that even if a lot of time has gone by, you just pick up where you left off? This isn't one of them.

"I'll be in the kitchen. I'm gonna try to get ahold of Marissa to let her know what happened," I add.

Michael simply nods. He doesn't ask about my daughter, his only niece. Instead, he turns from me and takes a seat beside the bed. Leaning forward, he props his elbows on the mattress. Mom's small hand disappears in his as he lowers his head and buries his face into what's left of her. There are murmured whispers, but I can't make out what he's saying. It's like he's a child again, asking for forgiveness after he'd done something wrong—but Mom's gone, and she can't forgive him . . . She can't forgive any of us anymore.

FOUR

BETH

I sip at a four-finger pour of Seagram's 7 whiskey. The apricot sweetness dissipates as soon as it touches my taste buds and is quickly overpowered by a flavor best described as weak rubbing alcohol. Another thing my mother enjoyed on the rarest of occasions. This swill was a treat for her. It's cheap, and it doesn't taste good. But sometimes it's the bad things in life that make us feel the most alive. I lean against the kitchen counter, waiting for a call back from my daughter. A fly buzzes around the sliced tomato I left out, the sandwich I never finished making. I consider killing it, but there's been enough death in this house for one day, so I let it frolic in the tomato water. At least someone is enjoying it.

I don't know what to do with myself right now, other than drink bad whiskey. Each gulp pushes the grief down a little further. I should be planning the funeral, but I don't even know what Mom wanted. Every time I brought it up, she'd say, "Let's talk about that later." Well, now there's no time to discuss it at all.

My phone rings. It's my daughter, Marissa.

"Hello," I say. There's static. We have a bad connection. Then again, we've had that for a long time.

"Hi, Mom. My sergeant told me you called. What's up?" she asks. It's noisy on her end. Heavy machinery, engines roaring, lots of chatter.

"You coming, Thomas?" a man yells. Marissa sounds farther away as she says, "Yeah, I'll be right there."

I can tell when the phone is pressed to her ear again because her voice is louder. "Mom, you still there?"

"Yeah, I'm here. How have you been?" I'm not ready to tell her about her grandma. I'm not even sure how much it'll affect her. They were close, up until seven years ago when my dad disappeared. That changed my mom. It made her detached and guarded all at the same time. It had the same effect on me. Someone choosing to leave your life is a hard thing to live with. And I didn't live with it well. I pushed Marissa away without even realizing. My mom did too, and I don't think we noticed, until the whole world was between us. Marissa's been stationed on a navy base in South Korea for over a year, and before that she was in training, so she hasn't even seen her grandma in over two years. She could have been stationed in the Great Lakes, close to home, but of course she chose a place as far away as she possibly could. If they would have offered to station her on the moon, I'm sure she would have said yes.

"Busy, real busy. Sorry I haven't rang in a while. Is that why you called?" she asks.

I sip the Seagram's again, holding it in my mouth for a moment before swallowing. I don't know why I do that. Maybe I'm punishing myself.

"No. I called because . . ." My eyes go back to the fly. It's flipped on its back in the tomato water. Dead. Too much of a good thing. "Your grandma passed today." There's a lump in my throat. It's a sob. I chug the rest of the whiskey, forcing it down again.

"What? Mom, I'm so sorry," she says—because it's my loss, not hers. "Are you okay? Do you want me to come home? I can see if they'll give me leave."

"I'm . . ." It takes me a moment to settle on the right word. *Okay*, no. *Good*, too flippant. *Fine*. That works. I am fine. I'm not okay. But I'm fine. It's the safety blanket of emotions. "Fine. And if you can come, I'd like that."

There's silence, and I worry the phone has cut out. I pull it from my ear and look at the display screen. The call time is still ticking away.

"Okay, Mom. I'll see what I can do." There's a beat of silence. "Does Dad know?" she adds. I know then she won't come. She's making sure there's someone here to comfort me. My ex-husband won't be jumping at that opportunity, and I wouldn't want him to. I haven't spoken to him since Marissa left for the navy. Plus, he gave up on us a year after my dad disappeared.

He didn't disappear.

"No, he doesn't know yet."

"What about Aunt Nicole?" she asks.

I'm taken back by the mention of my sister. I cut her out of my life nearly a year ago, after she became too unpredictable and too dangerous to be around. I never told Marissa how bad it was because I figured she was on the other side of the world anyway, so Nicole couldn't hurt her.

"I haven't been able to get ahold of her," I say frankly.

Silence.

"Have you talked to her recently?" I add.

"Umm . . . Aunt Nicole writes me letters," she says.

That doesn't surprise me. Nicole has always loved to write, mostly poems or short quotes. Her mind was truly a beautiful thing before the drugs ate away at it. I used to think she could get clean, but somewhere between the multiple rehab stints, the overdoses, the thefts, and the run-ins with the law, I lost all hope that I'd ever have my sister back.

"What does she write?"

"Just tells me about her life and asks me about the navy and South Korea." I can practically hear her smile. I do those things. I ask about her life. I tell her about mine. But when those words come from me, they don't make her smile. She connects better with my drug-addict sister than with me, her own mother. Something inside of me blossoms. Jealousy? I immediately push it away. Nicole is the last person I should be envious of.

"Hey, Mom. I'm really sorry about Grandma, but I gotta get going. I'll call back as soon as I can."

"Okay, honey . . ." Before I can finish my sentence, the line is dead and she's gone.

I let out a sigh and scroll through my texts. The one to my sister has been read but there is no reply. I type out a long message full of anger and grief. I tell her how mad I am for her not being here. I curse her for not visiting Mom before she passed. I accuse her of being selfish and weak. And then I delete the whole message and stow my phone back in my pocket. Some things are just better left unsaid.

There's movement in my peripheral, and I look up to find Michael standing in the doorframe. His face is flushed, and there's a sheen to his eyes, like he's been crying. I hold the Seagram's bottle and gesture toward him.

"Want some?"

He crumples his face in disgust but shrugs. "Yeah, why not."

A four-finger pour each. Michael takes the glass from me and holds it near his lips, staring at the dull gold liquid that resembles piss. He tosses his head back and chugs half of it. His whole body shivers and his face twists, like he's just sucked on a lemon. He's used to the finer things in life. I wonder what that's like. But I'd rather not know. It's better to be unaware of what you're missing out on, those things you'll never have access to and how *the one percent* lives—especially when you know it'd only be temporary.

"That's horrible," he says, coughing.

I take a long sip, peering over my glass at him while he tries to regain his composure.

"Yeah, it is."

Michael pulls out a chair and takes a seat, spinning the glass slowly in circles on the worn kitchen table. The wood is covered in gouges and scratches. I remember all of us sitting around this table: Mom and Dad on either end. Three of us in the middle with one empty chair. We never sat in the same spots, moving around based on who we were mad at and who we liked most that day. If I had to pick now, based on how I was feeling, I wouldn't even take a seat. But I'm not a teenager. Adults have to come to the table, so I sit on one of the short sides, directly across from Michael, in the spots our parents used to occupy.

"Were you able to get ahold of Marissa?" he asks.

I nod and take another sip.

"Is she coming home?"

"Probably not." A long exhale escapes through my nose. "She's stationed in South Korea."

Michael's eyes grow a little wide. "Wow, I didn't know that. Army?"

"Navy," I correct.

"Impressive," he says. I don't care about what impresses him. His watch clinks against the table. Half red, half blue. A luminescent silver band and the word *Rolex* in the center of the face. I know it cost more than my car, but he wears it like it came out of a quarter machine.

"What happened?" I ask, gesturing to the scar on his cheek.

He runs the tip of his finger over it. It's a couple inches in length, running vertically along his cheek. "Car accident."

"Why didn't you tell me?"

He cocks his head. "Would it have changed anything?"

My eyes narrow but I quickly relax them. Michael's right. It wouldn't have changed anything. I may have sent a text asking if he was okay. I may have even called. But that's it. I glance down at my chewed fingernails. I've bitten them since I was a child and no matter how many times I've tried to stop, they always find their way back to my mouth. Bad habits don't die.

"Are you all right now?" I ask.

Michael nods and sips his drink. He's clearly getting used to the taste because he doesn't react to it this time. I've learned you can get used to anything.

I'm glad one of us is all right. Mom died right before my eyes and, though I know I'll come to accept it, I don't know if I'll ever be all right again. Some things change you forever.

"What happens now?" Michael asks, briefly glancing over his shoulder toward the living room. Mom's body is covered with a sheet again. Only we know she's under there. Sharing this moment of grief with Michael feels hollow because he wasn't here when she passed. I stare at the outline of her face. A puff of air forces the sheet to expand. I blink several times. I'd imagined it. Wishful thinking, I guess. Or I'm going crazy. I've actually never understood that saying. *Going* crazy . . . because crazy isn't a place you go, it comes right to you.

"Beth," Michael says, pulling me from my thoughts.

I blink again. "Sorry. I'm not sure." I glance at the clock on the wall noting the time, thirty minutes past nine. "Cathy, Mom's hospice nurse, should be back from her break any minute. She'll tell us what happens next."

He sips his whiskey. "What about the funeral?"

"What about it?"

"Well, what did Mom want?"

"I don't know." A tear escapes the corner of my eye. I quickly wipe it away with the back of my hand. "She never told me."

Michael pulls his lips in, like he doesn't know what to say. He clears his throat. "So, what's new?" he asks, changing the subject.

It's been seven years since we last spoke, and I wish I could say, "Everything." It all should be new but it's not, because I've been stuck in place. I work at the same factory, live in the same house, drive the same car.

"I'm divorced," I finally land on. I'm not sad as I say it. I don't know if I ever loved my ex-husband. We met when I first started at the factory. I worked the line, and he was a machinery operator. I was just a nineteen-year-old with a dull future. When he asked me out, it gave me something to look forward to, other than a paycheck or a day off. And then I got pregnant and knew that marriage was the right thing to do, not for me—but for him and for our daughter.

Michael gives me a solemn look and mutters, "Sorry. How long ago?"

"Five years." I shrug. "But it was over long before that."

"What happened?"

"Life happened."

I'm not trying to be cryptic, but I know it's coming off that way. I take a deep breath and look him in the eye. "After Dad disappeared, I became 'obsessed,' as Tom would put it. It took a toll on my marriage, on my life, on my relationship with my daughter. I was so fixated on trying to find him that I lost everything else in the process."

Michael leans forward in his chair, propping his elbows on the table. If Mom were here, she'd scold him for that. "I'm sorry I wasn't here for you. I didn't know you were going through all that."

"Weren't you?"

He sinks back into his chair. "Wasn't I what?"

"Going through that too? Didn't you want to find Dad?" There are so many questions I want to ask him, but I know if I push too hard, he'll shut down. That's how he was as a kid, and most people don't change. He overthinks, overanalyzes, and then keeps it all to himself, amassing clever little secrets. It's probably why he's done so well with his life.

"Mom didn't want . . ." The front door creaks open, cutting him short.

Cathy pops her head in. She's tall and thin with black curly hair tied back into a low ponytail.

"Hi, Beth," she says, closing the door behind her. "How's Laura doing?"

My eyes instantly well up. If I keep saying she's gone, it makes it more real. I shake my head and lower it slightly. Cathy nods and delivers a sympathetic look. I wonder how she can do a job like this, meeting people in their final days just to watch them die. It has to take a toll on her. I think that as humans we can only carry so much death with us.

"I'm Michael, Beth's brother," he says, getting up from his chair and extending his hand.

"Cathy. I'm very sorry for your loss." She shakes his hand lightly. That's how greetings are during times of despair, fragile.

Cathy stands there awkwardly for a moment. She has worked as a hospice nurse for decades, but experience doesn't make this any easier. "I'm sorry I wasn't here," she finally says to me.

I'm glad she wasn't here but I don't say that. "Don't be."

"Have you both had your time with her?" Cathy glances at each of us.

We nod.

"Are you okay with me calling the funeral home for arrangements?"

I know what that means. They'll come and take her . . . well, not her. The body. The next time I see her, she'll have been injected with a couple gallons of formaldehyde to slow down the decay. She'll be wearing makeup for the first time since her wedding day. Her hair will be done up in a way she's never worn it before. She'll be dressed in her Sunday best. And she'd hate all of it.

When I don't answer, Michael steps in. "Yes, Cathy. You can make the arrangements."

She looks to me for confirmation, so I nod, and she backs out of the kitchen. Michael takes a seat kitty-corner to me and reaches for my hand, giving it a squeeze. I want to flick it away. But I need it more than I don't want it. I gulp the Seagram's. It's lost its flavor.

"It's gonna be okay," he says. I'm not sure I believe him.

My phone ringing startles me. *Unknown* is splayed across the top of the screen. I know it's bad news. Mom always said bad things came in threes. This is number two, I'm sure of it.

"Hello," I answer.

"Hi, is this Elizabeth Thomas?" The voice on the other end of the line is deep and authoritative.

"It is."

"I'm Officer Ross of the Beloit Police Department. Your sister, Nicole, was attacked about an hour ago, and she's currently being treated at Memorial Hospital."

"Is she okay?"

Michael's eyes go wide, and he leans toward me.

"She's demanding to leave but we need someone to release her to, given her injuries. Are you able to come and get her?" the officer asks.

"Yes, yes. Of course. I'm on my way. I can be there in twenty minutes."

"Thank you, Ms. Thomas. I'll see you shortly." The phone clicks off.

"What is it?" Michael asks.

I'm a little wobbly when I stand, and I immediately regret the alcohol I consumed. Typically, that's reserved for the morning after, but sometimes there is no gap between an action and a regret.

"It's Nicole. She's in the hospital. Can you take me there?"

Michael doesn't hesitate, immediately getting to his feet. I toss him the keys to my 2010 Toyota Camry. He catches them and looks at the tarnished keys like they're some sort of foreign object. He doesn't say anything, but I know what he's thinking. Money changes people the same way death does. If you don't know how to manage every aspect of it, it'll bring out the worst in you.

FIVE

NICOLE

It's funny how memory works. Our brain decides what's most important and retains it—the rest, it just lets go. Song lyrics we remember for years, decades even. Are they important? Most likely not. But they're tied to salient moments. I know all the words to "Californication" by the Red Hot Chili Peppers because I kissed the first boy I ever loved while listening to it back in 1999. I can recite all the lyrics to "Last Resort" by Papa Roach because that song was blaring through the speakers of my parent's car as I drove alone, right after getting my driver's license. It meant the world to me, freedom, or at least the first taste of it. And I remember the lyrics to "Hurt" by Nine Inch Nails because it was playing when I overdosed the first time, and I thought it would be the last thing I'd ever hear. I remember mouthing the words. My lips were the only thing I could move; they were coated in vomit, shifting back and forth and up and down. Then there are random memories permanently lodged in my mind, like phone numbers, despite the fact that cell phones store them for us now. I remember my dad's, though I haven't dialed it in years. And I remember my sister's. Two lifelines, but only one to call upon. Today, she picked up, and I'm surprised she did.

"How are you feeling, Nicole?" the nurse asks as she enters the hospital room where I'm laid up. She's young and vibrant with bright eyes and dewy skin. Actually, she's probably my age but I don't look like her. After all, time isn't the only thing that ages us. She smiles, not like she's happy to see me, but like she's happy she's not me. Pulling a clipboard from the end of my bed, she flips through several pages that must detail all the damage that was done. This isn't the first time I've been attacked. When you chase all the wrong things, you're bound to end up in the wrong place at the wrong time.

"I'm fine," I say, although I'm not.

My right arm is cocooned in a cast, not from today though. That injury happened four weeks ago, and the cast was supposed to be removed this week. But now the doctor wants to keep it on a little longer, just to be safe. My face is throbbing so I'm sure my skin is a swollen mix of colors. Several of my ribs are bruised. It hurts to inhale deeply, like I'm only sucking in enough air to survive, not enough to thrive. But I've felt that way about life for a long time. The doctor told me I was lucky my ribs weren't broken. I suppose he and I have different definitions of the word *lucky*.

A dose of methadone has helped to dull the withdrawal symptoms. I was supposed to get it earlier today. They asked me why I didn't go in for my treatment. I lied, making up an excuse about transportation or something like that. I *was* on my way to get my daily dose when I saw the text from my sister. I didn't read it fully, just the notification preview, just enough to get the gist as to why she was reaching out to me. *Mom is going to pass today*, it said. I'm on day twenty-nine of my sobriety, the longest I haven't used since my addiction started. I've tried and failed to stop more times than I care to admit. When I got the text, the craving intensified far beyond my control. Every ounce of my being wanted it . . . no, *needed* it, and I knew a dose of methadone wasn't going to cut it.

"How's your pain on a scale of one to ten?" the nurse asks.

I hesitate, deciding on the correct response and, by that, I don't mean the honest answer. They won't give me any more pain meds anyway because they know I'm an addict. Instead, I aim for a low number, one that'll get me out of here.

"Three," I say.

She scribbles it down on the chart, checks a few of my vitals, jots them down too, and returns the clipboard to the end of my bed. "The doctor is still advising that you stay overnight for observation. Are you sure we can't get you to stay?" The nurse tilts her head.

"I'm sure."

She slightly nods and delivers a sympathetic look. "Okay."

There's a knock on the door. It opens slowly and my older sister appears in the doorway. Although Beth's face is expressionless, her bloodshot, swollen eyes tell me she's been crying. *Mom's dead.* She doesn't even need to say it. The nurse greets her before slipping out of the room to get the doctor.

Beth stands awkwardly at the foot of my bed, uncomfortably adjusting her oversized navy green raincoat. Her dirty-blond hair is damp and hangs past her shoulders. She wears no makeup except a cherry-colored lip balm. Beth's always been pretty in an unassuming way. Her eyes skim over me, carefully noting each injury. It's how she always looks at me now, like a claims adjuster appraising the damage and deciding whether or not I'm salvageable. A year ago, she determined I wasn't worth saving. I can still hear her words. They cut deep, deeper than any physical injury I had ever endured.

I can't have you in my life, Nicole. I've tried to help you, but every time I do, I get burned worse than the last. I don't even know who you are anymore, because you sure as hell aren't my sister.

I remember Beth was calm when she said it. There was no emotion in her voice. No tears in her eyes. It was like she had already grieved the loss and was delivering the message to my ghost.

"How ya feeling?" she asks.

"Like a million bucks."

She nods, cracking a small smile. She's always liked my humor, but I think she's just humoring me right now because she feels bad for me.

"Money must have lost all value then," she quips.

I chuckle but stop myself when I feel a sharp pain in my ribs. I wince, holding my breath for a moment while pressing a hand against my abdomen.

Beth takes a step toward me. "You good?"

I blow the air out of my lungs. "Yeah. I'm surprised you came."

Her eyes are laser-focused on mine, the way Mom used to look at me when I came home late for curfew. "Yeah, I am too. So, what happened?" she asks.

I look away, focusing on the white wall behind her. I've never been fond of eye contact. It feels too intimate. It's a way to establish trust— but no one should trust me. I don't even trust myself.

When I don't answer, Beth continues, "Police said you got beat up pretty bad. Do you owe someone money?"

"No," I lie. "I was just in the wrong place at the wrong time."

She cocks her head. "Are you using?"

Even if I tell her no, she won't believe me. You can't trust people with an addiction because in many cases, like mine, their addiction is stronger than their word.

"Hello." Dr. Cline raps his knuckles against the partially open door. He's an older man with graying hair and a bulbous nose that keeps his glasses perfectly in place, despite his slick, oily skin.

He gives a routine smile and picks up the clipboard. "Pain level is down to three." He looks to me for confirmation.

I nod, and he continues. "Vitals look good. The radiologist reviewed your MRI scan and that came back normal as well."

I tried to refuse the MRI, but I was in and out of it when they brought me in, and they must have decided it was necessary. Now, I'll have pretty pictures of my brain, all for a whopping two thousand dollars. I should frame them like they're valuable pieces of artwork.

"Sounds like I'm good as new," I say.

"Not exactly. I want to see you back in two weeks so I can look at that cast. You have a mild concussion and several bruised ribs. So, no heavy lifting or strenuous exercise. Ice, ibuprofen, and rest. Just take it easy and keep up with your methadone treatments." Dr. Cline tilts his head.

I glance over at Beth. The whites of her eyes show at the mention of treatment. She's probably thinking she finally has her sister back. But I know that's not entirely true. Only part of me is here.

"Any questions?" he asks, slipping the clipboard back into its place.

"If you had to live with one leg or one arm, which would you choose, Doc?" I keep a straight face.

Beth stifles a laugh.

Dr. Cline raises an eyebrow. "I meant medical questions, but I suppose one arm," he says, cracking a smile. "I'll have the nurse get you checked out. Take care of yourself, Nicole." He nods and backs out of the room.

Beth looks to me, like that same claims adjuster, deciding there's still value, despite the damage. "How long?" she asks.

"Twenty-nine days."

"Good," she says with a nod. "Keep it up."

It's the most encouragement she's capable of offering me because I've let her down far too many times to warrant any more.

"Is Mom . . . ?" I don't finish my sentence, and I'm not sure why I even started it in the first place. I know the answer. But sometimes we question the things we already know.

Beth nods. "Yeah, she's gone."

I squeeze my eyes shut, picturing one of the last times Mom smiled at me. We were out shopping at rummage sales on a Saturday morning. She always loved a bargain and truly believed one man's garbage was another man's treasure. At a garage sale, I spotted a Remington Model 5 vintage typewriter. It was beautiful, priced at over four hundred dollars, less than half of what it was worth, but more than I could afford. I admired it for a few minutes before pulling myself away. Mom went up to pay for a small knickknack and tossed me the keys to her vehicle, telling me to turn on the air. She was going through menopause at the time and couldn't stand the humid Wisconsin summers paired with her hot flashes. Ten minutes later, she returned to the car carrying the typewriter and gifted it to me. I told her it was too much. She disagreed. I asked her how she could afford it. She told me not to worry about that. I told her I would pay her back. She smiled and said I could pay her back by writing a book. I promised her I would, but I never did, and years later, I sold the typewriter for drug money. She was as patient as a mother could be, but I wore it so thin, it became dust.

Beth rests her hand on mine. It's warm and comforting, something I haven't felt in what seems like forever. Day twenty-nine. I was one day away, just one day. I can hear my mother's words. The last ones she ever said to me. *Come back when you have a chip.*

SIX
BETH

Michael takes it slow down the long driveway. One of my headlights is burnt out, so only the right side is fully lit. The wind whips through my partially rolled-down window, and I can almost hear it carrying my mother's final words to me. I glance in the rearview mirror at Nicole. She sits quietly in the back seat, writing in her notepad. The pen scratches at the paper. She's always been that way. Rather than express how she's feeling outwardly, she writes it down, spinning poems and pithy lines out of her pain. She hasn't said more than *hello* to Michael when she greeted him in the car after leaving the hospital, so maybe she's writing about that.

The house is dark, and I know they've come and taken Mom away. This place used to be a home. Now I don't know what it is.

"Just park right here," I say.

Michael shuts off the engine and hands me the key. "I'll fix that headlight for you."

"You don't have to do that." I can't tell if he's being kind just because, or if it's because he feels sorry for me. Maybe there's no difference.

He presses his lips together and nods. "I know."

Inside the house, I turn on the lights. A bulb over the kitchen table flickers, signaling it's close to burning out, and I could say the same for myself. Without Mom, it feels empty in here now. Michael carries in a small bag of groceries he picked up while I was in the hospital with Nicole. At the doorway, she stops suddenly, like there's some sort of invisible force keeping her out. She looks down at her feet and inches one foot forward. A couple of large moths fly inside, darting toward the flickering light above the kitchen table. They swirl around one another, performing a synchronized air show of some sort.

"Nicole," I bark. She snaps out of it, looking to me with those big empty eyes. "Close the door. You're letting all the bugs in."

Her breath hitches as though she's bracing for impact and standing at the edge of an airplane door, thirty thousand feet above Earth with no parachute, rather than at the threshold of her childhood home. Nicole steps in quickly and closes the door behind her, letting out a sigh.

"Are you all right?" I ask.

She nods several times and swivels her cross-body bag behind her. She was robbed during the attack, so all that's in there are pads of paper and pens, but those are the most valuable things to her. I'd like to say I'm scared of losing her, but she's been living this way for so long that it feels like I already have, and I came to terms with that loss a year ago.

In the living room, there's an empty space where Mom used to be. The hospice bed is gone. The machines and IV stand are gone. She is gone. There are outlines where the items used to be, from where the dust has settled. If I concentrate hard enough, I can still see her lying there looking out the window. A chill runs down my spine. Nicole leans against the archway, using it to keep her frail self upright, while Michael stands stoic beside me. They take it all in, just as I am. But it's different for them. They haven't lived in this house the last few months. They haven't seen it transform from a home to a hospital to a memorial. They didn't watch Mom die slowly and then suddenly, all at once. And I hate them for that.

I swallow hard and cross the room, careful to walk around the bed that is no longer there, and take a seat on the floral-patterned couch.

Michael clears his throat. "I picked up some scotch. Do you want some?"

"Is Seagram's not good enough for you?" I tilt my head, half teasing but mostly serious.

"I'll have some," Nicole says.

I don't think it's a good idea, given her recovery, but I don't say anything. I'm not her mother, and she didn't listen to Mom anyway.

"All right, Port Charlotte for Nicole and me. Seagram's for Beth," Michaels says with a smirk.

"Give me your stupid fancy scotch," I huff.

He smiles and disappears into the kitchen. Several cupboards open and close. Ice cubes pop out of an ice tray and clink against glasses. Nicole sits down next to me. When the couch cushion barely sinks, I realize how thin she's gotten. She pulls the sleeves of her oversized sweatshirt over her thumbs and places her hands in her lap. Her posture is rigid, and I can't tell if it's from the pain she's in or if it's because she's uncomfortable being in this house.

"Do you want to lie down?" I ask.

Nicole shakes her head. "I can't believe she's gone," she says just above a whisper. She pushes her brown hair out of her face revealing green eyes she got from Mom and scarred skin she got from a lifetime of bad choices.

"I was planning to see her tomorrow." She's not looking directly at me when she speaks. Her eyes are focused a little above me, kind of how Mom was in her final moments.

I'm silent, waiting for my sister to say more, but she doesn't. Instead, her eyes well up and her breath hitches. Then she regains her composure, blinking the tears away and breathing through the impending sob, just like Dad taught us.

Michael reenters the living room, carrying three glasses of scotch. He hands us each one and takes a seat on the far end of the couch.

"Thanks," I say with a tight smile.

Nicole chugs half of hers. Michael shakes his head and delivers a disapproving look. "It's meant to be sipped."

She holds up the glass, flicks her pinky out, and takes the slowest sip she possibly can. "Is that better, Your Highness?" she mocks.

He cracks a smile and sips his drink. The scotch is equally smoky and sweet with flavors of honey, vanilla, and citrus.

"You have good taste, Michael," I say with a nod.

"Easy to have good taste when you have money," Nicole huffs. "But thanks," she quickly adds, tipping the glass toward him.

We drink in silence, exchanging glances. It seems like we all have something we want to say. The house creaks and moans. I like to think it's Mom, walking from room to room, making sure each one is in order like she used to do when we were young.

"Remember that time Mom caught us down in the valley with the camcorder making scary movies?" Nicole says, interrupting the silence. She lets out a laugh.

Growing up in a small town, there wasn't much to do. So, we made our own entertainment—building forts, swimming in the creek, filming movies with our family camcorder, going for bike rides, and turning just about everything into a game.

"You mean the *Blair Bitch Project*?" Michael chuckles into his glass.

"Yeah, I don't know why I had to play the Blair bitch," I scoff.

"You fit the part," Nicole quips.

I mock laugh and sip my drink. "Mom was so mad because she thought we were going to break the camcorder."

"Yeah . . . I bet it's still somewhere in this house," Michael says. He looks around the room, and then up at the ceiling where the attic is.

I'm sure it's up there too. Mom saved everything. She had lost so much in her life—her father, her sister, her mother, Dad—that she tried to hold on to anything and everything she could.

"Dad was even madder when he saw we were using his insect fogger for smoke effects," Nicole adds.

"Well, yeah. Because we were literally playing in poisonous gas." I shake my head and laugh.

"Remember Mom made us Oscar awards out of toilet paper rolls after our film debut?" Nicole looks to me and then Michael.

"I won Best Camcorder Holder." Michael smiles at the memory. "It should have been Director, but Mom didn't know the award categories."

Nicole grins. "I was Best Writer."

"Yeah, Best Actor here," I say. "That was really something special . . ." I trail off.

We sit in silence again, reminiscing about memories that feel like they happened both yesterday and more than a lifetime ago. It's funny how time works. I can remember Nicole before the drugs got into her. She was funny and bright, with so many goals and aspirations. And Michael, smart as a whip and the whole world at his fingertips. But he was the only one to truly grasp his dreams.

When our glasses are empty, Michael grabs the bottle from the kitchen and returns, pouring a generous amount in mine and his, and a little less in Nicole's. She either doesn't notice or doesn't say anything.

"Are you seeing anyone?" I look to Michael. I'm not sure why I ask the question, maybe because I'm curious to find out how much better his life is than mine. It's hard not to compare when we all had the same beginning.

"I was. But it ended a few months ago." He shrugs and sips his drink.

"Why?" Nicole asks.

"She wasn't happy with my workload."

"That doesn't seem like a real reason. My last boyfriend broke up with me because I sold his watch for drug money," Nicole says, nonchalantly. "Apparently, that was a deal-breaker for him."

Michael and I exchange worried looks. He glances at his wrist.

"I'm not going to steal your watch, Michael." She rolls her eyes.

"I didn't say you were," he says.

Nicole shifts in her seat and winces. "I'm fine," she says before either of us can ask. She positions a pillow behind her back, trying to get comfortable again. When she's settled, she looks to Michael and then me. "Do you think Dad will come back now?" She seems so young when she asks, as though she still believes in Santa, the tooth fairy, those monsters under the bed.

Michael hangs his head and stares at the dark-gold liquid in his glass.

Mom's final words return to me: *Your father. He didn't disappear. Don't trust.*

Nicole pulls her chin in when neither of us respond, as though she's embarrassed to have asked the question. I consider telling them what Mom said. But I don't. I'm not even sure it's worth mentioning. Maybe it meant nothing.

"If he knew Mom passed, he'd come home," I say. I'm not sure I believe those words, but I know Nicole needs them. Michael tosses back the golden liquid and pours himself another.

She nods and asks, "So, what next?"

"First, funeral arrangements. Then, we should get the house in order. Go through everything and decide what we're going to do with it all," I say.

"What do you mean? Like sell the house?" Nicole asks.

"Yeah. We either sell it or keep it."

Michael leans back into the cushion. "What are you thinking, Beth?"

I sigh. "I don't know. Maybe sell."

"I think you should sell it," Nicole says.

"Why?" I ask.

"Because I could use the money." Her eyes shift between Michael and me.

"For what, Nicole?" I tilt my head.

"To live on."

Michael raises a brow, but he doesn't say anything. He hasn't had to deal with Nicole's addiction like I have, so he can't understand how bad it's been.

"You know you can't be trusted with money, Nicole."

"What's that supposed to mean?" she spits.

"I think you know."

She stands quickly but winces and nearly falls over, spilling part of her drink onto Michael in the process. He groans and wipes at his pants.

"If you have something to say, Beth, then just fucking say it!" Nicole yells.

I'm used to her emotional outbursts. It comes with addiction, and it's why I put distance between us a year ago. I couldn't take it anymore. She'd call me every name in the book, tell me she hated me, that she wished I was dead. Sometimes, she even turned violent, lashing out at me or destroying whatever was around her when I told her no, that I wasn't giving her any more money. I'm not sure she even remembers any of those fights.

I look up at her and draw my brows together. "What would you spend that money on, Nicole?" My voice is calm.

Her mouth falls partially open. I can't help but think of Mom, her jaw lax after she passed. I close my eyes for a moment, willing my mind to bury that image. When I open them, Nicole is seated again—lips pressed firmly together, stewing. What I said was wrong but I'm also right, and she knows it. Sometimes right and wrong are interchangeable.

"We don't have to make any decisions now," Michael says.

"You're right," I say. "Let's just take it one day at a time."

Nicole nods but she's still stewing in her anger.

"I can only stay for a week though," Michael adds.

"And will it be another seven years until we see you again?" I ask.

"Let's hope not." He stands from the couch. "Good night, you two," he says, putting an end to the fight I was looking for.

Michael leaves the bottle but carries his glass with him as he heads down the hall to his old bedroom. His door closes with a thud, and my shoulders jump. It's been a long time since I've heard a door slam in this house, not since we were teens.

"Home sweet home," Nicole says sarcastically.

"Yep." I stand from my seat, deciding I don't want to fight after all, at least not tonight. I pick up the half-empty bottle of scotch because I don't want Nicole to feel tempted, and she doesn't need any more. "I'm going to turn in. Need anything?"

"No, I'm going to head to bed too," she says, draining the rest of her scotch.

She hands me her glass and gets to her feet, collecting her belongings. I rinse the glasses in the kitchen sink and hide the bottle of scotch in the lazy Susan cabinet before heading down to my bedroom. Nicole pads down the hall to her room but stops to look back at me. She tells me good night, and I tell her the same. Our bedroom doors close, and I make sure to lock mine. I worry about sleeping under the same roof as my sister. I know she can't be trusted.

SEVEN

NICOLE

Last week, I wrote a short story. It started out strong, lost its way in the middle, and never got back on track. The ending fell flat, the potential from the strong beginning faded, and it seemed un-salvageable. I rearranged words, deleted, added, but no matter what—it just wasn't what I intended it to be. I wanted more for it, but some things just can't be polished, so I threw it away.

Mom, is that how you felt about me? —Nicole

I tried to sleep but it's hard to turn my thoughts off. Writing helps. Gives me a place to put them, but I think I just have too many tonight. A soft knock on my childhood bedroom door startles me. I quickly close my notebook and sit up a little taller in bed, rearranging the comforter that's draped over my legs.

"Come in," I say.

It's Michael. He's changed into a T-shirt and a pair of sweatpants. There's no name brand on either but I can tell they're expensive. His hair sticks out in all directions like he fell asleep for a short time and woke again. Perhaps, like me, he has a hard time turning off his thoughts.

"What's up?" I ask because I don't know what else to say to him. My tone is flippant, and I think it's because I resent him. For leaving, for having a better life, for not being an addict like me, for having money, and for not being there when I needed him. I glance at the old worn carpet, and a memory comes plowing to the front of my mind.

When I was a kid, I was terrified of everything, so scared I couldn't sleep at night. My eyes would close, and I'd see monsters crawling out from beneath my bed, clawing at the sheets, trying to grab me and take me with them. My parents said I was cursed with an active imagination because I could close my eyes and imagine the worst possible thing happening. Maybe my mind wasn't overly active. Maybe it was preparing me for the broken life I'd live. I remember telling Michael I was too scared to sleep. I was twelve and he was ten. He dragged a comforter and pillows into my room, made himself a bed on my floor, and said he'd protect me. We talked until I dozed off. I had finally slept through the whole night. I felt safe, knowing he was there. But now I don't know how I feel. Because I'm not that scared little girl anymore, and he's not the brother he used to be.

Michael takes a couple of steps into my room, stopping in the center. A Walmart shopping bag hangs from his hand, his fingers looped through the plastic handles. He glances around my old bedroom. No one lives here anymore, but it holds the memory of the girl who called it home. That girl no longer exists. As we age, we shed layers of ourselves, disintegrating like any other organic material, but some of us just break down faster than others.

The walls of the room are painted a light purple, but they're bare now. Nail holes that were never patched hint at what the space used to look like. My bedroom furniture still fills the room—a bed, a desk, and a dresser. But all my belongings are gone. I lost them or sold them somewhere between eighteen and now. The ceiling is still covered in plastic glow-in-the-dark stars. I spent nearly a week sticking them up there when I was a teenager, but like me, they've lost their glow.

"Here, I got you something," Michael says, extending the bag. It swings mildly in the air.

I hesitate, not reaching out for it, because I don't want anything from him. He gives me a sympathetic look, also something I don't want from him. He inches closer to me, insisting that I take it. I finally do. Beggars can't be choosers as they say. Inside the bag, I find an iPhone and a purple case for it. Purple has always been my favorite color.

"What's this?" I ask.

"Yours was stolen so I figured you needed a new one."

I groan. "I had a flip phone, Michael. One of those pay-as-you-go. I can't afford this."

He slides his hands into his pockets and takes a step back. "I put you on my plan. It's covered, so you don't have to worry about it."

"I don't need your pity."

"Good, because you don't have it," he says, matter-of-factly. And I think I believe him. He turns and heads for the door.

"Thanks," I mutter.

Michael pauses, looking over his shoulder. His eyes try to meet mine, but they don't because I'm looking right through him. It's hard to see someone when the memory of them is stronger than the person standing directly in front of you.

"You're welcome, Nicole."

He closes the door behind him, leaving me to fend off the monsters on my own.

But they're not under the bed anymore.

They're in me.

EIGHT
BETH

The floor creaks beneath my feet like the house is waking up with me. Michael's bedroom door is open, and his bed is made. Nicole's door is closed, so I know she's still asleep. She's always been the last to bed and the last to rise. There's a pot of freshly brewed coffee in the kitchen. Counters are wiped down and everything is put away and tidy—not how I left it last night. I peek out the window above the sink. Michael's car is gone, and I wonder . . . *Gone for good? Just like Dad?* I pour a cup of coffee and inhale the nutty smell before taking it out to the back deck to enjoy.

The sky is a muted gray, dimly lit by the climbing sun. Birds chirp and peep a dawn chorus, while squirrels frolic in the bird feeders hung from old box elder and maple trees. The property dips into a hillside covered in trees. A valley carved through it sits off to the right, leading down to a small cabin and fire pit. Beyond that, a grassy plain, more trees, a hidden cemetery for the pets we've loved, and the twisting, bubbling creek. There's a pasture to the left covered in dandelions that look like little yellow explosions. The landscape is green and vibrant, but soon the colors will change, and the leaves will fall, and those chirping birds will fly south. That's life. It's a cycle until it's not anymore.

I shoot a text to Michael, asking him if he's on a flight home. He responds right away.

I went into town. Be back soon.

I'm not sure if I'm relieved or not to hear that he's coming back, but I suppose it's nice to have another person here to help clean up the mess and keep an eye on Nicole.

It's just after eight in the morning and for the first time in a long time, I don't know what to do with myself. If Mom were alive, I'd be making peanut butter toast and sitting down to watch *The Price Is Right* with her. But she's not. How do the living just keep living? I sip the hot coffee and clear my throat. It's much stronger than how I make it, almost like a thick bitter oil.

The roar of an engine pulls me from my thoughts. I make my way around the back of the house. As I turn a corner, I stumble into a tipped-over garbage can. *Damn raccoons.* I push the spilled contents back into the receptacle with my foot and stand it upright. A car nicer than mine but not as nice as Michael's rental is parked in front of the garage. The windows are darkly tinted, so I can't see who's in it. A man dressed in a gray suit steps out, lifts his chin, and waves.

"Can I help you?" I ask.

"Are you Elizabeth Thomas?"

"Yeah."

"I'm Craig Davidson, your mother's attorney," he says, walking around the front of his vehicle.

His introduction puzzles me. *Mom had a lawyer.* I had no idea. She never mentioned it, and I didn't think she had the money for one, especially since I was covering whatever bills she couldn't.

He extends a hand. "I'm very sorry for your loss." The sympathy seems robotic. Overusing words or phrases dulls their significance, and it's clear from how he speaks that he's said those words a thousand times.

"Thanks," I say, shaking his hand weakly.

Craig clears his throat. "I'm here to go over her will."

I'm even more puzzled by the mention of a will. She never brought it up, never talked about anything that would happen after she passed. So, I assumed she didn't have one. But I'm also a little relieved because now I'll know exactly what she wanted.

———

Nicole sits at the end of the table, a blanket wrapped around her shoulders, legs folded like a pretzel. Her hair is disheveled, and she switches between drinking water and coffee. I'm sure she's nursing a hangover because according to a Google search, she's not supposed to be consuming alcohol while on methadone treatments. And I'm sure she knows that too. But that's Nicole. She does what she wants when she wants. The lawyer, seated across from Michael and me, pulls a stack of folders from his briefcase. On top is a sealed manila envelope with the words *Thomas Children* written in black Sharpie. Michael taps his fingers against the table. His jaw is clenched and his eyes wander. He looks uncomfortable. But I'm sure we all do. There's nothing comforting about death.

Craig straightens out the papers. "Elizabeth, your mother has left most everything to you," he says, matter-of-factly.

My eyes flick to Nicole and then to Michael. His face is as tight as a drum. Hers is lax—a mix of disappointment and sadness, maybe something else.

I readjust myself in my seat. My fingers make their way to my teeth. I bite one nail before realizing that I'm biting it and quickly pull it away, folding my hands in my lap.

"What do you mean by *most everything*?" Nicole asks.

Craig scans the paper laid out in front of him. "The house and furniture go to Elizabeth, and so does this." He retrieves a small silver key and a Post-it Note. "The information for the lockbox is written down on the paper."

"What's in the box?" Michael asks. His eyes follow the key as it slides across the table toward me.

"Laura didn't say, so your guess is as good as mine," Craig explains.

I flip the key over and over in my hand. It's shiny and appears brand new. Is the lockbox also new? And what did Mom stow away? She's never had much, so I assume it contains little mementos that have no financial value but were treasures to her.

Craig drags his finger down the piece of paper. "Her car and journals go to Nicole," he says, flipping another page before continuing. "Your mother also kept most of your father's belongings. In here, she stipulates that Nicole and Elizabeth will have their choice of two of his items and the rest will go to Michael."

"Only two things?" Nicole groans.

"You can have whatever you want," Michael says with a shrug. I assume his generosity is because he has far more in life than me and Nicole will ever have.

"As far as your mother's personal belongings, they are to be divided between the three of you. Any questions?"

"How did you know my mother passed?" I ask.

Craig clears his throat. "I was alerted by her hospice nurse."

He rotates the paper toward us, clicks a pen, and places it on the table. "I'll need each of you to sign at the bottom. This just states that I went over everything."

Michael flicks his signature across it and slides it to me. I hesitate, the tip of the pen hovering an inch above the paper. It feels so uneventful. *Your mom's dead. Divide up all of her possessions. Sign here. Now, go about your own life.*

I force the pen to touch the paper and skid across it, leaving behind a blotchy signature that barely looks like mine. I pass it to Nicole, and she signs it without a thought.

The lawyer collects the paper, closes the folder, and opens another. "Your mother requests to be cremated, and she would like her ashes spread around the property." Craig looks to each of us to confirm our mom's wish will be honored.

Michael leans forward, tightening his eyes. "Seems a little disrespectful. This used to be farmland."

"It's not disrespectful. She wants to stay in the place she loved most," Nicole says.

The lawyer's gaze darts to me, "Is this going to be a problem?"

"No. That's what Mom wanted, so we'll carry out her wishes," I say with a nod. I'm relieved to know we're doing exactly what she asked for. Mom didn't get what she wanted in life, so the least I can do is give her what she wanted in death.

"Funerals aren't for the dead. They're for the living," Michael says. "Mom should be buried in a cemetery, so there's a place we can visit her."

"You didn't visit her when she was alive," I scoff.

"Beth!" Nicole scolds.

"What? I could say the same for you." I narrow my eyes at her.

"Just because you were here doesn't mean we didn't lose her too," Nicole argues. "She was just as much our mom as she was yours."

"Yeah, sure." I cock my head. "But I was the one that took care of her up until the moment she died. Where were you two?"

Michael shifts toward me. "Get off your high horse, Beth. You may have been here, but I was the one footing the bill for everything."

The lawyer quietly organizes his papers, trying to ignore the fight that's unfolding, but it's clear he's uncomfortable from the way his shoulders are pinned to his ears.

"No, you weren't," I practically yell. The rise in my own voice startles me.

"Oh great. So, we have Mr. Money Bags and Ms. I'm a Better Daughter Because I Watched Mom Die," Nicole says, rolling her eyes.

I almost add *and little miss drug addict*, but I stop myself.

"I put two thousand dollars in her account every month." Michael's voice is calm, making me, in contrast, look unhinged.

"That's a lie!" I'm nearly standing because I'm so mad. "I went through her finances. I was paying for anything Social Security didn't cover, which was practically everything. I was barely scraping by."

"You're both technically correct," Craig says quietly. The whites of his eyes show like he's anticipating one of us jumping down his throat.

"What?" I furrow my brow, slowly retaking my seat.

The lawyer flips through several pages. "Your mother had two checking accounts. One of them is what you're familiar with, Elizabeth. That's what she used to pay all of her bills . . . or some of them. The other was never touched. It has a balance of one hundred and thirty-two thousand dollars."

My eyes go wide, nearly splitting at the corners. Or at least that's how it feels. I can't believe it. I was struggling to cover my own bills and some of Mom's, and she was sitting on all that cash. Why would she do that to me?

"So, where's that money now?" Nicole asks.

"Your mother's wish was to donate that money to the Missing Persons Foundation," Craig says, glancing down at the will.

Michael balls up his fists and then stretches out his hands. His knuckles crack, and he groans. "I sent Mom that money to help her."

"You know Mom didn't take handouts, Michael," Nicole says. "But maybe since you—well, Mom—donated so much, they'll finally help us find Dad." She leans forward in her chair.

Nicole and I tried getting MPF to take Dad's case a few months after he disappeared. They told us his case didn't fit their criteria, and I think it was because they didn't believe he was missing. They thought he left on his own accord.

"Yeah, maybe," I say. My mother's final words echo in my head. *Your father. He didn't disappear.* She wants us to find him, I'm sure of it. But why didn't she donate that money before she passed, or at least . . . told me sooner? The rest of her words slither into my brain . . . *Don't trust.* Perhaps that's why. She was scared, but of what?

"Anything else?" Michael asks. He's agitated, and I guess I would be too if I were him. But when you give someone a gift, it's their choice as to what they do with it.

"There's one more thing," Craig says. He opens the manila envelope and removes three white letter-sized envelopes. They're sealed. He slides one to each of us. Written on the front are our names. The letters are smooth and round, each flowing seamlessly into the next. My mom always prided herself in her handwriting, and I wouldn't have been surprised if she'd practiced calligraphy at some point in her life.

"Your mother wrote each of you a letter, but she asked that you not open them until after her funeral."

Nicole holds her envelope up to the light, trying to see what's inside. "Why can't we open them now?" She sets it down in front of her and folds her noncasted arm in front of her chest. Her eyes dart between the lawyer and the envelope, and I can tell she's trying to resist the urge to rip it open.

"It's what she wanted," Craig says, gathering his papers and sliding them back into his briefcase.

I glance at the envelope on the table in front of me and trace my name with my finger. What did she want to say that she couldn't when she was alive? I flip it over. My skin tingles as I stare at the sealed flap.

"Any further questions?" the lawyer asks.

None of us say anything. He takes the silence as an answer and nods. Before closing his briefcase, he slides a business card to me. "Feel free to call with any questions. Otherwise, all remaining paperwork will be sent here within the next ten business days." Craig starts toward the door, making for a quick exit. *Of course.* Mom has already paid him, and there's no money left for him to make here. He's like a leech in salt.

"What happens if we open our envelopes before her funeral?" Nicole asks.

The lawyer pauses his quick exit, turns back, and lets out a sigh. "Probably nothing, but you should always respect the wishes of the dead."

His words send a chill down my spine, and I can't pinpoint why they have that effect.

The screen door slaps against the frame, punctuating his departure. My eyes flick to each of our envelopes, wondering what they contain. Michael hasn't even touched his. Maybe he knows what it says. Nicole looks at hers like it's her next fix, something she craves but will leave her damaged in the end. I can't imagine Mom had very nice parting words for her, given the hell she's put us through over the years. Regardless, I don't think her envelope will stay sealed for very long. But mine. I'm not sure I'll ever open it. I'm not even sure if I want to know what's inside. Final words make things final.

"Now what?" Nicole asks, never taking her eyes off her envelope. She presses the tips of her fingers together, some pressure to satisfy the urge to tamper with it.

I stand, sliding the key and Post-it Note into the front pocket of my jeans. I fold the envelope and slip it into my back pocket. "We do what Mom wanted."

NINE

NICOLE

Beth places a cardboard box labeled *Memories* on the living room floor beside me. I'm surrounded by my parents' belongings—boxes and totes strewn around, stacked three or four high. Mom kept them all these years, so they must have meant something. The ceiling creaks. Michael's up in the attic, carrying everything to the pull-down ladder that feeds into the hallway. He hands them to Beth, and she brings them to the living room. It's an assembly line of sorts, Beth's idea, thanks to working in a factory her entire adulthood. If I had two working arms, I'd be of more use, but instead I've been tasked with sorting everything into piles—garbage, donate, sell, and keep. I'm pretty sure my cast is more of a nuisance than it is helpful as I don't feel any pain in my arm. It's just my ribs and face that throb, but that wouldn't stop me from carrying boxes if I could. I'm used to feeling uncomfortable, so it doesn't faze me.

I open the *Memories* box and cough on a cloud of dust that swirls in the air. That's how memories are—dormant dust waiting to be stirred up. Inside are dozens of VHS tapes neatly stacked on their ends. Each one labeled with dates and short descriptions, like *Michael's 16th birthday*, *Christmas 1999*, and *Kids playing outside Summer of 1990*. The handwriting is neat and precise, just the way it is on our envelopes. My mother clearly cherished the memories on these tapes. I flip one over in my hand, running my fingers along the hard plastic edge. These little black rect-angles hold worlds I once lived in. I so badly wish I could jump inside one of them and take up residence, return to a time when I was whole.

I read through the labels, trying to conjure the memories on my own. Some are long gone. Some are crystal clear. But most are fuzzy, like when you wake up from a dream and can remember only fragments of it. I want to remember more. My eyes flick to the television in the corner of the room, where a dual VHS/DVD player sits on the shelf beneath it. A tingle runs through my hands, spreading to the tips of my fingers.

"Hurry up, Michael," Beth yells from the hallway. "You're taking forever."

"You're not the one up in this nasty attic, Beth. There's barely a floor up here, mostly ceiling beams to navigate." His voice carries through the house.

"How many more boxes?" she calls out.

Michael doesn't respond right away. But I hear his footsteps shuf-fle along the ceiling.

"How many?" Beth asks again. The ladder creaks, and I know she's scrambling up to see for herself. She's always been impatient.

"Here," he roars. "There's one more tote and a Christmas tree with outdoor decorations."

The ladder creaks again and a moment later Beth plops a box la-beled *Dad* on the floor. She lets out a huff while her eyes scan over the living room. It's an overwhelming sight, to say the least.

"What's all that?" Beth asks, gesturing to the tapes.

Right now, she looks so much like Mom. I'm taken back to when I was young, peering up at our mother, thinking she had the answers to all the questions in the world. We all look at our parents that way, until we don't. My dad could do no wrong, and then he ran out on us. I never thought he'd be the type to do that. I avert my eyes, staring back at the boxes in front of me before any tears escape.

"Home video tapes," I say.

Beth kneels and flips through a few, sliding them in and out of their flimsy cardboard sleeves. The inner reels rattle within the cassettes. She runs a finger along a tape labeled *Summer '99*. Beth would have been sixteen, I fifteen, and Michael thirteen. I don't remember much about that summer, but I do know that everything changed after it, only I don't know why.

"Seems so long ago," Beth says, staring at the tape.

"Yeah, a lifetime."

Heavy boots clomp down the hallway, and Michael emerges, carrying a tote. The old pair of Red Wing lace-up work boots he's wearing belong to Dad. I haven't seen them in years. They immediately conjure up a memory from my childhood: Dad coming home from work after a long day at the factory, plopping down in his recliner, feet kicked up. Beth and I would race to unlace his boots and remove them. Whoever was the fastest was declared the winner. She won most of the time. Dad always made chores and small tasks into games. I think he was trying to teach us that no matter how bad life was, it could still be fun. Maybe that was why he left us. He couldn't find the fun anymore.

"Was that fast enough for you, Queen Beth?" Michael asks in a teasing voice, as he walks into the room. He sets a bin labeled *Journals* on the floor and dusts off his hands.

Beth repeats his taunt right back to him, in a mocking voice. Michael cracks a smile and takes a few steps toward us. "Whatcha got there?"

She holds up the three tapes she plucked from the box. "Our home VHS tapes. Let's watch one. You pick, Michael. Summer '99, Nicole's birth, or Easter '96?"

"I'm vetoing my birth. I don't feel like watching the biggest regret of my life," I say with a laugh.

Beth chuckles and places that tape back in the box. "Okay, Michael. Summer '99 or Easter '96?"

He rubs his brow and bends over, opening up another box. "Let's just keep working."

"Oh, come on." I throw my nonbroken arm up in the air. "Just one tape."

Michael pulls children's clothes from a box and tosses them into a black garbage bag. "I really don't want to," he says.

"Why?" I ask.

He lets out a huff, directing his attention to me. "Digging up the past is depressing."

"We're not digging it up. We're revisiting it." I jump to my feet and swipe the *Summer '99* tape from Beth.

"Fine. Just one. We've got a lot more work to do," Michael says, picking up the TV remote.

I smile at him and carefully slide the tape from the box.

My hand shakes, the tape hovering right in front of the VCR. Maybe Michael's right, it's depressing to revisit the past and won't do any of us any good. It can't change anything. Or maybe it's just what we need. A new perspective. Closure, as they say, to a life we'll never live again. I push the tape into the VCR. It clicks, disappears inside, and then makes a humming sound while it settles into place. The TV screen flicks from black to static. And then it's 1999 and fifteen-year-old me is onscreen.

TEN
LAURA

1999

The camcorder sits heavily on my shoulder. It weighs nearly twenty pounds, but the burden is worth it because I want to capture everything I can. After losing my sister and my father before the age of fifteen, I know that no matter how powerful the brain is, it still forgets things. My kids hate it, always groaning at me to put away the camcorder, to stop taking photos. But one day they'll appreciate the time and effort I put into preserving our family memories. Whatever I don't capture through video and photos, I write about in journals, key points of each day that I cherish and even those I don't—it's important to remember both the good and the bad because together they keep us grateful and grounded.

I readjust the camcorder and flick my long hair over my shoulder to stop it from being pulled. You'd think they could make these things smaller. Maybe one day, they'll be as small as my hand. I press Record and walk slowly into the living room, panning from wall to wall so I can remember what it looks like. The white walls are adorned with family photos and the hanging shelves are filled with knickknacks I've picked up at resale shops and rummage sales. A tube television sits on a stand in the corner, playing a rerun of *The Fresh Prince of Bel-Air*. The drapes, couch, and chair are floral printed. I've always loved flowers. There's something special about their existence. They're how we greet the ones we love and say goodbye to the ones we've lost.

Nicole is seated on the couch dressed in wide-leg black jeans and a dragon graphic tee. She's listening to music on her Sony Discman with a pair of over-the-ear headphones. She saved up her allowance for months to buy that portable music machine. Her shoulder-length hair is crimped, her lids are covered in a heavy blue eye shadow, and her brows are overplucked. She's told me many times that it's style, and I can't really argue with her. I was born in the bra-burning decade, then sported bell-bottoms, crochet tops, and peasant blouses during my teen years.

"Nicole," I say. She doesn't respond because she's absorbed in her notebook, writing down poems and thoughts. She got that from me. There are some things we can't say out loud, and it's just easier to write them down. I call her name again, but her music is far too noisy. I've told her a hundred times she's going to blow her eardrums out, but it falls on deaf ears—perhaps my warning is already too late. Her head snaps up when she spots me in her peripheral view turning off the tele-vision she's not watching anyway. I'm constantly having to remind my kids that money doesn't grow on trees. She rolls her eyes so much I think they might pop out of her head.

"Mom, I was watching that," Nicole groans.

"Higher" by Creed blares from her headphones as she slips them off and clicks pause on her Discman. I know the song by heart at this point because she's listened to it so often. Her personality has always been all or nothing, which worries me sometimes. Zero or a hundred makes the middle, where everyday life exists, feel like a slump.

"Didn't look like it," I say, steadying the camcorder and keeping her in frame. "Now, how was your last day of freshman year?"

"Great," she says in a monotone voice.

I tightly smile.

"Because it's over," she adds with a smirk.

I pull my eye from the viewfinder and give her a disapproving look. "One day, you're gonna regret wishing your life away."

She leans back into the cushion, placing the palms of her hands on the back of her head, elbows propped up. "As if. When I'm a famous writer living in New York City, I'll be glad I wished high school away."

I want to tell her to have a backup plan, to be more realistic. But I know there's a fine line between keeping your children grounded and killing their dreams, so I smile a little wider instead. My own mother encouraged practicality to a fault. Get a job. Get married. Have kids. There was no room left in her plan for flights of fancy. I don't regret my decisions or the life I've made, though if I could go back, I'd dream a little more. But I still would like Nicole to understand how fast life passes, even if you're not wishing it away. That realization only sets in later in life, or in some cases, when it's cut short. When the seemingly impossible becomes the possible. It came early for me, twelve to be exact, when my sister and my father were ripped from this earth, killed by a drunk driver. My life was never the same after that. *I* was never the same after that.

Placing my eye back in the viewfinder, I center it on her. "Read me something you wrote today, Nicole."

Her cheeks flush. "Mom, no," she says.

"How are you going to be a writer if you don't want anyone to hear your words?"

She sighs, rolls her eyes again, and flips through a couple pages in her notebook. "Fine, just a small part," she says, looking up at me. She doesn't smile but her eyes do, and I'll take that. She buries her nose back in her journal and clears her throat.

"If you're afraid of falling, you'll never fly.
If you're afraid of failing, you'll never try.
If you're afraid of dying, you'll never truly be alive."

Closing up her journal, she shrugs. "It's rough. Not really that good."

"You don't need to be first, honey," I say, staring directly at her. I want my daughter to really hear me, to remember these words one day when she's stopped believing in herself. That day will come. It comes for all of us. And I want her to have the tools to get past that day and any other day like it.

Her brow furrows. "First?"

"The first to stand in your way. Other people are going to tell you no. They're going to tell you that you can't do something, you're not good enough, you're not worthy. You don't need to do that. Don't add to the noise. Because that's all it is . . . noise. You be a voice, a voice for yourself."

"Have you been reading those *Chicken Soup for the Soul* books, Mom?" Nicole teases.

She laughs but I see the seriousness in her eyes, so I hope my words stay with her. I'm not sure they will though. At fifteen, she sees me mostly as a buzzkill. I'm her drill instructor, her boss, an impediment to freedom, and a barrier to the life she wants to live. Everything cool, I am the opposite. This dynamic is a rite of passage for parents of teenagers. One day, she'll grow out of it. When that day comes, I might even miss her sass.

The sound of a door closing grabs my attention, and I aim the camcorder toward the kitchen. My oldest, Beth, rounds the corner. She stops and picks up two Blockbuster VHS rentals from the kitchen table and eyes them. Her hair is pulled back in a high ponytail and she's dressed in a pair of Soffe shorts and an oversized Backstreet Boys T-shirt. Her cheeks are flushed, and she's gasping, still catching her breath.

"What'd you rent?" she asks, holding them up.

"*Saving Private Ryan* and *A Night at the Roxbury*. Your dad's been wanting to see that first one, and I figured you kids would like that Roxbury one. It's a comedy," I say.

She nods and places them back on the table, and then fills a cup with water at the sink.

"I wish you would have rented *Psycho*," Nicole groans.

I pan the camcorder back to her. "They didn't have any more VHS rentals, only DVDs."

"Why don't we just get a DVD player then?"

"Because they're hundreds of dollars, and your father's convinced they're just a fad," I say.

"Yeah, but he also thought CDs were a fad, and he was wrong about that." Nicole gestures to her Sony Discman.

"Regardless, we can't afford it."

Beth carries in a half-full glass of water and plops down in the floral-patterned chair across from the couch, swinging her legs over the arm.

"Where have you been?" Nicole squints at her sister.

"On a run with Lucas."

"Why does Beth get to have a boyfriend and I don't?" Nicole asks.

Before I can answer, Beth quips, "Because you can't get one, loser." She laughs and gulps her water.

"How rude." Nicole shoots a glare at her sister.

I take a couple of steps back, so I can fit them both in the frame. "Beth, be nice. Nicole, you know the rules. No dating until you're sixteen."

Nicole crosses her arms in front of her chest. "Seems pretty arbitrary to me."

I've had this same conversation with her a dozen times, but she's too keen on growing up. I wish she'd learn to slow down. Because one day, she'll be my age, wishing for it back.

"You have your whole life to date, Nicole. Don't rush growing up because you can't go backward, only forward," I say.

"Yeah, and it's not like anyone is even interested in you," Beth teases.

"I said be nice," I warn, pursing my lips together.

"I can't be both nice and honest, Mom." My oldest rolls her eyes. "Would you rather me lie to her?"

I give Beth a stern look, and she straightens up in her seat. Nicole sticks her tongue out and immediately retracts it into her mouth when my eyes land on her. She acts nonchalant by fiddling with the black rubber band bracelets on her wrist.

There's a knock at the front door, interrupting their spat. Neither of my girls jump up to answer it, so I round the corner from the living room into the kitchen. Christie Roberts stands on the porch, hands cupped around her big brown eyes, peering in through the screen. She's around Beth's age and lives a couple streets over.

"Hey, Christie," I say, pushing open the door. "Smile for the camera."

She takes several steps back, delivers a crooked smile, and waves at the camcorder. "Hi, Mrs. Thomas." Her dark hair is greasy and un-combed, stopping right at her chin.

I return her smile and ask, "Whatcha up to?"

Christie rocks back on her heels, and I notice she's not wearing any shoes. She never does in the spring or summer. "I just wanted to see if Beth could come out and play?" Her smile doesn't falter. A camera hangs from a strap around her neck and a book bag is slung over her shoulders.

"Ummm, let me see what she's up to. I'll be right back."

She nods. The screen door closes behind me as I reenter the house, walking back into the living room.

"Christie's here," I say.

Beth shakes her head and whispers, "No, tell her I'm not here."

"Be nice," I whisper back. "Why don't you go hang out with her for a little bit?"

"No way. She followed me on my run, Mom."

"She just wants a friend." I keep my voice low.

Beth is adamant, shaking her head back and forth. "No, then you go be her friend," she says, slumping in her chair.

I look over at Nicole, hoping she'll offer to hang out with Christie or encourage her sister to, but her headphones are back over her ears, and she's writing in her notebook.

I sigh, accepting Beth's decision and feeling bad for Christie. I make my way back to the kitchen and push open the screen door again to find her waiting, still smiling. "Sorry, Christie. Beth just got back from a run, so she's going to shower, and we have plans as a family after that. But maybe tomorrow?" I say.

She nods. "Yeah, sure. I'll come back tomorrow." Her smile remains but it's strained now.

"Okay. Have a good night, Christie."

"You too, Mrs. Thomas," she says, turning on her foot. Her shoulders slump, and her head hangs forward as she walks up the driveway.

When I reenter the living room, Beth sits up straight in her chair. "Is she gone?"

I nod. "Yeah, but she'll be back tomorrow. You should be nice to Christie. It costs nothing to be kind."

Beth groans and flicks her head back dramatically. "Just my reputation."

Nicole notices her sister's displeasure and pulls her headphones off. "What's your problem?"

"Mom's forcing me to do things I don't want to do," Beth chides.

"What else is new?" Nicole rolls her eyes, teasing me.

The screen door slaps against the frame, interrupting the conversation. Shoes hit the wall with a thud as each one is kicked off. All of a sudden, my youngest child's arms are wrapped around my waist. I lean down, breathing him in. It's these moments I'll cherish forever.

"Mikey, how was school?" I ask. He pulls away and takes a couple of steps back, so I can get him in frame. He's tall for his age and lanky, sporting a bowl haircut his father gave him. I remind myself to take him to a salon next time.

"Da bomb! We had an ice cream party and our class played dodgeball against the eighth graders. Totally beat them too. Bunch of weaklings." He smiles wide.

"Hey now. No need to be a sore winner," I say.

"It's better than being a loser," Nicole chimes in.

I give her a disapproving look.

"You'd know because you are one," Beth says to Nicole.

"Mom!" Nicole whines.

I tell them to be nice to one another. Michael plops down next to Nicole on the couch. She ruffles his hair, and he pushes her playfully.

"Since it's the last day of school, your father and I are going to order in pizza tonight to celebrate." I smile.

Michael cheers, declaring he wants pepperoni.

"I don't eat meat," Nicole says.

"Since when?" Beth asks.

I have the same question because she ate the beef goulash I made yesterday, and she brought a ham and cheese sandwich to school today.

"It's a recent decision," Nicole says.

Another phase for my all-or-nothing girl. "I'll order a cheese pizza too," I say to appease her.

"I want sausage," Beth says.

"All right, one cheese, one sausage, one pepperoni, and one supreme for your dad."

I smile while mulling over the numbers in my head. I already know it's more than I budgeted for but figure I can lighten up groceries for the next two weeks to cover it. With Beth being a junior, there's only one more last day of school with all three of them together. And eventually, there won't be any more last school days. I know my children's futures are bright, but I want to live in the now—even if it is dimly lit, and we're barely scraping by. Because I know *now* is guaranteed, but tomorrow may never come.

ELEVEN

NICOLE

The television screen becomes white static and the younger versions of me, Beth, and Michael disappear. Mom's voice is back where it belongs . . . in the past. I glance over at Beth. Fat tears escape the corners of her eyes. She swipes them away with the back of her hand, but I've already seen them. The color in Michael's face has drained like he's seen a ghost. I guess we all have. Ghosts of the people we once were. He was right. This is depressing. Hearing Mom's voice again when she's no longer here feels wrong. Glimpsing at the past feels unnatural as though we're not supposed to be able to. It's like looking in a mirror, but I'm not the other person staring back. That version of myself no longer exists. I swallow hard, forcing the lump of grief in my throat back down where it belongs.

No one says anything. The only sound comes from the hum of the VCR as the tape continues. I get up and walk toward the television to eject it. Suddenly, the screen is black and the date in the bottom corner reads June 15, 1999. It feels significant, but I can't remember why it might be. I scoot away from the television, keeping my eyes glued to it. There's an outline of trees and a full moon illuminating the sky. An owl hoots from somewhere in the branches. The camcorder is unsteady as it scans the tree line.

"Where are you, little owl?" Mom says offscreen.

I grab the remote and crank up the volume. The speaker on the TV emits the sound of buzzing cicadas and squeaking bats. The camcorder zooms in slowly and scans the tree line again. Dark, thick branches reach in all directions like outstretched hands. Footsteps pound in the distance, growing louder. The camcorder swivels quickly to the right, going in and out of focus. All of a sudden, Dad's face fills the screen. He's panicked and gasping for air.

"Jesus, Brian! You scared the hell out of me," Mom huffs. The lens zooms out again, so Dad is in the frame from his waist up.

His hand grips a flashlight and, like the video camera, it's also shaky. He's large and burly with a full beard. Red is smeared across his white T-shirt, right around his barrel-sized chest. His eyes are wide and the whites of them glow in the moonlight. I've never seen him look so scared before.

"Laura, I need your help now," he says, out of breath.

"What? What is it?" Mom's voice matches his panic.

"Shut that off," he yells as he turns and heads in the direction he just came from.

Several buttons click as Mom removes the camcorder from her shoulder. It's still recording though. The picture onscreen is a shaky blur of trees, grass, and shadows. The camera is pointed at Mom's white sneakers as they travel down the concrete steps that cut through the valley. They pass the cabin and the fire pit, through the green pasture, and the wooded area at the bottom of the property. She follows Dad along the bank of the creek. There's a splash, and Mom stops abruptly. The camcorder swivels toward the direction of the sound. A fish leaps in the air from the creek and splashes back into the water. She lets out a sigh.

"Laura, this way," Dad says.

He's in frame again, ten yards ahead. Mom follows the path of the creek and stops a few feet behind Dad under the bridge of Highway X. He scans his flashlight along the ground. The camcorder's focus goes in and out as it tries to pick up on something. Then, all of a sudden, the picture becomes clear. A body. Head cocked to the right. Lips blue and bloated. Skin pale as freshly fallen snow. Damp blond hair streaked with mud and blood. Wet clothes, a pair of blue jean shorts and a Britney Spears T-shirt, hug her small body.

Mom screams. The light disappears. The screen is black again, like a nightmare you can't wake yourself up from and all you can see is the back of your eyelids.

Dad shushes her, telling her to stay calm, but even he isn't calm.

"Oh my God!" Mom cries out. The camcorder hits the ground. The image of the young girl is sideways, taking her in from a new angle. Her blue eyes are clouded like they've been submerged in milk, two Hope Diamonds, fluttering to the bottom of the sea, lost forever. They stare into the lens of the camera and it's as though she's looking directly at me, calling out for help, twenty-three years too late—like the light of a star that's already exploded, finally reaching our eyes.

"What happened?" Mom's voice is a mix of fear, anger, and sadness.

"It was an accident," Dad explains, but he doesn't sound convinced.

"We need to call the police," she cries.

Every muscle in my body is taught, tightened as much as the membrane pulled over a drum. My breaths are shallow, almost nonexistent. I'm sure they're barely registering with my lungs.

"No, we can't," Dad says firmly.

"What? Why? You said it was an accident, Brian."

"They won't see it that way."

There's a long pause between the two of them. And the only sound is the buzzing cicadas, the squeaking bats, and water moving through the twisted creek.

"Tell me what happened," Mom says. Although she's normally calm, the way her tone rises and falls tells a different story.

"The less you know, the better."

There's shuffling offscreen. Shoes trudging through mud. The camcorder is suspended, aimed up at the night sky. The little dead girl disappears and a moment later Dad is onscreen. It's a close-up of him, as he's holding the video camera.

"Jesus, Laura. This thing is still on. How do you erase it?"

"Hit the Rewind button. I'll have to record over it," Mom says in a panic.

Tears cling to his eyes, but they don't escape. There's a look of confusion on his face as he fiddles with the device, and then the screen goes black.

June 15, 1999, is in the past again.

But I know it won't stay there.

TWELVE
BETH

A burst of air escapes my mouth as I try to catch my breath, reeling from what I just witnessed. I don't think I breathed at all while the tape played. *It's real*, I keep telling myself, although my mind is rejecting that notion, instead registering the video as fiction, as though I'd just watched a movie. But I know it's real. Because I know the girl in the video. The little dead girl. The one that's been missing for more than half of my life.

Her name is Emma Harper. Well, I guess it *was* Emma Harper. She was twelve when she disappeared. She was our next-door neighbor, the younger sister of my high school sweetheart, Lucas. Everyone looked for her when she went missing the summer of 1999. We searched high and low for days, weeks, months. Even then, her family didn't give up. In those early days, when she'd first gone, we combed the local nature trail, an abandoned railroad track without the tracks that runs six miles between the Grove and Clinton. We searched nearby towns: Darien, Delavan, Sharon, Elkhorn, all of them. Flyers with her sixth-grade class picture were plastered on trees, telephone poles, and front windows of local businesses. But Emma was never found. And no one knew what happened to her . . . I can barely finish the thought. No one knew what happened to Emma Harper, except my parents.

On the day she went missing, there was a carnival at the park in the center of town. They called it Groovin' in the Grove. My mom was the event's lead organizer. She wanted Allen's Grove to shine because that was how she saw our town, like coal before it's compressed and heated enough to form a diamond. There were games, vendors, food fried and double fried, farm animals, even a few janky carnival rides. The *Dukes of Hazzard*-themed bar called Boar's Nest that sits kitty-corner to the park, across Highway X, had live local bands and drinks flowing all day for the adults. It was the biggest event this little town had ever seen.

Groovin' in the Grove was a fundraiser for the park, so they could purchase playground equipment, picnic tables, and a shade shelter as well as provide ongoing maintenance. People from surrounding towns showed up, at least five hundred, tripling the size of our town's population. And sometime that day, June 15, 1999, Emma went missing. The police figured some creep slipped through the crowd, and with all the noise and excitement, they were able to kidnap a child in plain sight. No one noticed. It wasn't the first time it's happened, and it certainly wasn't the last. But it was the first time it had happened here, and it left a stain on the community that could never be removed.

The Grove was a place where children could ride their bikes past dark, play ghost in the graveyard in the woods, hike the nature trail, swim the crayfish-and-leech-infested creek, and even trespass on farmland without the worry of farmers shooting at them. Parents expected their children to return home in one piece. Because children didn't go missing in a place like Allen's Grove . . . until one did.

I remember everything changed after that day, not only for the town but for our family. I'd always believed Emma's disappearance hit too close to home, just across the street, or that my mother blamed herself for planning the whole event. I never in a million years would have thought my parents had anything to do with it. After all, they searched for her, alongside Nicole, Michael, and me. Shoulder to shoulder, we all walked the nature trail, the fields, and the wood. We hung missing person posters and made phone calls. We did everything we could. I remember their reassurances: "Don't worry, we'll find her." The very thought of what they'd said sends a shiver down my spine. Mom even donated part of the fundraising money from the event to Emma's family. The park got its swing set, monkey bars, slide, shade shelter, picnic tables, basketball court, and several flower beds. But the Harper family never got Emma back, and they never found out what happened to her.

There they are again . . . those words . . . right at the forefront of my mind.

Your father. He didn't disappear. Don't trust.

Disappear . . . That sticks out even more now. Maybe my mom wasn't offering hope that our father would return. Maybe it was a warning. Did Dad do something to Emma? Had he lied to Mom about it being an accident? Is that why she left me with those cryptic final words?

My eyes flick to Nicole. She's frozen, hand on the remote, shoulders tense, eyes wide. I saw her like this once, the first time she overdosed. But she's not dying, I remind myself. Still, this is life-altering. How she sees the world is perishing. Michael is frozen too. Nothing on him moves, not even a blink or a twitch of an eyebrow. But there's a sheen to his eyes, like he's holding his emotions in, trying to keep them caged.

"That . . . that can't be real. It must be some prank Mom and Dad were playing," Nicole says. "Right?" Her eyes are still wide, but now they're staring right at me.

"Did either of you know about this?" Michael asks. He studies our faces, like he's waiting for one of us to reveal a tell.

I shake my head, unable to utter a single word.

"You think it's real?" Nicole asks.

"Of course, it's real. That's Emma Harper on that tape, and that's the day she disappeared." Michael gestures to the TV.

Even though it's a blank screen, I can still see the image of her lying in the mud, covered in blood. Her lifeless eyes staring into the lens of the camera, while insects crawl over her porcelain skin. How could Mom take this secret to her grave? How could she bring Emma's family casseroles, invite them over for dinners, go on daily walks with Susan to search for her daughter, all the while knowing she was dead?

Nicole stands abruptly. "I don't believe it," she says, pacing the living room. Her footsteps are as heavy as the past.

"You saw it with your own eyes," I finally say, trying to convince myself more so than her.

Michael shakes his head and gets up from his seat, disappearing into the kitchen.

"Mom would never . . ." Nicole's voice cracks and her bottom lip trembles. "And Dad . . ." She doesn't finish that sentence, but I know what she was going to say. Dad would never hurt anyone. But he did. He hurt all of us when he picked up and left.

Michael returns a moment later with three plastic cups stacked on top of one another and the bottle of scotch. He pours more for me and him and less for Nicole, and then passes them out. We each take a gulp before speaking.

"Is that . . . I mean, do you think that's why Dad left?" Nicole's question isn't directed at either of us.

"Maybe he couldn't deal with the guilt anymore," Michael says.

I furrow my brow. "But this happened back in 1999, and he left in 2015. That doesn't make any sense."

Michael's eyes meet mine. "Guilt can eat you slowly or swallow you whole."

He's right about that.

Nicole swigs more than a mouthful of scotch. Some of the liquid slithers out of her lips and dribbles down her chin. She doesn't wipe it away. Either she doesn't notice or doesn't care. "In the video, Dad said it was an accident," she says, pointing at the television.

I lean forward in my chair, clutching the cup with both hands. "If it were an accident, why wouldn't he just call the police?"

"Maybe he thought he'd be held liable because it happened on his property, and he and Mom would lose everything?" Michael offers.

"Or maybe it wasn't an accident, and he just told Mom it was." As soon as the words leave my mouth, I want to suck them back in. I had the thought but saying it out loud feels wrong. Just because Dad walked out on us doesn't make him a murderer. But perhaps I didn't know him after all.

A montage of memories plays out in front of my eyes, a private viewing just for myself. Dad teaching me how to ride a bike. Dad sitting in the bleachers at my track meets. His face painted with my high school colors, blue and yellow, like he was cheering on his Green Bay Packers rather than me run 'round and 'round the track. Dad helping me reel in a bass from the creek. Dad crying with me when I blew my knee out senior year due to overtraining and malnourishment. Dad telling me just because my future wasn't going to include a full-ride scholarship anymore, that didn't mean it wasn't going to be bright. Dad walking me down the aisle. Dad holding his granddaughter. And then Dad . . . standing over the body of Emma Harper.

I shake the memories away and focus on my surroundings, trying to ground myself in the present rather than be overtaken by the past. My parents' belongings are scattered all over the floor. I wonder if any of them hold clues about what really happened the night of June 15, 1999. And then there are my siblings, who are more like strangers to me than family. Michael sits on the couch, massaging his forehead. Nicole fidgets with her fingers and continues to pace.

She stops suddenly and snaps her head in my direction. "Where's Emma's body now?"

I hadn't thought of that. What could they have possibly done with it? We all look at one another, eyes darting back and forth.

"Wherever it is, it must be long gone, since no one ever found her," Michael says. "Maybe they buried it, or weighted it and sent it down the creek, or maybe they cut it up and threw her away one piece at a time."

"What the fuck is wrong with you, Michael?" I practically spit.

He throws a hand up defensively. "What? Nicole's the one that asked the question."

"Yeah, but you're so crass. Do you really think Mom and Dad would dismember a child's body?" I narrow my eyes.

"I don't know, Beth. Clearly, they did something with it," he huffs.

We all exhale like we're releasing everything we thought we knew.

"What do we do now?" Nicole asks.

I don't answer because I really don't know. On one hand, I think the Harper family deserves to know what happened to Emma. But on the other, will it do them any good? Lucas moved away after high school, and his father died in a hunting accident shortly thereafter. Emma's mother, Susan, still lives in the house across the street. Her health has been declining for years. I guess it's hard to stay healthy when you have a broken heart. Mom was close with Susan, and I think knowing what Mom kept from her all these years would kill her. So maybe the truth would do more harm than good at this point.

A knock at the front door startles us, three knocks to be exact. They're quick and loud, the urgency reverberating through the door. My shoulders practically collide with my ears. Nicole freezes in place, staring wildly at the kitchen. Michael swallows hard, his Adam's apple rocking up and down, like a snake that's consumed too large of prey.

Mom and Dad may have buried a body, but they didn't bury the past . . . and now, it's clearly caught up with us.

THIRTEEN
BETH

My hand moves to the door handle almost in slow motion, my frame of reference shaky, like an old horror film being shot in first person. If it were a movie, surely the ghost of Emma Harper would be on the other side of the door, or someone who knows the terrible secret my father ran off with and my mother took to her grave.

"Who is it?" Nicole whispers from the other room.

I shush her and focus on the door, my hand hovering less than an inch away from the knob, cupped, ready to grab, twist, and swing it open. I can see the outline of a person through the four square opaque windows. Our visitor is tall, at least six foot two, with broad shoulders, shifting side to side, seemingly nervous. If they can see me, I'm sure I appear the same way to them . . . nervous. I don't think when I switch on the porch light and swing open the door. Shutting off the brain is sometimes the only way to get past fear.

Moths and tiny insects swarm to the golden light that hangs from the ceiling above his head. My stomach drops then flutters up toward my lungs. My heart races faster than I used to be able to run. And my skin perspires despite the cool night air seeping through the thousands of cut-out aluminum squares on the screen that separates me from him. It's been years, more than years, and he hasn't changed. But I think when you fall in love with a person and never fall out of love, they always look the same as how you first saw them. There's that sharp jawline I always joked could cut through diamond, and those blue eyes that I imagined the ocean looked like up close. He delivers a faint smile, and I think I return one back. But I'm not sure how my face looks to him.

"Hey, Beth," he says.

"Hi, Lucas." My words come out breathy. I clear my throat and shift my stance, unsure of what to say or how to act.

He extends his hand and in it is a loaf of homemade banana bread packaged in Saran wrap.

"I . . ." he stammers. We were once closer than two humans could possibly be, and now we're practically strangers, but there's a familiarity that strings us together, making this encounter all the more complicated. "I heard about your mom. I'm so sorry." The corners of his eyes crinkle, and he drops his chin.

The mention of Mom first makes my heart ache and then is a punch to the gut as I'm shot back to reality, remembering what I just saw on the TV screen. My breathing changes. It's fast and short and uneven, like my mom's final breaths. My eyes fill with tears. I try to breathe through it, blink it away, but I don't think I'll be able to this time. I want to tell him what I just found out about his sister. I want to show him the tape, but I know it'll be like picking a scab, uncovering something that was already in the process of healing. And the video doesn't provide anything substantial. It doesn't tell us where her body is. It just reveals that my father had something to do with her death—whether it was an accident or not—and that my parents knew what happened to Emma Harper. Rather than reporting it, they covered it up. I need to know more before I can tell Lucas, if I ever can.

Finally, I nod several times and retrieve the loaf of bread from him.

"It's my mom's recipe." He shoves his hands into the front pockets of his jeans. It's like he doesn't know what to do with them. "I made it, so if it doesn't taste good, that's on me," Lucas adds, rocking back on his heels. He cracks a half smile but it quickly fades, and I assume that's because of me. I'm sure I have the look of a person being interrogated for a crime they did commit.

"Thanks," is all I manage to say.

When I realize I'm squeezing the soft bread, I loosen my grip, causing it to fall to the ground. I quickly bend down to pick it up. The loaf is dented and crushed where I clutched it too tightly. That's how he and I are—a misshapen thing that was once made with love and molded to perfection. Even the most perfect things crumble under pressure.

"Sorry," I mutter.

"Probably for the best. I may have accidentally used salt when the recipe called for sugar," he jokes, shoving his hands deeper into his pockets.

A laugh escapes me, and it feels foreign and wrong. I don't deserve the relief.

"How's your mom doing?" I ask.

He blows out his cheeks and glances to the right briefly. "Some days are better than others. That's why I'm back . . . to take care of her. Hearing of Laura's passing really broke her today." He shuffles his feet.

I didn't realize he was back in town. Last I heard, he was married and living in Wausau, a city a few hours north of the Grove. I'm not surprised he and Susan heard about my mom's passing. News travels fast around here and bad news travels even faster. Everyone knew she wasn't doing well and that her days were numbered. Some nosey neighbor must have seen the funeral home come collect her body.

"How are ya holding up?" he adds when I don't say anything.

"I'm okay." I'm not, but that's just what you say.

He delivers a sympathetic look because he knows I'm not okay. He won't pry any further. Even though we haven't spoken in a very long time, at the core we still know each other. But my core isn't the same. It's rotten now—thanks to the sins of my parents. As I look at him, all I can see is his little sister lying dead down by the creek. I avert my gaze, first at my feet and then back at him, no, above his head. I can't look him in the eyes. He'll see right through me.

"Well, I just wanted to stop by and see how you're doing, so I'll leave you to it," Lucas says, rocking back on his heels again.

He starts to turn, and it's then that I feel this strong pull, like we're two magnets drawn to one another. They say you should live life with no regrets, but I've lived a lifetime of them and my biggest one is standing right in front of me.

"Do you want to go for a walk with me tomorrow morning?" I ask before I can even think about what that'll entail.

Lucas stops and looks back at me. He and I used to go for morning runs, but after I blew my knee out, it was never the same. So many parts of ourselves stay raw like that, never fully healing.

The corner of his lip lifts. "Yeah. How about I stop over at seven?"

I nod but don't smile. I can't force my lips up. "That sounds good to me."

"It's a date then." His cheeks flush. "I mean a walk," he says with a nod. "Good night, Beth." He jogs down the porch steps, tossing another glance at me.

I watch him walk down the sidewalk and up our long driveway, waiting to close the door until he's more than halfway up it.

I exhale, hoping the guilt will expire too. But it doesn't. It's still there, sitting in the pit of my stomach like a tumor, festering and growing. I can barely live with myself, and I've only known for an hour. How did Mom live more than twenty years with that terrible secret?

FOURTEEN

NICOLE

I flop the slice of cheese pizza onto my plate. It doesn't taste the way pizza should. It's bland with crust that has the consistency of cardboard. Although the cheese is gooey and greasy, it brings me no joy. My taste buds are barely registering it as food, and I know it has nothing to do with the quality of the pizza. It has to do with the video of Emma Harper. I think everything is going to taste different now.

Michael sits at the other end of the table, chewing on his second slice. Maybe it tastes the same to him. He swigs from a can of PBR after every two bites, so perhaps he's just forcing it down. Beth's eaten one slice but stopped short of the crust. She's never liked the crust—the crunchiest, hardest part of the pizza that offers nothing more than cooked dough. I think that people dislike something for one of two reasons: we truly dislike it, or we dislike it because it gives us an opportunity to value something else more. And when you don't have much in life, there isn't much you're able to detest before you run out of things to, well, detest. So, Beth chose crust. Michael chose this town. And I chose myself.

I sip from a cup half filled with the red wine Beth found in one of the cupboards. It tastes like vinegar, but I don't mind. My veins tingle. They always do now. A needle sliding into one that hasn't collapsed yet would be divine. It would make all my problems go away. One bump would erase the guilt, the pain, the grief. I know Michael and Beth are thinking about the VHS tape, but I wonder how disgusted they would be if they knew what was going through my mind. I need to distract myself before my thoughts lead to action, so I look to Beth.

"So, you're hanging out with Lucas tomorrow morning. Think that's a good idea?" I ask.

"I don't know what good is anymore," she says with a shrug and sips from her glass. It's filled with warm Seagram's. She didn't even add ice, and I'm sure she's just trying to numb the pain.

I shift in my chair, refolding my legs into a pretzel. "Are you going to tell him about the video?"

"I don't know," she says, staring into her glass.

Michael leans back in his chair. "We need to really think about what we're going to do."

Beth's eyes dart to him. "What do you mean?"

"I mean, do we keep Mom and Dad's secret, or do we tell someone?"

"It would give Lucas and Susan closure," Beth says.

I squint at her. "Will it though? Or will it bring them more pain, knowing it wasn't a stranger who killed Emma; it was their neighbors, their friends?"

"Wouldn't you give anything in the world to know what happened to Dad?" she asks.

"If you would have asked me an hour ago, I'd say yes." I lower my head, staring down at my lap. "But after seeing what Mom and Dad did, I'm not so sure I want to know what happened to him."

"Dad said it was an accident on the tape," Beth argues.

Michael rolls his eyes. "Yeah, let's trust the guy that ran out on this family."

"He's still our dad." Her voice comes out meek and unconfident.

"Just because you're a parent doesn't mean you can't do bad things. Ted Bundy had a daughter and so did the BTK killer. I'm sure their children told themselves, *But he's our dad. He could never . . .* Anyone can do anything at any time," I say, staring directly at my sister.

"You're not seriously comparing Dad to two of the most notorious serial killers in the world." She scoffs and shakes her head.

"I'm just saying." I shrug.

Beth bites at her pinky nail, ripping off a sliver of it. She pulls it from her teeth and flicks it away. "I think we should tell Susan. She deserves to know."

"It'll probably kill her," Michael says.

"He's right," I add with a nod.

"But it's the right thing to do," Beth says, though there's very little conviction in her voice.

This is one of those situations where there isn't a right or wrong answer. You just have to pick one and convince yourself later that it was the best decision at that time.

My eyes swing to Michael. "What do you think?"

"I'm not sure because we don't really know what happened."

"We know enough," Beth says. Each word comes out slow and punctuated.

Michael drops his gaze to the beer clutched in his hands. "I think we have to consider the ramifications this would have on us and on Mom and Dad before we make any decisions."

"What do you mean?" Beth's eyes are slits.

"Think about it, Beth. Do you want to be known as the daughter of Brian and Laura Thomas, the couple that may have killed a child and then got rid of the body? If this gets out, you'll never be anything else." Michael swigs his drink.

"I don't care," she says.

"Well, I do." He sets the beer bottle down with a little force. It thuds against the table.

I'm about to agree with Michael, but Beth cuts in. "Oh, screw off, Michael. You'll scurry back to your big home in California, sip your expensive fucking scotch, and go on with your life, never having been affected by this, just like you did before."

He hangs his head. A single tear runs down his cheek. It falls slowly, like a person trudging through land that has never been traversed. It zigzags a little, touches the corner of his lip, then dribbles the rest of the way to his chin, clinging to his jawline, refusing to drop.

"I agree with Michael," I say. "I don't want to be known for that."

"It's a step-up from being a junkie," Beth mutters.

I stand abruptly from my seat, sending the old wooden chair reeling backward. It smacks against the hardwood floor, causing one of the spindles to crack and break into two pieces. "Screw you, Beth. You think you're so great? You work on an assembly line, putting bags of frozen vegetables into boxes. Your own daughter won't even talk to you, so I'd say it would be a step-up for you too."

"Don't you fucking dare talk about my daughter, you crackhead," Beth shouts, pointing her finger at me.

"Enough!" Michael slams his fist against the table, startling the both of us.

Beth's eyes are wide, and her mouth is partially open like she's about to yell at him too, but she doesn't. Michael's tear has disappeared, either fallen onto his shirt and absorbed by the expensive material or evaporated into thin air. I take a deep breath, pick up the broken chair, and retake my seat, leaving the splintered spindle on the floor.

"Fighting with each other isn't going to help. Let's just finish going through everything, and if we find enough to give us an idea of what actually happened to Emma or where her body is, we'll report it. If not, we'll move on with our lives and forget we ever saw that tape," he says with a firm tone.

Beth closes her mouth and purses her lips.

Michael's eyes flick between us. "Deal?"

I nod because that sounds right to me. Why tell anyone when we really don't have much to tell?

Michael looks to Beth, waiting for a response. She chugs the rest of her drink and sets the glass down with force. "Fine," she says reluctantly.

"And if we find nothing, we take it to our graves just like Mom did, right?" he adds, ensuring she agrees and understands.

Beth stares back at him with slightly narrowed eyes. "Okay." The word comes out raspy with very little conviction. I'm not sure I believe her.

She's never stopped loving Lucas, even when she was married, even after all these years, and even though she hadn't seen him in more than a decade before today. I trust Michael though. He'll honor whichever way this goes.

"Good, we're all in agreement then." He nods.

I leave the table and make my way to the living room where the box labeled *Journals* is located. It's one of the few things left specifically to me.

"What are you doing?" Beth calls out.

"If there are any clues as to what happened to Emma Harper, it'll be somewhere in here," I say as I take a seat on the floor and pull open the cardboard box.

She delivers the faintest smile as though she's thanking me for helping her. But I'm not doing this for her. I'm doing it for me.

FIFTEEN
LAURA

JUNE 15, 1999

It's just after noon, and the sun is set high in the sky, shining bright on our little event. Perfect weather for a perfect day. I slip eight one-dollar bills into the cashbox and smile back at a family of four I've never met before. They collect their raffle tickets and make their way around the admission booth to the park.

A hand taps my shoulder. "Great turnout," Susan says, beaming.

Her blond hair stops an inch below her chin, and her blue eyes look like two robin eggs sitting in a nest, waiting to hatch. We've been next-door neighbors since 1990, when she, her husband, and their two children moved into the house across the street. I remember liking Susan right away. She has one of those warm personalities that makes you feel like you're standing directly under sunlight, even when you're not.

I nod and glance out at the park. It's around the size of a football field, located in the center of town, sprinkled with large ash and white oak trees. Today, it's buzzing with people and excitement. The Grove feels like one of those big cities I've seen in movies and TV shows. Hundreds of people from surrounding towns have descended upon our small unincorporated community to attend the Groovin' in the Grove fundraiser.

"Can't believe we pulled it off," I say, looking around, trying to take it all in. There are carnival games, food stands, a rickety roller coaster ride for children, and a Tilt-A-Whirl. A clown inflates balloons, twisting them into swords and poodles for the kids. Brian's voice, amplified by a microphone, cuts through all the noise. He calls out B9, as ten tables full of people all ages focus on their player cards, marking their bingo sheets with dabbers.

"*You* pulled it off." Susan bumps her shoulder against me.

"Couldn't have done it without you."

"I think you could have, but I'll accept the compliment." She laughs, crinkling up her nose.

"Hey, let's get a quick photo," I say, gesturing for her to come closer. I remove the thick strap hanging from my neck. It's attached to a Nikon 28Ti camera, not one we could afford. Brian surprised me with it last Christmas. I told him to take it back, that it was too much, but he claimed to have lost the receipt. I knew he was lying. He's always been a terrible liar. But he was lying for my sake because he knew I'd never spend that kind of money on myself. So, I let him lie to me, and I kept the camera.

"Cheese," I say, holding it out as far as I can from us. We stand next to one another, arms wrapped around each other's shoulders, and smile. The camera clicks and makes a winding noise.

I loop the strap back around my neck, letting the camera hang freely, just above my belly button.

"I want a copy of that," Susan says.

"Of course, I'll make sure to get double prints."

She thanks me, and we turn to observe the park again.

I spot Nicole dressed in a Nirvana tee and jean cutoffs that used to be a nice pair of pants. One of her father's flannel button-downs is tied around her waist. She counts down for the start of a sack race, while a line of children and even some adults stand shoulder to shoulder waiting for her to say *Go*. Their hands clutch the potato sacks, holding them up to their waist, feet and legs snuggled inside. Nicole started the counting at twenty rather than three like we talked about, and people are starting to groan. Finally, she says *Go* and the competitors hop forward.

"Look at Emma!" Susan beams. My eyes find her daughter, wearing a Britney Spears tee and a determined look. She quickly takes the lead, smiling and laughing, while others fall behind or fall to the ground.

"Go, Emma!" Susan cheers.

"She's fast," I say.

"Yeah, I can barely keep up with her most days." Susan chuckles and claps for her daughter.

Christie Roberts gets a burst of momentum and catches up to Emma. She's got five years and over a foot on her, so she has the advantage, but Emma is beyond intent on winning. The two are neck and neck, that is until Christie slips and tumbles face-first into the grass. Emma's blond hair blows in all directions as she crosses the finish line, taking first place. She hops out of her potato sack, and Nicole holds up her arm, declaring Emma the Groovin' in the Grove sack race champion.

I scan the park again, searching for my other two children. Although Michael is at the far end with his back turned toward me, I know it's him. I can spot my children from anywhere, regardless of the distance, even if my eyes were blindfolded. Mothers just know. He's in the fenced-in petting zoo, feeding a baby goat hay pellets. In the far-right corner of the park, a local band kicks off their set with "Chattahoochee" by Alan Jackson. The stage they're performing on was supplied by the local Boar's Nest dive bar. Bartenders serve cold beer from fresh kegs while people swig from their Solo cups, swaying and dancing to the music.

"Mom, Mom!" Emma calls out, running full speed at Susan. "Look what I won." She holds up her hand, showing off a First Place blue ribbon. A mood ring colored orange sits loosely on her slender finger.

"Wow! You gotta display this proudly," Susan says, pinning the ribbon to her daughter's T-shirt.

"We saw you out there." I raise an eyebrow and smile. "You even beat a few teenage boys."

"And they say boys are stronger than girls." Emma giggles and slaps her knee.

"The egg toss is about to start. Are you playing?" Susan points to a group of people halfway across the park, who are in the process of pairing up and filing into two lines.

"Yeah, I'm going to collect all the blue ribbons today," Emma says with a firm nod. She has the confidence of a girl three times her age, and I can already picture her taking on the whole world one day.

"You better get out there and find a partner then," Susan says, giving her a pat on the back.

Emma turns on her heel and bolts toward the egg toss, switching between a casual skip and a full-on sprint.

I scan the park again, looking for my oldest daughter, hoping she hasn't run off with her boyfriend.

"Have you seen Beth or Lucas?" I ask.

"Not since earlier, when we were setting everything up. They should be around here somewhere," she says, flicking her hand.

Susan doesn't worry like I do, and I envy her for that. She hasn't encountered loss like I have, so she can't fathom it. But I know the worst things always happen in an instant, and once you've experienced it, you'll forever be on the lookout, bracing yourself for it to happen again. It's both a blessing and a curse because it forces you to live in the moment while also fearing the next.

Susan places her hand on my shoulder. "Why don't you go and mingle? It's my turn to watch admissions."

"Are you sure?"

"Yeah, go, I'll be fine."

"All right. I won't be long, and I'll bring you back a corn dog," I say.

"A beer would be great too." She laughs, but I know she's serious.

I head deeper into the park, exchanging greetings and smiles with several people from the Grove. Many compliment the event, and I respond the same way to each of them, that I couldn't have done it without all the volunteers, donations, and the others who helped organize the whole thing. A hand taps my shoulder, startling me. I turn to find Nicole.

"Can I hang out with my friends now, Mom?" Her arms are folded across her chest, her way of telling me she's over this. Nicole wasn't one of my willing volunteers, but she agreed when I promised to buy her that new Blink-182 CD she's been wanting.

I scan the park again. Michael isn't near the petting zoo anymore. I spot him lining up for the egg toss game. Brian calls out B4 to a group of bingo players. He adds, "I hope one of you wins B4 the keg taps out." It garners a handful of chuckles. I shake my head and laugh at his cheesy joke.

"Mom!" Nicole groans, stealing my attention.

"Where's your sister?"

"How the heck am I supposed to know? She's probably off getting jiggy with Lucas."

I give her a stern look and let out a heavy sigh, hoping she's yanking my chain and there's no truth to it. Beth is almost seventeen, and I know how teens can be, but I'm just not ready for my little girl to grow up yet.

Scrutinizing the park once more, I finally spot Beth. She's slow dancing with Lucas in front of the stage, while a local band performs "Amazed" by Lonestar. Her hands are draped around his neck and his arms are wrapped around her waist. They sway back and forth to the music, their eyes never leaving one another. It may be young love but that doesn't mean it's not real love. I looked at Brian the same way at her age and still do.

I hold up the camera, placing my eye over the viewfinder, and snap a photo of the two of them and then a few others—an egg splatting against Michael's chest, Brian pulling a ball from the bingo machine, and Nicole grimacing right in front of me.

"Mom, stop being a buzzkill."

I release the camera, allowing it to hang from its strap again, and focus on my wild child.

"So . . . can I hang out with my friends now?"

"Fine, but make sure you're home before dinner, and keep an eye on your brother."

"Yeah, yeah, yeah," she mutters as she runs toward a table full of teens her age. They're dressed similarly to her—grunge, as they call it. I only recognize one of them, a boy named Casey Dunn. He and Nicole have been friends since middle school, and he seems to be a good influence on her. The rest of them I'm not so sure.

"Mom!" Michael whines, stealing my attention. Egg yolk is splashed across his shirt. "Look what they did," he says, gesturing to the mess. There are tears in his eyes, but they don't escape. He's trying not to cry.

"Oh, honey," I say, getting eye level with him and patting his shoulder. "Why don't you go home and change quick? Just throw the dirty shirt in the washing machine, and I'll take care of it later."

"But I'm going to miss the water balloon toss," he groans.

"No, you won't. And bring another shirt just in case," I tease.

He stomps his foot, letting his head fall forward. I place my hand under his chin, lifting it, and promise him cotton candy when he returns. That garners a smile and gets him moving. He takes off across the street and down our road. I can see the mailbox from here, so I keep an eye on him until he reaches the driveway.

"Hey, babe," Brian calls from behind me.

I turn to find him holding two cups of beer and wearing that boyish grin I fell in love with twenty years earlier. Dressed in a white T-shirt and a pair of Wrangler jeans, he closes the distance and leans down, planting a warm kiss on my lips. A swarm of butterflies flap their wings inside my stomach. Brian always has that effect on me.

"I'm proud of you," he whispers.

"Thanks," I say, smiling up at him.

He hands me a beer. The thick foamy head clings to my lip when I take a gulp.

"Need any help?" he asks.

I look past him out at the park. My eyes land on Charles, a tall, gangly man with a horseshoe mustache, long thin hair, and a slight hunchback. He's in his forties and lives on the corner of our street. Not only is he an eyesore but so is his yard, which is filled with run-down vehicles he refuses to get rid of. He stands alone, staring at a group of teen girls who are attempting to create a human pyramid. A beer is clutched in one hand and a lit Marlboro cigarette is in his other, pinched between his pointer finger and thumb.

"Can you just keep an eye on things?" I say to Brian.

By *things*, I mean Charles, but I don't specify.

"Yeah, sure. Where are the kids?" Brian asks.

I tell him Michael ran home to change his shirt, and then I point toward the stage where Beth and Lucas are.

"For crying out loud!" I groan.

My gaze swings to Nicole. "Damn it."

"What?" Brian asks.

His eyes follow my finger first to Beth who is making out with her boyfriend in front of the whole damn town, and then to Nicole, who is seated at a picnic table, sipping a beer. I take a step forward, ready to march over and yell at both of them, but Brian stops me.

"I'll take care of it, Laura."

Letting out a heavy sigh, I throw my hands on my hips. "Those girls are going to send me to an early grave."

"Now you know how your mother felt when you and I were that age and sneaking off, knocking boots, drinking beer down by the nature trail." Brian waggles his eyebrows.

"Oh, stop. We weren't that bad."

He kisses my forehead and whispers, "I remember you being pretty bad."

I giggle and smack my hand playfully against his chest. For a moment, it feels like we're teenagers again. But I like what we have now more—the deep connection threaded through decades, children, a home, and a life we've built together. I wouldn't give it up for the world.

"All right, time to put my stern father face on," he says, forcing his expression to turn serious. Brian plods toward Nicole like he's on a mission. He throws a silly look over his shoulder, and I can't help but laugh.

"Here, Mom!" Michael yells.

Just as I turn around, a balled-up shirt is hurling in my direction, but I catch it before it hits my face.

"What's this?"

"My extra shirt because you think I'm going to drop the water balloon too." He rolls his eyes.

"I don't think that, Michael. It's just better to be prepared," I say, unfolding the shirt and hanging it over my shoulder.

"Whatever." He shrugs and runs away, heading toward the water balloon toss.

Observing the park again, my eyes stop on Charles. He flicks his cigarette butt and steps on it with his old dirty work boot, grinding it into the ground. The flapping butterflies are gone from my stomach, the ones that Brian always conjures up. In their place is a sinking feeling, a warning that something bad is about to happen. I know this because I've felt it before . . .

SIXTEEN
BETH

The house is eerily quiet as I slide out of bed and slip into a hoodie and a pair of sweatpants. I don't think I slept more than a few hours last night. And even when I did, I dreamed of Mom and Dad, and those dreams quickly morphed into nightmares I couldn't wake from. The white envelope on the nightstand catches my eye, the one with my name scrawled across it in Mom's handwriting. I want to open it, find out what she had to say, but I can't. The lawyer's words return to me, *You should always respect the wishes of the dead.* And so, I will. We'll spread her ashes around the property the day after tomorrow, and I'll read it then.

The silver key sits beside the envelope, glinting when the light from the bedside table lamp catches it. There were no rules or last wishes surrounding the lockbox. I could open that at any time but I'm afraid of what I'll find. I'm worried, too, about keeping our family's dark secret. It feels a little easier today, which is concerning. Yesterday I thought I'd spew it all over the place like projectile vomit. Today it's more like heartburn, crawling up my esophagus. Maybe tomorrow it'll sit in my stomach, heavy, like overprocessed food that refuses to be digested.

The front door slams, startling me, and then it's quiet again. I'm sure it's Michael leaving to run errands or to get some work done at a café. I heard Nicole come out of her room sometime in the middle of the night.

She rifled through some boxes and cupboards in the kitchen. I'm not sure what she was searching for, but hopefully she didn't steal anything.

I retrieve the key from the bedside table, holding it in front of my eyes, examining it closely, and considering what to do with it. When I can't decide, I slide it between the mattress and the box spring, hiding it not only from myself but also from my siblings. You can never be too careful. It was something my mother used to say, though I'm beginning to think she hadn't followed her own advice.

Out in the kitchen, I pour myself a cup of coffee. Michael made it and, once again, it's too strong, coating my tongue like a thick oil. I don't how he could possibly enjoy it. I glance at the clock on the wall, noting the time. Lucas will be here soon, and I'm both looking forward to it and dreading it. I want to be around him, but I don't know if I can be, not really. Physically, yes. Mentally, I am somewhere else entirely, and I'm not sure I'll ever get back to . . . here.

The rising sun seeps through the window in the living room, bathing the stacks of boxes with a warm glow. They're spread out all over the floor, some empty, some open, some still sealed. We got through about a third of them, but none of the contents gave us any further insight as to what happened the night of June 15, 1999—except *that* tape. It sits on top of the VHS/DVD player, exposed and out in the open. Anyone could walk in, pop it into the player, and see a buried truth. I consider hiding it or stowing it away, but I don't have the energy to hide anything else, and maybe I want someone to see it. This secret feels almost too heavy for the three of us to shoulder.

Last night I watched that tape twelve times, searching for a clue, something to tell me what happened before Dad led Mom to Emma's body or what may have occurred after the recording stopped. I thought the more I watched, the more I would be desensitized to it. But I wasn't. Each viewing shocked and rattled me more than the last. I guess there are some things you can't get used to. I noticed something different each time I watched it. Dad's eyes were bloodshot like he had been crying or maybe it was from too much drinking that night. He was never much of a drinker though, a couple beers here or there. Mom's breathing was shallow and uncontrolled. It could have been from running from the house down to the creek or she might have been in the midst of a panic attack. And Emma's hair was caked in blood. Some of it was dry and some of it was wet as though it was still pooling from her head.

Knuckles rap softly against the screen door, and I meet Lucas at the threshold. He's wearing a zip-up hoodie, a baseball cap, and a pair of faded blue jeans. In each hand is a thermos, one purple, one blue. They're the same ones we used when we were teens. His smile reaches his eyes, crinkling the corners of them.

"Morning," Lucas says. His voice is clear, not raspy, so I know he's been up for a while.

He extends the purple thermos to me. It's cold. He remembered. I prefer my coffee iced, but I never drink it that way anymore. Too much work. Too much planning. Too many ice cubes to freeze. I involuntarily smile.

"Cold and black," he adds.

"Just like my heart."

We both laugh . . . for old time's sake.

"Shall we?" he asks, gesturing.

I nod and together we walk side by side down the porch steps and up the driveway. The air is cool and damp, and the sky is a gray blanket, the sun seeping through its weakest seams. Our steps are in stride, as though they never went out of sync. At the top of the driveway, I briefly look across the street where his childhood home sits. Only it's no longer a home. It's a house. A home has joy, but they were robbed of theirs back in 1999.

"So," Lucas says with a quick glance at me. He tips back his thermos. He used to take his coffee hot with two sugars, and I wonder if he still does. Or maybe he drinks it the same way his wife does. I wonder where she is. Perhaps at their home, waiting for him to return.

"So," I say.

There are only three houses on this road. Ours, the Harpers', and Charles Gallagher's. Ever since my dad disappeared, I got the feeling this dead-end street was cursed, given what happened to each family that lived on it. At the stop sign, Lucas takes a sharp right. He's clearly avoiding the park. His jaw clenches and doesn't relax until we turn left on another road, leaving the park behind us.

The Grove is quiet. Even the birds don't sing and chirp today. Houses in this town are, for the most part, modest-sized. Many are ranch style with large yards and tall trees sprinkled throughout. It's like any other unincorporated community you couldn't find on a map. It's just a place you're either born in or you stumble upon and wonder, *Who could live here?* as you pass through.

"Is your wife joining you?" I ask. It comes out meek and awkward, and I immediately regret the question. I remember seeing his wedding photos on my Facebook feed, and although they were beautiful, I cried over them. I mourned a future he and I could have had if things happened otherwise, and then I deleted my account. I didn't have much to share with the world anyway and seeing others happy just made me sadder.

He looks over at me, gauging my expression. "No, we divorced two years ago." His face remains neutral like he's neither happy nor sad about it.

"I'm sorry," I say, and I think I mean it.

"Nothing to be sorry about. We just wanted different things, and I'm sorry about yours too."

I nod and press my lips together. I'd assumed Lucas knew about my divorce. My mom would have told his mom back when it happened. I never heard from him though, not that I expected to. We tread carefully down North Road. It's steep and our feet carry us faster than we intend. Growing up, this was the place to ride your bike because it felt like you were flying, a moment of magic for a child. The entrance to the nature trail is at the bottom of the hill, and I assume that's where Lucas is leading me. Because that was our spot.

"What did you want?" I ask.

"It's not what I wanted. It's what I didn't want."

I steal a glance, taking in his sharp jawline covered in stubble and those lips. I remember them being soft and warm. "And what didn't you want?"

"Kids," he says, matter-of-factly.

I take a sip from my thermos, unsure of how to respond. I don't remember thinking about having kids before I had one. I was only nineteen when I got pregnant with Marissa. I became a mom before I ever had a chance to consider what I wanted. But now I couldn't imagine not being one. Although our relationship is strained, and my daughter is living on the other side of the world, she and I will always be connected. It's a bond that can never be severed, for the love between a mother and her child is infinite. I still feel my mom's love even though she's gone and even after learning what she did to Emma. Our arms brush against one another. I swallow hard, pushing the dark secret down again.

We enter the nature trail, which is like a tunnel cut through woods, an old railroad track without the tracks. The ground is a mix of dirt, grass, and small rocks. Large trees on either side arch over it, creating a canopy. There's a stream off to one side—but it's dried up in most areas. Nothing lasts forever. The silence between us stretches so long that I figure the subject of kids will be changed, but then Lucas continues.

"After seeing what my mother and father went through when Emma disappeared, I just couldn't. My father didn't survive it, and my mom . . . I watched her die over and over again. Not in the literal sense, in the real sense." He pauses, glancing over at me. "Feeling dead while your body still walks this earth is far worse than being dead."

He doesn't have to explain what he means because I know.

"The day she went missing, the police kept saying the first forty-eight hours are the most critical, and then it came and went, and they never mentioned it again. My mother died at the one-month mark, the one year, and every year since. Maybe it's the cynic in me, but I figured if I didn't have kids, I couldn't lose them."

I give him a sympathetic look. It's easy to become a cynic when you live in a cynical world, where best intentions are not true intentions, where trust feels more like a religion—not one you practice, just one you go along with in case there is a God in the end.

"Do you ever wish you knew what happened to her . . . Emma, I mean?" I can't look at him when I ask the question.

"No. Because I know she's dead," he says matter-of-factly.

My breathing changes—short, fast, and uncontrolled. I inhale deeply, trying to even it out and steal a glimpse of him. His eyes are narrowed, staring at the long, dark tunnel ahead of us. There is no light at the end of it.

"She's been missing for twenty-three years, and it's highly unlikely she's just out there living her life. There's an ounce of me that believes otherwise, but if I knew what happened to her, I'd lose that crumb of hope."

My eyes feel wet, and I blink until the moisture dries up. Maybe Nicole and Michael are right. It's best to leave the past in the past because knowing what's true doesn't change anything. I drink from the thermos, pushing down whatever it is that feels stuck in my throat. It could be guilt, grief, remorse. It might even be the truth, my body trying to regurgitate it like it's a poison it needs to rid itself of.

"Mom keeps asking about her too. With the dementia, sometimes she forgets Emma ever went missing. I've had to remind her a few times. Watch her grieve that loss over and over." Lucas shakes his head. "But lately, I lie. Tell her she's at a friend's house or out riding her bike. They're tiny moments of reprieve for her, but I think they're more for me. She'll smile and talk about Emma like she's been here the whole time. Maybe I'm wrong for that." He shrugs.

"I don't think you're wrong. If I could have done the same for my mom, I would have."

He blows out his cheeks, and it's my turn to receive a sympathetic look. "Yeah, your dad. I'm really sorry, Beth."

I don't say anything because there's really nothing to say.

"It's been seven years, right?" he asks. It's specific, too specific. He clearly knows it's been that long.

I nod.

Neither of us say anything for nearly a minute. We just walk. Branches sway in the wind. Leaves let go one by one, cascading to the ground, finally accepting their fate. They'll break down, creating a layer of rot and decay at a tree's base, which will protect it through the winter—absorbing rainfall and providing nutrients. Even in death, they still have a purpose.

A black cat darts out of the woods ten yards in front of us and stops suddenly, lifting a front paw and craning its neck in our direction. Its yellow eyes glow like fireflies. It continues its route, scurrying into the woods again. A black cat crossed my path the day my dad went missing too. I remember thinking to myself, *I should turn back.* At least, that's what people say you're supposed to do, otherwise, bad luck will find you . . . and it did.

Lucas finally speaks. "Do you ever wish you knew what happened to your dad?"

"Yeah." I pause, looking over at him. "It's the not knowing that kills me. A mixture of hope and grief is toxic, like combining ammonia and bleach. On their own, you can stand it at least for a little while, but together, it's deadly."

I quickly look away from him as soon as I utter the word *deadly*. The image of Emma's lifeless body lying down by the creek flashes before my eyes. It's horrifying. Something I'll never be able to unsee.

He doesn't say anything, and I wonder if I said the wrong thing. We cut out of the nature trail through a small clearing that feeds into the Dead End. They call it that because it's the main road in town, and it just stops like there was no point in going any farther. It's where this side of the Grove ends. The other side ends on our street, just one mile away.

Asphalt forms a circle large enough for a vehicle to turn around and go back, designed specifically for a school bus. A guardrail wraps around half of it, a warning not to venture past the barricade where the grass and trees grow wild and untamed. As children, adults told us that those who'd gone in there never came back. We didn't listen though. We used to climb over the guardrail and dare one another to venture farther and farther. Nothing ever happened. We always came back in one piece. But it was here where they found Emma's bicycle, pink with white tassels hanging from each handlebar. It appeared months after she went missing, like the wild grass and woods had spit it up. Kids stopped crossing the guardrail after that, fearing that the warnings from our parents were true. I know now it was all a lie. All of it.

"I write an email to my dad every week," I say, and I don't even know why I mention it. I've never told anyone, not even Mom, because I'm embarrassed. It's like I'm a child too old to still believe in Santa Claus.

"Does it help?" Lucas asks as we head down the main road, back toward our houses.

"I don't know."

The Grove is still asleep. Cars sit idle in driveways. Drapes are drawn. Fog lingers over dewy yards. It's both peaceful and haunting.

"What do you write to him?"

"Stupid stuff really. Basically what I would tell him if he were here. Movies or shows I'm watching, books I'm reading. Things that have happened around me or to me."

"That's not stupid. At the very least, it must be cathartic."

I think Lucas is just being nice. Because who sends over three hundred emails without ever getting a response? My ex would say a crazy person, someone who isn't grounded in reality, someone frozen in time. And maybe he's right. Maybe I'm all of those things.

"Yeah, I guess. I like to think he's reading them even though he's never replied."

Lucas nods and drinks from his thermos.

"I sent him one last night, telling him about Mom." My voice cracks just mentioning her. "If he doesn't reply, I'll finally know that he's gone for good, and I'll let him go."

The weight of my words forces my shoulders to drop and my lip to quiver. It's hard to swallow again, and I feel my eyes filling with tears. I don't want to cry. But it feels like I have to, like I don't have a choice in the matter. I read about crying once, when I couldn't stop after Dad left. I wanted to know why it happens or what the point of it is. What I learned is that no one knows for sure. One theory is that it tells others we're in pain, triggering a human connection. Emotional tears are thicker, fatty sacks of protein. They fall slowly, clinging to our cheeks, declaring to those around us that we need help, that we cannot cope on our own. And I think that's where I'm at. It's where I've been for a very long time—stuck, unable to endure, to persist, to live.

Lucas places a hand on my shoulder and turns to face me. He looks into my eyes, but I'm not looking back. I can't. Those fat emotional tears escape, telling him more than I could ever say with words, but he understands and he pulls me into his chest, resting his chin on my head as he holds me. I sob, my body quaking and trembling against his.

And although I'm falling apart—somehow, I feel whole in his arms.

That is why we cry.

SEVENTEEN
NICOLE

I thought I knew everything about my mother until I started reading her journals. You can know a person your whole life but never really *know* them. Because they only have to show you what they want you to see. I didn't know she felt insecure as a mother. I didn't know she was afraid she'd raise us wrong, make a mistake that would permanently damage us in some way or another. I didn't know she blamed herself for my addiction. And I didn't know how much she truly loved us. She doesn't write about the night of June 15, 1999. She alludes to it, but the entry is hieroglyphically cryptic. She refers to it as the night everything changed, the night that made her question every moment of her life that led up to it, the night that shook her faith, and, most terrifying of all, the night she realized monsters walk among us.

I pick up my mug of coffee from the kitchen table and take a drink. It's lukewarm now but I don't mind because I just want the caffeine—another drug to distract my brain from craving a much stronger one. My hand trembles as I set the cup back down and flip another page. I read every word deliberately because I know each one was written for a reason, whether it was hastily scribbled down or not. Mom's journals are sometimes like a word dump as though she's just trying to get it all out.

Other times, it's poetic like she's taking her time, making sure it's just right. A few lines jump out at me.

Even if I could dig a hole deep enough to reach the center of the earth, I still couldn't bury this.

I always tried to do the right thing but somewhere along the way, it all went wrong.

You don't believe in monsters until you're living with one . . . and even then, you don't believe until you're looking in the mirror, realizing you've become one of them.

I notice there are pages missing, specifically around June 15. The frayed edges caught in the metal spiral are evidence of written truths tossed away. Why'd she even write them down to begin with? Perhaps it was cathartic to tell someone her story, even if it was just a blank page. I can understand that. There are many truths that I have written only for myself. Because some stories aren't meant to be shared.

The front screen door squeaks open. I lift my head to find Beth walking in and kicking off her shoes. Her face is flushed and puffy, and her bloodshot eyes look like baseballs with red stitching. She's been crying, and I'd ask her what's wrong but I'm still mad at her for calling me a junkie and a crackhead. It's true but that doesn't mean she should say it.

"How was your walk with Lucas?"

I study her face, trying to gauge her expression. Did she tell Lucas about Emma? She said she wouldn't unless we found something more concrete, but I'm not sure I believe her.

"Fine." She retrieves a glass from a cupboard and fills it with tap water. "And no, I didn't tell him about Emma," she says, not looking at me.

"I didn't ask."

"You didn't have to." She tips the glass back and drinks almost half of it.

It's nearly impossible to hide anything from Beth. She was the first one to even suspect my addiction. I think she knew before me, if that makes any sense. I thought I was just having fun and didn't realize I wasn't until the chase became my whole life and the high was just a means to an end. My mother knew next, but it took her longer. Parents have a blind spot for their children.

Beth takes a couple of steps toward the kitchen table, eyeing the spirals laid out before me. "Find anything interesting?" she asks.

Interesting isn't the right word, so I'm not sure how to answer her. I'd use that word to describe a new fact I discovered. Like when I learned that three days after death, the enzymes that help break down a person's food begin to eat their own body. I thought that was interesting. These journals are different though, and I don't think there's a word to describe them.

"No," I say. "But some of the pages are missing around . . . that night."

Beth raises a brow. "Did she tear them out?"

"She must have."

I consider offering her a journal to read but Mom left them to me. I didn't get much, just these and her old car that I'm not sure even runs anymore. If Mom wanted anyone else to read them, she would have split them up, given a third to each of us, but she didn't. So, they're mine.

"Maybe they're around here somewhere." Beth looks at all the boxes in the living room—some opened, some closed, some empty, some full.

"Yeah, maybe," I say, stacking up the journals. I need a break from them. I fell asleep reading her words and when I woke up this morning, I returned to them.

"Is Michael back?" she asks.

I shake my head.

"Should we start without him?"

"Actually, I need to go in for my . . ." I pause, searching for the right word, "Treatment?" I'm not sure that's the right one either. I'm still taking opiates, synthetic ones, just in smaller doses. The doctor is hopeful that I'll only need it for a year. But I wonder, will I be able to live without the methadone too?

"Can you take me?" I add.

I don't want to ask her for help, because I know she grew tired of helping me a year ago. I can't blame her though. I've always had a tendency to look for the highs in life, even before the car accident. In my twenties, it was weed, alcohol, and cocaine, whenever I could get my hands on it. But I was functioning, until I got a taste for something stronger—much stronger than myself. It was the oxy the doctors prescribed. They kept me on it for far too long, and then they cut me off cold turkey without a plan in place. So, I made a plan of my own. *Get high or die trying.* And I almost did many times. But that didn't stop me. Addiction is like having your arm in a vise. You can't loosen the grip. You can't pull away. You just have to learn to live with it.

Addiction has made me do the worst things to the people I love most—Beth being one of them. So, like I said, I can't blame her for no longer wanting to help me, but I can still hate her for it. Maybe that's the addiction talking. I really don't know anymore.

"Sure," Beth says. Her voice is soft, and the word comes out slow like she had to force it out. "Let me change quick," she adds.

Let me change quick . . . I wish that applied to more than just outfits.

EIGHTEEN
BETH

The car idles outside of the run-down treatment center. It sits in a strip mall a couple towns over, positioned between a Dollar General and one of those scammy quick loan places where your interest seems to accrue by the minute. One of the windows has been boarded up with plywood. I assume someone wanted their treatment after hours. The rest of the windows have the shades drawn, providing privacy—or hiding what goes on behind those doors. People far more broken than my sister enter and exit the clouded glass door. From what I've read online, most of them will relapse. Nicole unbuckles her seat belt and climbs out of the vehicle.

"Want me to come in with you?" I offer.

"No, I won't be long," she says.

"You sure?"

She slams the door shut. Either she didn't hear me, or she didn't care to respond. She disappears inside the clinic. I tap my fingers against the steering wheel just to busy them, keep my mind focused before it strays. There's a light drizzle. Beads of rain hit the windshield, slithering down the glass. They stop when the liquid is depleted, nothing else to keep the momentum going. I pull out my cell phone and first check my missed calls. I tried calling Marissa last night, but it went to voice mail, and I didn't leave a message. She hasn't returned my call. I check my email next. It's the ninth time I've looked at it this morning. It's all junk, minus an email from HR, asking if I have an update as to when I'll return to work from FMLA leave. There's no reply from my father. He and I used to email back when my parents got a computer for the family—well, it was mostly for Michael, but we all used it. I remember him telling me it helped with his typing skills. Dad went from pecking to actually having all his fingers on the keyboard. As he improved, his emails got longer. The first couple dozen he sent were only a few sentences in length, but I'm sure they took an hour each. They were riddled with typos and sometimes, I could barely understand what he was trying to tell me. He'd send one in the wee hours of the morning before he left for the factory, and then I'd have to wait until he got home from work to ask him about his cryptic emails. He'd laugh and tell me I'd understand the next one better. And I always did until they stopped.

I glance up at the door leading to the treatment center. Another broken person scurries in and another exits. It's been fifteen minutes. I shut the car off and cautiously get out of the vehicle, clutching my keys in my hand. This isn't a good part of town. Honestly, I don't think there are any good parts in any town. Some areas just hide their indiscretions better. I make my way inside so quickly the rain barely touches me. There's a line of people, waiting for their next fix in order to halt the withdrawals. Nicole's not in it, so I cut to the front. A man growls at me. I apologize and tell him I'll be quick.

"I'm looking for my sister, Nicole Thomas," I say to the woman sitting behind a bulletproof window. She wears a scowl like it's tattooed on her face. I don't blame her though. This wouldn't be an easy place to work.

The woman inputs her name into the computer. "She went in for her dose ten minutes ago, so she should have come out already. Must have left through the back." The woman points to the hallway off to her side.

Before I can thank her, she's already yelling, "Next," and shooing me away.

I pass by medical staff and patients. Every one of them looks tired, and I don't believe it's from a lack of sleep. I think they're tired of life.

Sometimes life gets old before we do. There's a parking lot in the back for the staff. I pull my hood up and scan the area. There she is at the far corner. She's talking with a man. He's tall, towering over my sister, dressed in a rain jacket and dark jeans. Then there's some sort of an exchange. He hands her a large manila envelope. She glances around and quickly shoves it into her bag.

"Nicole!" I scream as I run across the lot toward her. My damaged knee throbs, but I ignore the pain.

Her head snaps in my direction, eyes wide. The man turns to look at me and then moves to the side, so he's standing next to Nicole rather than in front of her.

"What the hell are you doing?" I yell at her the same way Mom used to whenever she came home late from curfew. I don't even look at the man. He's insignificant, just a bridge to her addiction. "Are you fucking using again?"

"What? No!" she says, vehemently. Her eyes are wild, and her jaw moves from side to side.

I grab at her bag. She tries to fight me, swinging aimlessly with her arm that's cocooned in a fiberglass cast, but I'm bigger and stronger. Nearly a decade of drug use has made both her mind and her body weak.

"Then what the hell is this?" I snatch the manila envelope from inside her bag and hold it up. It's thick and heavy.

"Give that back to me!" she yells, reaching for it, trying to swipe it away.

"What is it, Nicole?"

"It's the goddamn case file for Emma Harper's disappearance," she huffs.

Her fleshy lids narrow, hiding those green eyes that have clouded over the years. She reaches for it again, but this time I let her take it from my hand.

I take a step back and finally look at the man standing next to her. I recognize him immediately. Casey Dunn. He was a grade below me and a grade above Nicole. They were friends in high school, just friends, but everyone knew there was something more between them. They just never figured it out. The two of them bonded over their love for the written word. I was surprised when he went on to become a deputy for the Walworth County Sheriff's Office. I'm sure he's much higher up now. But I always figured he'd be an English professor or a writer or something like that. I thought the same for Nicole, but obviously, she took a very different path than anyone expected. We all did.

"Hey, Beth," he says. His voice is deep, and there's an air of authority behind it. He's not that skinny little teenage boy anymore. He's filled out now with wide shoulders and a thick neck. His face is clean-shaven, free of the acne that speckled it in high school, and he's traded in that shaggy hair for a buzz cut.

I deliver a tight smile. "Nice to see you, Casey."

Nicole crosses her arms in front of her chest and juts out her bony hip. *Sorry* isn't enough for her, but of course that's where my mind went. Why else would she be meeting someone in the back parking lot of a methadone clinic?

"How have you been?" Casey asks. "I mean . . . never mind. That was a stupid question." He rubs his brow and mutters, "I'm sorry about your mom."

It's not a stupid question though. It's what people ask. And the answer is always *fine* or *good*, because no one wants to actually hear how you're doing.

"Thanks." I fold in my lips. "Are you still with the Walworth County Sheriff's Office?"

He nods. "Yep. Going on nearly twenty years. I'm actually in the Detective Bureau now."

My eyes flick to Nicole for a moment. She and Michael fought me on telling anyone about the tape and now she's going out of her way to uncover what happened. I wonder if Casey finds it suspicious that she's interested in the case after all these years. What did she tell him? What reason did she give him for wanting that information?

"Congrats," I say, though I'm not even sure that's the right thing to say. My gaze bounces back and forth between Nicole and Casey. It's like we're in a standoff but no one has a gun. Well, actually there's probably one hiding beneath Casey's raincoat, tucked in the waist of his jeans, or nestled in a holster. But in this case, the gun is the truth and only Nicole and I are holding it.

"Are you done?" Nicole directs her question at me. Her tone is full of attitude, and she taps her foot against the pavement.

"What's with the case file?" I need to know how she convinced him to swipe it.

"Nicole messaged me, asking if I had access to it and if I could get it for her," Casey starts to explain, but Nicole interrupts. "Yeah, for the true crime book I'm writing about Emma Harper's disappearance. *Remember*, Beth?" She raises an eyebrow—her way of telling me to go along with her story.

"Oh, yeah, that. I thought it was just an idea. I didn't know you were serious about it." My words weave together, forming a somewhat convincing lie. I glance at Casey. His face is unchanged, so I think he's buying it.

"Now you know." Nicole cocks her head.

Casey clears his throat. "It's great that you're doing that. Obviously, we were teens when she disappeared, but I always thought it was sad that they never found out what happened to her," he says. "Things like buttons and keys go missing. People shouldn't." He shakes his head and then gestures to the envelope. "At one point in time, that was the most important case file in this county. Now, no one even noticed me taking it. It's like a toy a child's lost interest in."

We stand there in silence, unsure of what to say. It's true. The case went cold after the first year. People forgot. Children played in the streets past dark again. It was like it never happened.

Casey pushes his sleeve up to check the time. "I've gotta get going," he says to Nicole. "It was good seeing you, Beth."

"Likewise."

"And Nicole." His eyes swing to her, and his face softens. "Let me know if you need anything else. I mean anything. I'm here."

Nicole smiles. "Thanks, Casey." She leaves unsaid the words I know she wants to say. "I'll text you."

He nods and heads to his vehicle. I don't say anything until he's out of earshot.

"You could have just told me, Nicole."

"I don't have to tell you anything," she says, stomping back toward the treatment center.

Nicole's always been that way, closed off, almost sneaky. She's lied for so long about her addiction and the things she's done that I don't think she knows where the truth starts and ends.

NINETEEN
LAURA

JUNE 15, 1999

There's a knock at the front door. It's frantic, and I know immediately something is very wrong. My eyes go to Nicole, who is on the couch writing in her journal. Michael and Beth are lying on the floor, bellies down, elbows propped up, playing *Zombies Ate My Neighbors* on Sega. Brian is seated in his recliner, half watching the video game, half reading the newspaper opened in his lap. It's after eight p.m., and my family is all accounted for. My mind always goes there . . . always. I set my book down and jump from my seat.

"If it's Christie, tell her I'm not home," Beth calls over her shoulder, never taking her eyes off the TV screen. I groan at her teenage callousness as I make my way to the front door.

The knocking continues, harder and faster.

I swing it open to find Susan standing on the other side. Her face is a crumpled, wet mess and her bottom lip trembles.

"Susan, what's going on? Are you okay?"

"Emma's missing," she cries. "Have you seen her? Is she here?" Her words come out like the knocks on the door, hard and fast and frantic.

"What? What do you mean? No, she's not here."

She lets out a howl of a cry. "Eddie and I can't find her."

I pull Susan in for a hug and hold her tightly. A missing child is every parent's worst nightmare—and although it's not happening to me, I'm terrified.

"What is it?" Brian's voice calls out.

I glance over my shoulder to find him standing behind me with a look of bewilderment. "They can't find Emma." Suddenly, I'm crying too.

Brian shoves his feet into his work boots, forgoing lacing them up, and grabs the keys to his truck. "Did you call the police?"

Susan lets go of me and nods several times. "They're on their way."

"When was the last time you saw her?" he asks. His eyes are slits, focusing on Susan, waiting for her response.

"I don't know." Her voice is basically a whisper. "Sometime at the fundraiser, after the sack race but before the egg toss, I think. Her bike is missing too. She was there and then I assumed . . . I . . . I don't know what I assumed. I was so preoccupied with everything. I should have been watching her. I should have never taken my eyes off of her. But Allen's Grove is a small town and nothing bad happens here. It's safe." Susan cries harder.

Anything can happen anywhere at any time. That's the thought that crosses my mind, but I don't say it out loud.

"It's not your fault," I say instead, rubbing my hand on her shoulder, trying to reassure her, but I know the only comfort will come from bringing Emma home. "We're going to find her. She's probably just out riding her bike."

"What's going on?" Beth asks, standing just behind her father. Her eyes are wide, darting between me and Susan. Nicole and Michael are positioned beside her, giving me the same look.

"When was the last time any of you saw Emma?" I ask.

Beth answers first, "At the fundraiser."

"When she won the sack race," Nicole adds.

Michael nods. "The water balloon toss," he says. "Her team got second place."

The image of Emma slapping her knee and giggling at her joke of being better than the boys comes to mind. The First Place blue ribbon pinned to her shirt. The orange mood ring adorning her small finger. And then her sprinting away to compete in another game, determined to win all the contests.

"Where's Lucas?" Beth asks.

"He's out looking for her." Susan sniffles, trying to compose herself, but it's no use. There is no composure in these situations.

Beth slips on her tennis shoes and asks, "Where?"

"He went to check the nature trail," Susan says.

"Can I go?" Beth's eyes dart to me. They're almost pleading. I know she wants to comfort Lucas, to be there for him, to help him. They're a package deal, have been for years.

"Take Nicole with you and stay together. I mean it."

The two of them nod, and within thirty seconds, they're bolting out the door with Nicole trailing behind.

"I'm going to drive around and see if I spot her," Brian says, planting a quick kiss on the side of my head. He places his hand on Susan's shoulder. "We're going to find her."

She nods but the tears still fall. Brian leaves quickly with Michael following him.

"Let's go back to your house and wait for the police to arrive," I say to Susan, steering her out the door. She nods again, but I don't think she's listening. I hope Emma is out just riding her bike, and that she'll walk through their door with a smile on her face and some fun stories of her adventures. But something deep in my gut tells me otherwise.

TWENTY

BETH

Nicole hasn't said a word to me the whole ride home. She's mad that I thought she was trying to score drugs. Can she blame me? A memory from a year ago comes to mind: Nicole banging on my front door, demanding money. I stood still on the other side listening to her scream and cry and thrash. A car idled in my driveway. Someone, not a friend, maybe another junkie had driven her to my house. When I didn't answer, she kicked the door repeatedly, calling me every name in the book, even threatening my life if I didn't give in to her demands. I ignored her because it wasn't her. It was her addiction. Then she picked up one of my flowerpots and threw it across the porch. She tossed another one into my front yard. She smashed the wooden rocking chair, a gift Mom had gotten me from a rummage sale, one of the last presents she ever gave me. The minutes stretched on until she finally tired herself out and left in the car she'd arrived in. I didn't see her again until the day our mom died.

I blink several times, leaving the memory in the past, and look over at her. She stares out the passenger-side window. I would wonder what she's thinking about, but I already know. The case file rests in her lap. I'm surprised she hasn't started reading through it. I figured she'd be anxious to, but maybe she's scared of what she'll find.

We enter the Grove, and I turn slowly onto our road. Up ahead,

Michael's car is veering into our driveway. *Perfect timing.* He's already parked and stepping out of his vehicle when we pull in. Michael delivers a small wave and a smaller smile when he spots us. He swings his messenger bag over his shoulder and grabs a Walmart shopping bag from his back seat. I park my old car next to his, and we exit.

"Where were you two?" he asks, putting a hand up to his brow to shield his eyes from the sun.

"Treatment," Nicole says. "And you?"

"Oh . . ." he pauses and appraises her, like he's checking her over. "You good?"

She tells him yeah. He doesn't ask about the manila envelope clutched in her hand, and she doesn't offer an explanation for it.

He extends the Walmart bag to me. "I picked up a new headlight for you while I was in town. I can install it later, if you'd like."

"Thanks," I say, taking it from him. "You didn't have to do that."

"I know but I wanted to."

It's hard to see Michael as a full-grown man, when he's always been my little brother. I don't know what I was expecting when I saw him again. I wanted to hate him, still do. But he's making it hard. So maybe the only person I actually hate is myself.

"Well," I say, gesturing to the house. "Shall we get back to work?" My brother and sister nod and follow behind, their shoes shuffling against the concrete. I pull open the screen door; the hinges squeak, but then I stop. Something's not right.

"What the hell," I say, noticing the busted doorjamb and splintered wood near the handle. The door is ajar, just an inch or so.

"What? What is it?" Michael asks.

"Beth," Nicole says.

"Someone broke in."

"Move." Michael shuffles me aside so he can enter first. He doesn't say it in a rude way. He's being protective.

He pushes the door open slowly, peeks his head in, and pauses to listen before entering.

"Should we call the police?" I ask.

Neither Nicole nor Michael responds. I creep in behind Michael, despite him motioning for us to stay back. The cupboards and drawers in the kitchen have been pulled open. Items are strewn everywhere like someone was looking for something. The living room is a bigger mess. All the boxes have been emptied, even the ones we had already sorted through. Michael grabs the broom and wields it like a sword while he moves through the house, room by room. Nicole tiptoes into the living room, letting out a heavy sigh when she sees the mess.

"Who would do this?" I ask. "And why?"

My eyes flick to the VCR. The tape with the deadly secret is still sitting on top of it, seemingly untouched, unlike all the others. They're scattered across the floor, mixed in with all of our parents' other belongings.

The ladder to the attic creaks as it's pulled open. Then there are footsteps up the ladder and on the floor above. My shoulders tense as I glance at the ceiling.

"All clear," Michael yells.

I exhale. The ceiling creaks and moans as he makes his way through the attic and back down the ladder. It closes, smacking back into place with a thud.

"What about the other rooms?" I ask as Michael enters the living room. He lets out a heavy sigh, then leans the broom against the wall.

"They were ransacked too."

"Is anything missing?" I ask.

"I don't know. I can't tell because they tore this place apart, and I'm not even sure what's all in here."

Nicole is frozen in place, picking at the plaster on her cast and staring off at nothing.

"Should we call the police?" I ask again.

"Yeah, probably. Just in case anything was taken," Michael says with a shrug.

I shake my head. "I don't understand who would do this."

"What if someone knows?" Nicole asks, still staring off. She snaps out of it, the gravity of the situation pulling her back to us. She looks to me and then Michael. "About Emma and what Mom and Dad did."

"Why would they ransack the house? Wouldn't they just go to the police?" I furrow my brow.

Michael nods in agreement.

"Maybe they were looking for evidence, or maybe . . . this was a warning."

My eyes dart to the tape placed on top of the VCR. If that was the case, the evidence was right there, and they missed it. Then again, we would have too if we hadn't randomly picked that particular tape and watched it.

"But how would anyone know?" Michael squints.

"What if Mom had something set up? A fail-safe for when she passed, like someone would be alerted as to what she and Dad did. The pages in her journal from that time are missing. Maybe she tore them out and sent them to someone. Told them to wait to open it until after she died," Nicole says. The words come slowly like she's trying to piece together a theory as she speaks.

"You really think Mom is capable of that? A grand fail-safe plan in the event of her death?" Michael asks.

"She hired a lawyer and put together a will without me even knowing," I say, clinging to Nicole's theory.

"And she hid the money you wired to her, Michael. Beth had no idea she had another checking account," Nicole adds.

Michael rubs his forehead. "But who would she tell?"

"Susan," Nicole offers.

"She's too feeble to do something like this," he says, gesturing to the ransacked room.

"Lucas?" Nicole looks to me.

"He would never do this," I say.

Michael raises a brow. "Even if he found out Mom and Dad were involved in his sister's disappearance?"

I close my eyes for a second. I can't say he wouldn't. Because I don't know what he would do if he knew the truth. They say the truth will set you free, but they don't tell you it can set you free in the same way death does.

"Okay, who else is there?" Nicole asks.

Mom's final words echo in my head. *Your father. He didn't disappear. Don't trust . . .*

I swallow hard, pushing them down again. Maybe she wasn't trying to tell me what happened. Maybe she was trying to warn me because she had already told someone or had plans to, and she knew they'd come looking for answers.

"Maybe someone from the Grove?"

"Like who?" Michael tilts his head.

"I don't know. But whoever it is, do you think they'll come back?" I ask.

"If they didn't find what they were looking for, I'm sure they will," he says.

"What do we do then?" The color from Nicole's face has drained, and I'm not sure if it's from the methadone or fear.

"I've got Dad's pistol," Michael says with a serious look. "It was in one of the boxes Mom left to me. Luckily, I had already stowed it away for safekeeping, so whoever broke in didn't find it. And if they come back, well, they'll wish they hadn't."

"You're not actually going to shoot someone, Michael," I scoff.

"I would if I had to."

I don't question him again, because I believe him. I hope it doesn't come to that. I'd like to say this was just a random burglary. But that doesn't happen in a town this size. Everything that happens here happens for a reason.

The sound of something thudding against the hardwood floor steals our attention. Nicole bends down to pick up the fat manila envelope that slipped from her hand.

"What's that?" Michael asks.

She holds it against her chest. A guilty look slithers across her face. I know he's not going to like what she's about to tell him. I didn't like it either. Her actions were careless and messy, even more so now, with the break-in.

"Emma Harper's case file," she says.

Michael blows out his cheeks. "Where'd you get it?"

"From a friend." She shrugs, trying to act nonchalant.

"Why?" he asks.

"You said if we didn't find anything then we wouldn't tell anyone, but we can't find anything if we don't look," Nicole argues.

She was fine leaving the past in the past yesterday, so it wouldn't "tarnish" her reputation. I'm not sure where the change of heart came from. Perhaps it finally sank in that there wasn't anything left to tarnish.

"I meant find something here." He gestures to our parents' belongings scattered across the floor. "Not playing Nancy Drew and stealing files from the police station."

"I didn't steal anything."

"Did your 'friend' steal it?" Michael makes air quotes around the word *friend*.

"He borrowed it," she says, raising her chin.

"Oh, I didn't realize the police had a library system for their unsolved case files." He rolls his eyes and starts off toward the kitchen.

The fridge opens, glass clinks against glass, and a moment later he returns with a bottle of Miller Lite perched to his lips. He swigs nearly half of it. Michael's been gone a long time and isn't used to dealing with someone like Nicole. She does things the way she wants. Sometimes you gotta give her an inch, but make sure to reel her back in before she takes a mile.

"Since we already have the case file, it doesn't hurt to look it over," I offer, knowing that it'll keep Nicole occupied.

"And what if someone notices it's missing?" Michael asks.

"They won't," Nicole says.

"But if they do?"

"Case files go missing all the time," she says.

Michael furrows his brow. "How would you know that?"

"I've seen a lot of police procedural shows."

"This isn't an episode of *NCIS*, Nicole. This is real life, and it has real consequences," he lectures.

"I know that. I'm not stupid."

"Well, you're acting like it." He shakes his head.

"Oh, piss off, Michael. Just because you went to some fancy college and work at some fancy tech firm doesn't mean you're smarter than me. So, stop pretending like you are." She narrows her eyes at him.

"I don't have to pretend, Nicole." He drinks his beer and turns his back to her, walking farther into the living room, careful not to step on anything.

Nicole's face is flushed and her hand makes a fist. My phone dings and I retrieve it from my back pocket to check the notification.

When Nicole can't contain her anger anymore, she marches toward him. "You know what, Michael? I'm so sick of your—"

"Oh my God," I cry out.

Nicole stops midrant and snaps her head in my direction. "What? What is it?"

"Beth," Michael says, drawing his brows together.

"It's Dad," I say. "He's alive."

FROM: brianthomas1@yahoo.com
TO: elizabeth.thomas3@yahoo.com
SUBJECT: LONG OVERDUE

Beth,

I'm sorry I haven't written you in so long. Trust me. It was for the best that I stayed away. There are things I've done that I'm not proud of. Unspeakable things. But know that not a day has gone by that I don't think about you, Nicole, Michael, and my Laura. I can't believe she's gone, and I'm so sorry I can't be there for you all right now. I wish I could have been a better father, grandfather, and husband. But sometimes we're not the people we want to be. We just are. I know you worry about me. But don't. I am safe. I am well. And I'm closer than you think I am. Give Michael and Nicole my love. And please forget about me because I am not a man worth remembering.

Love,

Dad

TWENTY-ONE
BETH

I've always wanted Dad to write back to me and now that he has—I wish he hadn't. I'm not sure why I ever thought I needed his words to begin with. Everything he had to say, he said when he walked out of our lives seven years ago. Michael sits on the other end of the couch with a fresh beer in hand, rotating it as if he's actually reading the label. I'm not sure if he usually drinks this much or if this is out of the ordinary for him. But then again, grief is like an airport. There are no rules or social norms. You just do what you gotta do to pass the time until you reach your next destination. Nicole clutches my phone in her hand. Her brows are knitted together as she rereads the email over and over again.

"Why would he write you now after all these years?" she asks.

"Because Mom passed," I say. That had to be the only reason why he'd choose to respond now. All of my other emails went unanswered.

Michael lifts his beer bottle and swigs. "Or he knew we found out."

"How?" I look to Michael and then Nicole.

She lifts her head. "Maybe he thought Mom told us."

I swallow hard as my mother's words return to me. *Your father. He didn't disappear. Don't trust . . .*

Michael raises a brow. "Mom didn't say anything to you before she passed, did she?" He's staring at me.

Nicole is too now.

"No," I lie again. I don't know why I don't just come out and tell them. But they weren't here. They knew she was dying, and they still didn't come, so they don't deserve Mom's last words.

A line from Dad's email jumps to the front of my mind. *I'm closer than you think I am.*

It's creepy. Or maybe it isn't? I don't know. The police figured he fled to Mexico given where his truck was found—a little over ten miles from the border. Now I'm not so sure. Mom's words echo in my head. *He didn't disappear.* And then Dad's. *I'm closer than you think I am.* Maybe she knew he'd reach out after she passed. Maybe Mom was the one that kept him away.

I try to think back to when he left. I remember Mom coming to terms with the fact that he was gone rather quickly. She always tried to get me to stop looking for him and would say things like, *If he wanted to be here, he would.* It wasn't like when Emma went missing. Susan, Eddie, and Lucas held out hope that she would return. They never stopped looking for her. But Mom stopped looking for Dad. Maybe because she knew exactly where he was this whole time, and she wanted him to stay there.

My eyes dart between Michael and Nicole again.

"She did say one thing." The words fall out of my mouth. I only say it because I don't think I can figure it out on my own. Perhaps they can help solve Mom's riddle and Dad's cryptic email. Michael's smart. He's always been the brains of the family. And Nicole sees things through a different lens, like the world is presented uniquely to her. If I put an apple in front of her face and asked her to describe it, she wouldn't say it was red or shiny or round. She'd tell me about its natural wax, the layer of protection that slows down its decay. She'd point out a weak spot, perhaps discoloration or a bruised, mushy area caused by impact or too much compression. By the end, she wouldn't even be describing the apple anymore.

Michael leans forward in his seat, squaring up with me in a way. "What did she tell you?"

Nicole purses her lips, holding in the words she clearly wants to yell at me. She crosses one leg over the other and bounces her foot, showing how little patience she has for me. They're waiting for me to say more, to admit that I lied to them, and to reveal what exactly I lied to them about. This undercurrent is why we can't trust each other.

"She said Dad didn't disappear." I leave out the *Don't trust* part, and I don't know why I do. Maybe I want to keep it for myself. Something just for me. Or maybe I don't want to lose hope that my dad is a good man.

"Why wouldn't you tell us that?" Michael scoffs. "What else did she say?"

"Nothing. That was it," I lie again. *The more you lie the easier it becomes.*

Nicole tilts her head in an accusatory way. "How do we know you're telling the truth?" She's good at catching a lie, because she does it all the time . . . lying, I mean.

"Why would I?"

She shoots a glare at me. "Why would you lie about Mom saying something to you in the first place?"

"I . . . I don't know. I just didn't understand what Mom meant, so I thought it was nothing." My words come out choppy and unconvincing.

I always knew it was meaningful. People don't use their last breaths on worthless words.

Michael leans back in his seat and sips his beer. "Well, clearly it meant something." He appears nonchalant but I can practically see his brain working overtime, trying to put the pieces together.

Nicole squints in concentration. She wants to be the one that figures this out. When you have nothing, you have everything to prove.

"Yeah, but what?" I ask. "With the email from Dad, it seems like she was warning me . . . like she knew he'd come back."

"Wait, can't you track an email?" Nicole asks. "Like an IP address or something?" She glances at me, but I don't have the answer. And then we both look at Michael.

"Sometimes, yeah," he says.

"Well, do that. His email said he's closer than we think." Nicole practically jumps from her seat.

Michael furrows his brow. "And what, we're just supposed to go find him?"

"Why not? I mean, if he's close, we may as well." Nicole hands the phone to him.

Don't trust . . . Do I tell them Mom's warning? No, I can't. I don't know who she was referring to. Don't trust Dad? Don't trust anyone? I've already lied to them twice. I can't just be like, *Well, Mom actually said a little more*, so I keep my mouth shut. They're not going to find him anyway. I spent years searching, turning over every rock, and still came up empty-handed.

"Please," Nicole begs. Her eyes develop a sheen.

Michael looks to me, but I offer nothing. His gaze falls on Nicole. She's good at getting her way, and he's not used to telling her no. It took me years to finally say no to her because saying that to an addict takes practice. Finally, he lets out a huff and gets up from his seat, heading toward the hallway.

"Where are you going?" she calls after him.

"I'm getting my laptop."

Her face lights up. I knew he wouldn't be able to say no to her, though I think he should have. False hope is the worst kind of hope.

"I can't believe it. I can't believe we're close to finding Dad," she says.

I can't believe it either, because I know it can't be true.

"Yeah," is all I'm able to muster up.

"Aren't you excited or at least relieved?" she asks.

"Even if we did find him, it wouldn't change anything."

"But he could tell us what happened to Emma, and he could be in our lives again."

"But what if . . . ?" I pause, not wanting to say the words but feeling I need to, especially with Mom's warning rolling around my brain like a ball in a pinball machine. "What if he's dangerous?"

She snaps her head back, and her eyes go wide. "How could you even think that?"

"Because he's been gone a long time, and I don't know him anymore. The dad I knew wouldn't walk out on Mom after over thirty years of marriage. He wouldn't walk out on his kids. He wouldn't not be in his granddaughter's life. He wouldn't show up after seven years via a fucking cryptic email. I don't know who sent that email, but it didn't come from the dad I knew."

Nicole's eyes well up. "You give up on people so easily."

I know she's not talking about Dad.

Before I can respond and yell at her and ask her how dare she say something like that to me, Michael walks into the living room with his laptop in hand. I was the one that was there for Nicole. I gave her money. I gave her food. I gave her clothes. And I gave her a place to stay until I couldn't trust sleeping under the same roof as her anymore.

He pauses for a moment. "Am I interrupting something?"

I cross my arms over my chest and shake my head.

"No, just see if you can find out where the email was sent from," Nicole says.

Michael takes a seat and flips open his laptop. "Forward the email to me," he says, and then he rattles off his email address.

Nicole presses several buttons on my phone. "Done." She tosses it back to me. Her eyes have lost their sheen and are now clouded with a mix of anger and hope. The former directed at me.

The problem with Nicole is she doesn't remember the past seven or so years. For her, it's like Dad left yesterday because her addiction has stolen so many of her memories. I noticed it first . . . the addiction. She was prescribed oxycodone after getting into a car accident back in 2015. The sad thing is, she was driving around looking for Dad when it happened. Another car T-boned her, leaving her in critical condition, and she spent nearly a year healing via meds, physical therapy, and hope. But when the pain finally went away, the addiction took its place. She convinced the doctor her body still needed the meds, but really it was her brain that craved them.

Michael's fingers are fast and furious as they tap against the keyboard. I'm sure Nicole and I have melted away as he's laser-focused on his computer screen. Nicole stares, waiting for the answer to the question she's been asking herself for years. *Where's Dad?*

"Got it," Michael finally says, lifting his head.

"Where is he?" Nicole asks. She's ready to run out the door and find our missing father.

"Juda, Wisconsin. About an hour west of here."

"Can you tell exactly where he sent it from?" Her eyes seem to brighten.

"Not always, but I pulled the latitude and longitude for the IP address and cross-checked it with Google Maps; there's only one house within a three-mile radius, so it's gotta be that one, and it was sent via a private internet connection."

Nicole tilts her head. "What's that mean?"

"Meaning he wasn't at a Starbucks or a library or some other business."

"Let's go then. Let's find him." She smiles, like Dad's location is "X marks the spot" on a treasure map. I feel so sorry for her. Even if she finds him, finds exactly what she's looking for, he won't be the father she remembers. He just can't be.

Michael looks to me. I think he's expecting me to be on board, to jump for joy like Nicole practically is, but I'm not. Dad has disappointed me far too many times, and I can't do it anymore.

"I'm not going," I say.

Her smile fades and a scowl replaces it. "What do you mean you're not going?"

"I mean I'm not going."

"Don't you want to find him?" Nicole eyes me cautiously.

"No, I don't."

"Why?" she asks.

"I just don't." I'm not going to explain myself to her because she wouldn't understand anyway.

She shakes her head, as if I'll change my mind and jump up and join her, but I won't. I lost everything looking for him. Even though there's nothing else for me to lose, I'm not willing to gamble it for a sliver of hope. She looks to Michael. He raises his shoulders slightly and drops them, a weak shrug.

"Michael?" she says. Her voice is meek and soft.

He closes his laptop, pausing before he answers. I don't think either of us know what he's going to say. He's always held his cards close. "All right, I'll drive."

Her lips curve into a smile, and she bolts toward the front door. It brings me back to when we were kids and Mom would call out, "Dad's home," on Friday nights. We'd be so excited, and we'd all come running to greet him. Only one of us is running to him now, and that's only because she's running away from everything else.

Michael stands from his seat and tilts his chin. "Are you sure you don't want to come, Beth?"

"I'm sure," I say. "But I do hope you find him."

"Will you be fine here on your own? Given the break-in . . ." His eyes scan the living room and then land back on me.

"Yeah."

Michael nods, accepting my answer. I can't tell if he's disappointed in my response, if he understands it, or if he's happy that I took a stance. He leaves the house without another word. And that silence is exactly what I need.

TWENTY-TWO
NICOLE

Michael's rental car drives smoothly, absorbing the shock from bumpy roads and streets riddled with potholes. I think that's how his life has been too, equivalent to a ride in a luxury vehicle, untouchable from the ups and downs of existence. I haven't owned a car in a while, but I did have an old Toyota Camry, before I couldn't afford the insurance or even the gas in the tank, and I remember the drives were never smooth.

His hand rests on the bottom of the steering wheel while his other lies in his lap. There's no tension, no worry, nothing. It's all very laid-back. We're maybe five minutes away, and we haven't spoken the whole ride. I'm not sure either of us know what to say. What do you say to a person you used to know? It'd be easier to talk to him if I didn't know him at all.

"Thanks for coming," I finally land on.

Michael glances over at me. "Of course. I couldn't let you go alone."

"Beth could." I briefly meet his gaze before breaking away and looking out the passenger-side window.

A blur of harvested cornfields and pastures scattered with dairy cows pass by. The sky is a light gray, like a dirty sheet has been pulled over it. It's looked like that since Mom passed. Maybe she took the sunshine with her.

"I wouldn't take it personally," he says. His eyes are back on the road ahead.

"How else am I supposed to take it?"

"Did you take it personally when I stopped coming around after Dad went missing?"

It's the first time he's mentioned his absence.

"Yes," I say without hesitation.

"Why?"

"Because we're family, and we needed you."

"Mom didn't."

I study his profile. He has Dad's nose and chin, strong and pronounced. His eyes are a mix of both our parents', not blue, not green, but hazel. His hair is dark like Dad's with specks of gray, but he keeps it cut short on the sides and a little longer on top.

"What do you mean *Mom didn't*?"

He clenches his jaw slightly, like he's chewing on the words that he hasn't uttered yet, clasping them with his back molars and deciding whether or not to release them.

"She told me not to come back," he says.

"Why would she tell you that?"

He swallows hard; his Adam's apple rocks up and down, covering nearly the full length of his neck.

"Because when she called to tell me about Dad leaving, I said it was probably for the best."

"Why would you say that to her?"

"Why wouldn't I say that? She said he left a note. That means he chose to leave, and honestly, he and I hadn't been good for a long time. Ever since I moved out to California, he lost interest in my life. I think he resented me for doing more than he ever did, which is pretty fucked up. Our parents pushed us to be the best, but when I did better than Dad, he shut me out."

I deliver a sympathetic look but Michael doesn't see it. His eyes are focused on the road. I didn't know there were issues between him and Dad.

"I'm sorry, Michael," I say.

He shrugs and mutters, "Thanks."

"If it makes you feel any better, you get the same treatment if you do worse than your parents too," I say.

"What do you mean?" he asks.

"I hadn't seen Mom in over a year before her death."

"Why?"

"She told me not to come back too . . . not until I had a chip." A tear escapes the corner of my eye. "The day she died, I was one day away from getting my chip, the closest I ever was to it. But she passed before I could get it, before I could see her again. I tried. I really did." I shake my head. "But I was too late. I was too fucking late," I say, nearly choking on my words.

He sighs. "I'm sorry, Nicole."

I wipe away my tear and attempt to compose myself. "It makes sense now, why Mom donated the money you gave her to the Missing Persons Foundation."

He makes a *humph* sound, mixed with the *ha* of a laugh. "Even in death, she just had to teach me one last lesson."

"Same here. I almost feel like she knew I was one day away from being clean, so she died on purpose as a way of saying, 'You should have tried sooner and harder.'"

"You really believe that?" he asks, raising a brow.

I let on a small smile. "Not really."

He smiles back and slows the car down, turning into a gravel driveway that leads to a ranch-style house. The shutters have fallen off the windows, and several are boarded up. The grass is unkempt, patchy in some areas and overgrown in others. It looks abandoned. I bite at my lower lip. It's chapped, and my teeth tear off a sliver of dry skin.

My breathing changes, switching to short and fast.

Michael shuts off the engine. "This is it," he says.

"It looks like no one lives here."

"Which makes it the perfect place to hide out." He raises a brow, opens his door, and gets out of the vehicle.

I exit on my side, and our shoes crunch over the gravel as we walk toward the house. Michael knocks on the door, but it's already ajar. The force of his knock pushes it farther open. He pokes his head in and calls out, "Hello." The sound echoes throughout the empty home.

I force my way past Michael, running into the dark, quiet house. It smells stale and musty. There's an old stained mattress on the living room floor, like someone had been camping out here. Empty food wrappers and cans of soda are scattered around. Cobwebs cling to every corner and light fixture.

"Dad," I call out, running room to room, each one emptier than the last. The house repeats *Dad* each time I yell it, taunting me. I stand in the center of a room at the end of the hall. I'm sure it used to be a bedroom, but without a bed it's just a room. Closing my eyes, I take several deep breaths, inhaling through my nose and exhaling through my mouth. The craving is strong . . . stronger than it's been in a long time. I imagine the tip of the needle disappearing into my skin. Pressing down on the plunger. And then that almost instant euphoria. Like being bathed in warm honey. Feeling everything and nothing at the same time. It's the closest I've gotten to heaven or at least how I picture heaven to be. My heart races. My skin tingles and perspires. And then there's a tremble so deep inside of me. It starts off small, but I can feel it growing . . .

"Nicole," Michael says.

I open my eyes and turn quickly to find him standing in the doorway.

"Are you all right?" he asks.

"You said he'd be here." My voice cracks, exposing my weakness.

"I'm sorry, Nicole. Tracking IP addresses isn't black-and-white. They're not always accurate. He could have used a VPN or something else." Michael presses his lips together and looks down at his feet.

Every muscle in my face is pulled tight by deep disappointment. It almost feels like each ligament could snap at any moment. Or maybe I will.

"Are you okay to head out now?"

I shake my head and tell him, "I guess."

Michael starts down the hallway.

"Hey," I call out. "Mind if we make a pit stop in Beloit?"

He pauses and turns back. "For what?"

"I was staying with a friend at a motel there. Just temporarily until I could find something more permanent. She texted me earlier saying she was leaving and that I should come get my stuff, if I still wanted it. It's just some clothes and personal hygiene items and whatnot."

Michael nods. "Yeah, that's not a problem."

"Thanks," I say, not making eye contact. Because if I do, he'll know I'm lying.

TWENTY-THREE
MICHAEL

I pull the car into the parking lot of a run-down place called Motel 5. I think it's supposed to be a joke, one step below a Motel 6. But it's far worse than that. It's a long one-story building offering private entrances for each room. Several windowpanes are cracked, and the siding has been graffitied. I take the lot slowly, keeping my eyes peeled. People are camped out and strung out; some lean against the building, others are bent over, barely standing. Loud music blares from a couple of idled cars. Beefy men sit in the driver's seats, staring at the motel rooms in front of them like they're security, but I know the only thing they're securing is their illegal activities. I can't believe this is where my sister has been staying. Nicole points to the far left and tells me to park. I do as she says, even though I want to drive off and tell her I'll replace everything she's left here.

I park in front of the last motel room but keep the engine running.

"Want me to come in?" I ask.

Nicole's already stepping out of the car. "No, I'll just be a minute," she says, slamming the door behind her.

I look off to the right, making sure no one is approaching. The strung-out ones couldn't if they tried. Their movements are slow, almost zombielike. My eyes go to the vehicle parked twenty yards away. The burly man sitting in the driver's seat glances in my direction. He nods, but I know it's not a friendly nod.

The motel room door Nicole's standing at opens six inches or so, and she quickly slips inside.

I sit and wait in silence. The seconds morph into minutes and then it starts to feel like a long time has passed, but maybe it just feels that way in a place like this. I hear a noise, first a loud thud, then yelling. It's muffled but is undeniably the sounds of anger and fear helixing around one another. Something crashes inside of the motel room. I rip the car door open and sprint toward it. I can hear the words being yelled clearly now.

"Where's the money, you stupid bitch!"

"I don't have any money!"

"That stupid dead mother of yours didn't have anything valuable in her house either. So, the real question is, how are you gonna get me my fucking money!"

I drop my shoulder into the center of the door without even thinking and charge forward. The slam of the knob piercing drywall puts a punctuation on the room and for a moment, time freezes. A man stares back at me as he hovers over my sister on the bed. One hand around her shirt collar, the other raised in the air with limitless possibilities, all of them bad. Then it's as if someone pressed Play on a remote control. The hard sound of a hand slapping across a face brings us all back into motion.

There's no time for words. No reasoning with a man like this. The good news is that he looks just as strung out as Nicole at her worst— gaunt, weak, shaking for the fix he has yet to find. My mind goes blank, and I begin to run.

I plow through him and send him flying off the bed, into the wall. I run over and grab his collar, just like he was doing to Nicole and raise my fist, slamming it into his face. First his cheek, then his forehead, then his eye, then I break his nose and the blood pours like I turned on a faucet. He gags, spitting blood onto my clothing, and I can only imagine the sick and vile things swimming around his bodily fluid. I punch again, this time knocking his teeth in. He's barely conscious when I stop.

Getting to my feet, I turn to Nicole who is stricken with fear and shame. My heart is racing, and adrenaline is coursing through my veins so fast that I don't feel anything at the moment. I'm sure I broke bones in my hand or, at the very least, severely bruised it, but nothing registers except the crumpled form of my sister, sobbing on the bed.

"How much do you owe him?"

Nicole looks up, bewildered that this is the question I ask first.

"Five hundred dollars," she manages to choke out through tears and sucking breaths.

I reach into my pocket and pull out my wallet. It's a beautiful piece from Hermès, calfskin, handmade in France. It's worth more than the money Nicole owes this piece of shit. I take out a wad of cash and throw it at his battered face. Some of it sticks to the blood that has pooled around his nose and mouth.

"Here. Now she owes you nothing," I say, crouching down. I put my lips near his ear and whisper, "If you come near my sister again, next time I won't stop. Do you understand?"

He nods and moans.

"Good."

I stand again and kick him in the ribs just to make sure he truly understands. It sounds like a child breaking a stick over their knee. He sucks in a high-pitched squeal as he rolls over on his side.

I help Nicole, and she sobs as we walk out of the motel room, back into the light of the world. Opening the passenger door, I help guide her into her seat.

"I'm sorry, Michael. I'm so sorry."

"You have nothing to be sorry for," I reassure her.

"I'm not strong enough," she sobs.

"Yes, you are."

Nicole lifts her head. "Thank you . . ." Her eyes say more than that, and I know exactly what she is thanking me for.

"Please don't tell Beth about this," she adds.

"I won't."

I close her door, hop in the driver's seat, and put the car in Reverse. As I begin to accelerate out of the parking lot, I turn to look at the man sitting in the dark SUV. He smiles and lifts his chin. This time, I know it's friendly.

BETH

Michael and Nicole have been gone a while, which gave me all afternoon to get most everything in the living room and kitchen cleaned up and put away. Many of the fragile items were destroyed, so I tossed them. Some things you can't fix.

I push a VHS tape labeled *November 1999* into the VCR. It clicks into place and the machine makes a winding noise. This tape is the next one in chronological order after June 15, 1999. There was a gap, months without a tape, and that made sense. Mom clearly didn't want to capture any of the memories following Emma's disappearance. It also explains why she forgot to record over the clip from that evening—she couldn't face what happened. The screen is gray static and then it flicks to blue before an image appears. The date on the bottom right corner reads November 13, 1999. Michael is seated at the kitchen table. A birthday cake decorated with an edible image of a computer monitor rests in front of him. Across the top of the cake, *Happy 13th Birthday, Michael* is styled in green icing like computer code, and there are thirteen lit candles surrounding the message. The flames flicker and dance.

We haven't celebrated Michael's birthday since he moved to California. And I haven't wished him a happy birthday in years, so it's not something I usually remember, but he'll be thirty-six next month.

Onscreen, Dad sits next to Michael at the kitchen table, smiling and singing "Happy Birthday." There's little evidence on his face of the horrible thing he'd done, but he does appear to have aged a few years in the five months since the previous tape. Gray hair peppers his burly beard and new wrinkles crowd the corners of his eyes. Nicole and I stand on either side of our brother, belting out the same lyrics. Mom isn't in view, so I know she's the one holding the camcorder. She was almost always the one holding the camcorder, which is why hardly any photos or videos of her exist. Strangely, although the microphone is right next to her, it barely picks up the sound of her singing. It's like she's whispering the words, not fully committed to them.

When the song finishes, Michael squeezes his eyes shut, conjuring up a wish, and then he extinguishes all the flames with one gust of air. Wax drips down the candles, seeping into the cake. My siblings and I don't waste even a second before we pull the candles and suck the frosting off the ends.

"What'd you wish for?" Dad asks.

"I can't tell you," Michael says.

"Oh, come on. You can trust me." Dad forces a laugh and nudges him.

The camcorder makes a whirring sound, and the lens zooms in on Dad, closer and closer, until the center of his face fills the whole screen. Although the video is blurry, the intensity in his green eyes is clear as day. The camcorder stays zoomed in on him for a few seconds before the lens retracts, bringing me and my siblings back into frame.

"If you tell him, it won't come true," Mom says. Her tone isn't playful. It's serious. But no one seems to notice.

Michael juts out his chin. "Yeah, I can't tell you."

"You can tell me anything," Dad says with another forced laugh, playfully ruffling Michael's hair. My brother pulls away, flicking his locks back into place, while Dad flashes a smile in Mom's direction. I don't think she returns it, because he quickly averts his attention back to us three, asking, "Who wants cake?"

"I do," we all say in unison.

Dad cuts it into slices and divvies them up. Mom declines.

No one notices. She keeps the camera focused, so all of us are in the shot. It seems like a birthday celebration that any other family would have, and I don't remember noticing anything out of the ordinary that day. But that's because I was seeing it through my eyes, not Mom's.

The camcorder whirs as the lens zooms in again. First, it's on me. My face fills the screen as I shove a forkful of white birthday cake into my mouth. My skin is youthful and glowing, slightly tan from the sun. Then it's Nicole's turn. She fills the frame. Her skin is oily with a smattering of teen acne. You wouldn't notice it though unless you were standing an inch away from her because it's those big green eyes that grab your attention and never let go. The camcorder moves to Michael. Frosting clings to his top lip, and he smiles wide, swiveling his head to flick the shaggy brown hair out of his eyes. Then it's on Dad again, and it lingers on him far longer than the rest of us. All I see is Dad onscreen, nothing out of the ordinary, but it's clear Mom sees something different, perhaps the facade he's putting on. There's nothing typical about this home video tape or how it was filmed. Mom wasn't capturing the moment. She was studying us.

"Can I open my presents now?" Michael asks. His tone is high-pitched because puberty hasn't set in yet.

"Laura, is it present time?" Dad says to Mom, giving her a strained look. He doesn't realize the camcorder is only on him. The lens zooms out slowly, and we're all back onscreen again.

"Sure," Mom says. Her voice lacks enthusiasm. No one notices.

Michael claps his hands and pushes his plate to the side, freeing up the space in front of him.

"Hold on." Dad backs his chair out and stands from the table, walking toward Mom.

"Michael's going to flip over this. Make sure you get his reaction," he whispers to her before leaving the room.

Mom says nothing.

A few moments later Dad appears back onscreen carrying a large wrapped box. "This is from the whole family," he says, placing the gift on the table and beaming at his son.

"The whole family?" Nicole laughs. "I got him a yo-yo. I don't know anything about this huge present."

It's true. Nicole and I didn't know what was in the box.

Michael tears through the wrapping paper, revealing a Compaq ProSignia desktop computer, or at least that's what it says on the side of the cardboard box.

He squeals and a string of words fly out of his mouth. "Awesome. This is da bomb. I can't believe it. This is for me? Thank you, Mom and Dad. I love it so much." He rotates the box, taking it all in.

"I hope this means I'm getting a car for my birthday," younger me says, her eyes darting to Dad and then directly at the camcorder.

Dad pats the box with his hand. "Well, this is so Michael can do Java-Script coding at home. But since it's the only computer in the house, we're going to set it up in the front room so everyone can use it. Understand?"

We all nod but Nicole and I exchange a look. And I remember what it meant. Michael getting that sizable gift seemed so unfair to us and completely out of the norm. They didn't have money for something like that, but now it makes sense. Michael's birthday was the first of ours since Emma went missing. Mine is in April and Nicole's is in March. Maybe this was their way of distracting us, keeping us from seeing the cracks in our own family or from uncovering the truth of what they had done. Busy minds don't wander.

A knock at the front door startles me, pulling me from the past. I quickly eject the tape, slide it back into its sleeve, and place it with the others. Well, except for the one that's been left out, set on top of the VCR. That one doesn't belong with the others.

Out on the porch, I find Lucas. He's wearing a gray knit beanie that I'm sure his mother made. His hands are slipped into the front pockets of his jeans, and he smiles at me. It's the kind of smile that makes the eyes sparkle. No one's looked at me like that in a very long time. Despite the temperature outside hovering in the fifties, my skin feels warm to the touch.

"Hey," I say, pushing open the screen door so there's nothing between us—well, except for that secret that feels more like a brick wall stacked five miles high. "Everything all right?" It's the question you ask when you've gotten more bad news than good in your life.

"Yeah, everything's fine." He pauses for a moment. "Oh, what happened here?" Lucas gestures to where the door's wood has splintered.

I glance at it. *The break-in.* But I can't tell him that, because it might have something to do with his sister and what our parents did. "Oh . . . we were hauling a piece of furniture out to donate to Goodwill and, well, that happened. Another thing to fix, I guess." I shrug and offer the tightest smile. "Did you need something?" I quickly add, trying to make sure the subject of the broken door is changed.

His eyes linger on the door for a moment before swinging back to me. "No," he says. "Umm . . . I just wanted some fresh air and to see if you had time for a walk?"

"Sure." I nod. "Let me grab my coat."

He smiles again. It's smaller this time.

I shove my feet into a pair of old tennis shoes and grab the nearest coat hung on the rack. It's a faded old denim jacket—*Mom's.* I consider putting it back and picking another, but I don't. I just slip it on. Some things you have to wear, like guilt and grief and old jackets left behind by loved ones who've passed.

"Where to?" I ask, closing the broken door behind me.

Lucas looks left, where our long driveway leads to the road. Then he looks right, where the curved waterway followed by concrete steps cuts through the hillside.

"How about down to the creek? I haven't seen it in ages."

I swallow hard but agree to his suggestion. It would be odd if I said I didn't want to go down there.

We walk side by side, following the path of the waterway my dad poured when we were kids. It was his design, a means to ensure heavy storms didn't erode his land when the rain ran downhill. Dad was always worried about losing things. He didn't have much, which made what he had all the more valuable, even the dirt on his land. Both of my parents were that way. My mom due to loss. My dad due to having little to begin with.

There's a drop-off a few feet high where a wall was created out of cement and rocks collected on the property. When the rain is heavy, it flows over it and crashes to the pavement, making a sound like a waterfall.

Lucas jumps first, his feet landing firmly on the concrete. He turns and holds out his hand to help me, just like he did when we were young. But unlike back then, I actually need the help now. I take his hand, bend at the knees, and hop off the ledge. When my shoes hit the pavement, my bad knee gives out, and I nearly tumble over. His hands grab the sides of my waist, keeping me in place so I don't fall.

"I got you," he says.

I look up at him, studying his face. There's a thousand words I want to say to him but the only one I let out is, "Thanks."

We exchange smiles. Mine is tight like a rubber band stretched to its limit. His is the opposite.

The concrete steps leading down the valley are large, so we take them slowly. They're lined with rocks and boulders, also collected from the land, five feet wide on either side. On the left, three lamp posts are positioned equally in distance to one another. Beyond the concrete and the rocks are hillsides covered in old trees; wild, untamed weeds; and fallen leaves and branches. Lucas holds my hand until we're at the bottom. When his fingers slip away, I can still feel them cradled in mine like a phantom limb.

The valley feeds into a clearing enclosed by hefty box elder and ash trees. From where we're standing, it looks like the tips of them are touching the dull gray sky. Leaves ranging in colors from yellow to orange to brown dance through the crisp air, falling one by one before settling onto the ground.

"I forgot how incredible it is down here," he says, scanning the area.

"It really is," I say.

"Where are your siblings?"

I sigh. "They went to find my dad."

He furrows his brow. "What do you mean?"

"You know those emails I told you about, the ones I send to my dad every week?"

Lucas nods.

"He wrote back."

"Wow, that's . . . unbelievable." He scratches the back of his neck and glances down at his shoes.

"It is."

"Why would he write back after all this time?"

"Maybe because Mom passed, and he felt obligated to reply." I shrug.

"What did he say?"

"Not much. Just that he couldn't be here for us."

"Why even send the email then?"

"I don't know. But Nicole wanted to find him, so she had Michael track down the IP address to where he sent the email from."

"And you didn't want to go?"

"No, because I can't get my hopes up again."

"I'm sorry, Beth," Lucas says, and I'm not exactly sure what he's apologizing for, but I tilt my head and nod. The wind whispers through the trees as though it has something it wants to say. We all do.

Lucas clears his throat. "How are the funeral arrangements coming along?" He obviously wants to change the topic of conversation. Death is an easier subject than the unknown.

"It's tomorrow. She asked to be cremated and have her ashes spread around the property." I look to him. "You know how my mom was. She never wanted anyone to make a fuss over her. Even her final wishes were as hassle-free as she could be."

"Yeah. I remember bringing her flowers on her birthday, and after she thanked me, she scolded me for wasting my money." He lets out a small laugh.

"That was Mom," I say, shaking my head and smiling at the memory. "She gave everything, and she wanted nothing in return." I pull the jean jacket a little tighter around my body, and for a split second, it feels like a hug from her.

"Would you mind if my mom and I stopped by to pay our respects?" he asks. "We won't stay long, only ten minutes or so since she's not doing well. But I know she'd like that."

I lower my head, looking down at my old tennis shoes. I've probably walked fifty miles in them, but all they've gotten me is here. I should say no. I should make up a reason as to why they can't come. But there is no good reason—at least not one I can tell Lucas.

His lips sit partially open, waiting for an answer.

"Of course. It's at sunset. That's when she wanted it to be."

He smiles and nods. "Shall we?" Lucas gestures to the field of overgrown grass.

I return the nod, but not the smile, and walk in step with him. Dad used to keep it cut short. But now the grass comes up past my knees. Lucas and I used to race each other from one fence to the other. I was faster than him until sophomore year of high school, but even then, he'd still let me win, pretending to trip and fall just before he reached the finish line. No matter what I was going through, whether I was feeling on top of the world or hitting rock bottom, Lucas always made me feel like I was a winner.

We trudge through the unmaintained land carefully, watching out for holes that gophers and groundhogs have burrowed in. The grass rustles against our pants as we leave the field and enter a wide path that cuts through the woods. To the left, it's thick and dark with a smattering of smaller trees fighting with one another for space and nutrients. To the right, the trees are spread out, larger with robust trunks and sprawling roots, demanding ample room around them.

Before we reach the creek, I can hear it. It burbles along its bed and trickles around the trees and branches that have succumbed to it. Finally, we're standing at the bank of the stream that severs my parents' land. The water is brown. It sounds prettier than it looks. Across the creek, several weeping willows lean into it while their long, graceful branches graze over the babbling water. The only way to get to the other side is by crossing the stream or walking up the steep side of Highway X and taking the bridge across.

Lucas stands beside me, feet shoulder width apart, chin slightly lifted, hands tucked into the front pockets of his jeans. I scan the creek until my eyes lock onto the arch of the highway underpass. The water under the bridge is shallow, causing the creek to narrow and create a bed of sludge. I blink and I see her there, covered in blood and mud. Clouded eyes that see no future. Her skin pale and cold. I wonder what they did with her. Where is Emma now? I blink again, and she's gone.

Lucas rests a hand on my shoulder. "Are you all right?"

I shake my head and say, "Yeah." He doesn't notice my body tells the truth while my mouth lies.

"Thought I lost you there."

"No, I'm still here." I avert my gaze because I can barely look at him.

"Good," he says. "Because I miss this," he adds with a faint smile.

My eyes find their way back to him like magnets to metal. "Miss what?"

"Us."

My body speaks before my brain can shut it down and say it's not a good idea. My arms snake around his neck, and my hands settle on his back. He pulls me into him. Although I haven't kissed him in decades, when our lips touch it feels like everything I've ever lost has been safely returned home. It starts off slow and soft and warm. When the pressure builds, our tongues take over, flicking and swirling around one another. My teeth sink into his fleshy lip. I can't get enough, and I wonder how I ever let him go to begin with. It feels like a first kiss or a final one. But I fear it might be the latter, thanks to the deadly secret sewn to my heart. I want to tell him but if I do, I think it'll destroy us again and this time, I won't survive it.

TWENTY-FIVE
LAURA

JUNE 16, 1999

I didn't sleep last night. How could I? How could I close my eyes and fall into a dream knowing what I had done? Within a matter of hours, I went from consoling Susan and telling her we'd find Emma, that her daughter would return to her, to knowing she never would. Brian lays beside me, under the covers, sleeping on and off. He won't tell me what happened. He said he wasn't even sure what all happened yet. He said he needed to know more before he could tell me. Then he said the less I knew, the better. I don't believe it, and I don't think I can live with a half-truth. A half-truth is just a whole lie.

Brian told me we had to get rid of Emma's body. That there was no other way. Telling the police would destroy us. He swears he didn't do anything, that he hadn't harmed her. That he never would. But why not just go to the police then? I asked him that same question a dozen-plus times. And each time I asked, the words became quieter, losing their conviction. Finally, I went along with it. I'm not sure why I did. Maybe I was in shock. Maybe I feared discovering what my husband is capable of. Or maybe I care for him too much. So, I went through the motions. I had to hide one thing or lose everything. By the time we were done, it was the wee hours of the morning, three a.m. or so. No one's awake at that time unless you work third shift or you're up to no good.

I glance over at the clock on my nightstand. The numbers are bold and red as they should be. Life is a countdown, but it doesn't end at zero. Sometimes the destination is twelve, like Emma; or forty, like my father; or fifteen, like my sister.

It's a little after nine in the morning. Footsteps clamor through the house, so I know the kids are up. It should just be a normal Sunday. But it's not, and I don't think I'll ever have a normal day again. Brian shifts, turning over from one side to the other, facing me now. I crane my neck toward him. His eyes are closed, sleep gathering at the corners of them. He's rested somewhat well, and I don't know how he managed that. We've been married for sixteen years, and I thought we knew everything about one another. Now, I'm not so sure. The man I fell in love with would never ask me to help him get rid of a body, and I never thought I'd agree to a request like that. But my family is too important to me, and if I lost Brian, it would all fall apart.

"Mom," Beth calls from the other side of our bedroom door.

Brian stirs. His eyes shoot open. They're green with yellow flecks. I used to get lost in them, but now I'm just lost.

"Hey." His voice is hoarse, just above a whisper. His large hand emerges from beneath the covers, finding mine. He holds it, squeezing three times. It means *I love you*. I don't squeeze back. Not because I don't love him but because I don't love him in this moment. I stare into those eyes, wondering what they witnessed. What did they see that backed him into a corner where the only thing he could do was the wrong thing? Or his hand, the one that mine is engulfed in. What did it do?

"Are you okay?" he asks.

He knows the answer, but he wants me to lie to him, and I can't do that right now.

"I don't know what I am," I say.

"Laura, we did what we had to do."

That's what he keeps saying.

Yesterday I saw him as the man I fell madly in love with two decades before. But now I notice changes from when I met him, the kind you don't notice when you spend every day with a person, the subtle vicissitudes: The gray hairs stippled throughout his full beard and mustache. The small dark spots spattered across his skin from too much time spent in the sun. The faded scar on his forehead that disappears into his hairline, four or so inches in length. I remember the day he got it. We were out on a walk when the kids were young. They were on bicycles, all of them equipped with training wheels except for Beth's. She had just learned how to ride without them—not well, but well enough. She was weaving in and out of the center of the road, which doesn't matter in a place the size of the Grove. But a car came along. Someone from out of town. Someone who didn't respect the speed limit in a small community. We were all laughing and chatting and didn't notice the car. But Brian did, almost too late. He pushed Beth out of the way and took the hit like any parent would. His head cracked against the windshield. Blood poured from the wound, trickling down his face in a steady stream. I remember him saying he was fine as he crawled to a crying Beth with scuffed-up knees. He didn't care about his own well-being. He only cared about hers. It took thirty-six stitches to close the wound. And even when it did, it left behind a scar that served as a reminder of the type of man he is. One that would do anything to protect the people he loves most. I cling to that reminder in this moment. Because it's all I have.

"Mom," Beth yells again.

"What is it, Beth?" Brian answers for me.

"Can I go with Lucas to search for Emma?"

Brian lets out a heavy sigh. What will we tell our children when she never returns? Will we keep searching? Will we pretend to have hope when we know there is none? There's no right answer. Because you can't give a correct answer to a wrong question.

"Yeah, but be careful and make sure you're home for lunch," he says.

"Thanks, Dad." Her footsteps pound down the hallway, growing quieter as she moves through the house. The front door slams closed, startling me.

"Should we really have Beth out looking for . . . ?" I can't say her name out loud.

"It'd be odd if we didn't let her help. Don't you think that would raise suspicions?" He looks at me, staring into my eyes, and I wonder how I look to him. His thumb slides back and forth, grazing over the top of my hand. His touch used to be comforting but now it feels like a needle dragging across my skin, perforating it.

"I don't know. It just feels wrong having her search for someone she'll never find."

He presses his lips together. "I know. But there's nothing we can do now."

"We could tell Susan and Eddie the truth."

"We can't. It's too late. We got rid of her body. That's a felony," he explains, but he doesn't explain enough, like why we had to hide it in the first place.

"I still don't understand. Why couldn't we just call the police?"

Brian exhales deeply, and I think maybe he just might exhale the truth too. "Laura, please stop asking me that."

His eyes search mine, but there's nothing for him to find. I'm not the one hiding secrets—well, at least not from him . . . yet.

"Can't you just tell me? I know you said it's better that I don't know. But that can't be true." My mouth is so dry it feels like I swallowed sand. But maybe that's how guilt tastes when you have to swallow it—grainy, flavorless, bitter.

"I can't. You just have to trust me. We did the right thing for us."

If you have to qualify *right* with a pronoun, then it's not right.

"You do believe me?" he asks.

I pull my hand from his. "I don't have a choice."

His brows knit together and a sliver of his green eyes disappear behind his lids. We've both done a bad thing. It binds us to one another, more than any other connection we've ever had—more than this house we built together, more than our marriage, and more than our children. He and I share the darkest of secrets.

"Brian, when you love someone as much as I love you, you believe them. You always believe them," I say.

He smiles warmly, and his thumb grazes over my hand again. It feels like a razor blade, but I don't wince.

It doesn't matter if I trust him. It only matters that he thinks I trust him.

TWENTY-SIX

MICHAEL

On the way home, we stopped at the clinic for Nicole to get her methadone treatment. She's apparently supposed to go every day, but she's been going every other day or every two days, trying to get clean faster. It clearly isn't working, because there are no shortcuts in life. Nicole hasn't learned that yet, and I'm not so sure she ever will.

"You promise you won't tell Beth?" she says again as I park the car in front of the garage.

"Yeah," I say, but I don't know if that's true or not. Maybe I should tell Beth, though arguably it's none of my business and it's not Beth's either.

"Thanks," she says, sliding out of the car.

"Wait, why don't you want Beth to know?" I ask.

"Because she'd probably kill me."

I almost crack a smile but stop myself when I realize she's being serious. Nicole slams the car door behind her and stands there waiting for me to get out. It's like she's scared to go inside the house alone.

My knuckles are an angry red. Two of them are split open, but the blood has dried and the skin has begun to bruise. They throb, so I flex my fingers and shake them out.

I get out of the vehicle and go in through the front door with Nicole trailing behind me. Beth kept herself busy while we were gone because the kitchen looks like it did before the break-in. Nicole grabs a stack of journals from the table and tells me she'll be in her room before disappearing down the hall. She's probably trying to avoid Beth until she's more composed and capable of covering up her lies.

I make my way into the living room, which also shows no evidence of the break-in. Beth sits on the floor, surrounded by neat stacks of boxes, carefully going through each one. She spends time with every object as though they're an extension of our parents. I don't see the point. They're just things.

She pauses her sorting. "I'm guessing it didn't go well."

"What gave it away?"

"Nicole darting to her room."

"She didn't dart," I say, taking a seat on the couch. "She just needs a little time to herself."

Beth raises a brow, but quickly lowers it and goes back to sorting. She unravels an item wrapped in old newspaper. It's an empty can of A&W root beer from the seventies. It doesn't have the curvature that soda cans have these days. The shape is more like a soup can. I don't remember much from my childhood, but I remember the story behind that root beer can because Mom told it to us many times. Dad bought it for her on their very first date. The two of them had gone for a walk, and they stopped at the corner store that used to sit directly across from the park. The soda was ten cents, but it meant the world to Mom, and she saved it all these years later. Most people would look at it and see a piece of garbage, but for her, it represented a new beginning. Beth looks at the can fondly. I know she remembers the story too. She places it off to the side, as though she's unable to determine whether she should keep it or toss it. If it were up to me, it'd be in the trash like most everything in this house. I think it's important to get rid of things from the past because they hold us back from going forward, and that's the only way to live.

"So, what happened?" she asks.

I shrug. "Nothing really. It was an abandoned house. Maybe he was there and left, or maybe he'd never been there. He could have used a VPN or something like that to change his IP address."

She rummages through a box and pulls out more items. "Is Nicole okay?"

I pause and consider telling Beth what happened earlier at the motel, but Nicole's words linger in my mind. *Because she'd probably kill me.*

"Yeah, she's fine," I land on.

Beth looks to the entrance of the hallway and back at me. "We should probably keep a close eye on her. I'm scared she's going to re-lapse again."

I'm not scared because I know that she most likely will. It's hard to be scared of something you can see coming. Nicole would have re-lapsed today if it weren't for me, but I can't watch her all the time and neither can Beth.

I nod and tilt my head. "Have you thought any more about what you're going to do with the house?"

"I don't know. Why?"

"I was just thinking, since Nicole doesn't have a place to stay. Maybe it would be a good idea to keep the house and let her live in it."

"She can't afford this place."

"It's paid off, so it's just upkeep, property taxes, and utilities, which I could cover until she gets back on her feet."

Beth lifts a brow. It's almost accusatory, and I don't know where it's coming from.

"I was thinking of selling."

"You'd told us you weren't sure yet," I say, crossing my arms over my chest.

"I'm not, but the money I'd get for it would be life-changing."

I raise my brow, matching hers. I'd estimate the place is worth three hundred grand or so, not life-changing by any means. But she doesn't know that because it's more money than she's ever seen. It's enough to make you comfortable for a time, not enough to change your life.

"What about Nicole?" I ask.

"Don't," she says, shaking her head.

"Don't what?"

She grits her teeth and speaks in a low voice. "Don't come here and lecture me about Nicole. You aren't the one who's had to deal with her over the years. You aren't the one she stole from, called every name in the book, threatened, nor the one she's been violent with. So, I don't wanna hear it from you."

"She's sick, Beth."

"I know, but you can't help someone that won't help themself." She unravels a porcelain horse from a spool of rolled-up newspaper. Two of the legs are broken, but she sets it in the keep pile anyway.

"Very cliché, Beth."

"It's cliché because it's true," she argues.

I let out a sigh and survey the room, taking note of everything we have left to do. We may share the same DNA, the same last name, the same parents, but that's all. I rub the bridge of my nose with my pointer finger and thumb, pressing on the sides.

"Just because you weren't able to help Nicole, doesn't mean I can't," I say.

Her eyes narrow. "You're a real piece of work, Michael."

"How so?"

"You've been gone seven years, and the only person you've helped is yourself. I'm the one that took care of Mom and Nicole."

"Yeah, well, Mom's dead and Nicole's in the process. So, who have you really helped?"

"Screw you. You show up here in your fancy car, wearing your expensive clothes and designer watch, and have the nerve to look down on me. You may have money, but that's all you have." She gets to her feet and aggressively tosses items into a garbage bag.

"And you hate me for it. Don't you, Beth?" I stare at her.

"No, I hate you because you got everything."

"What's that supposed to mean?" I ask. "We all had the same beginnings."

"No, we didn't. You got the computer summer camps, private coding lessons, expensive tech equipment, trips for academic competitions. So, of course you're better off than Nicole and me. Mom and Dad set you up for success." She spews out the words she's clearly been holding in for a long time. A green-eyed monster, trying to rationalize her own failures and shortcomings.

"I don't know what you're talking about, Beth. Mom and Dad supported your interest in running and track. It's not their fault you blew out your knee. They supported Nicole and her writing, and it's not their fault she became an addict. So, stop blaming everyone else for why your lives turned out the way they did."

"You're an entitled asshole." Her voice cracks because she knows what I'm saying is true.

"And you're a miserable bitch. But at least I don't hold it against you."

Footsteps explode down the hallway, pulling our attention from the hatred we feel for one another at this moment.

"You guys!" Nicole yells in a panic.

She bursts into the living room, carrying a journal and a stack of papers.

"What is it?" I ask, half standing from my seat.

Her eyes are wild, showing the whites around her green irises.

"I don't think Emma Harper was the only body Mom and Dad got rid of."

MISSING TEEN:
POLICE ASK FOR PUBLIC'S
HELP TO FIND 17-YEAR-OLD GIRL

OCTOBER 31, 1999

ALLEN'S GROVE, Wis. —Walworth County Sheriff's Office is seeking the public's help to locate Christie Roberts, 17, of Allen's Grove.

According to a press release from the Walworth County Sheriff's Office, Roberts is believed to have left on foot from her family's home located on Hill Street at 5 p.m. on October 26. Roberts is 5'3", approximately 120 pounds with shoulder-length dark brown hair. She was last seen wearing an Old Navy branded sweatshirt, jeans, and New Balance sneakers.

It is believed Roberts left willingly and may be a possible runaway. Roberts's parents are concerned for her safety.

You can notify the Walworth County Sheriff's Office dispatch center at 262-741-3300 if you know of Roberts's whereabouts or have any information that may help police locate her.

TWENTY-SEVEN
LAURA

NOVEMBER 1, 1999

Another girl went missing this week. In a town this size, even one is too many. She's been deemed a runaway, but I think Brian had something to do with it. He sits across from me at the head of the table, shoveling a forkful of food into his mouth. I made ramen, mixed with chunks of thick-cut ham, scrambled eggs, and fried onions. It's cheap but everyone enjoys it. Brian smiles at me as he twists the fork in his bowl, entangling a wad of noodles between the tines. I don't feel so different than the ramen.

I force a smile back, as I look to my children. Michael and Beth sit on the right side of the table. Michael has already stained his shirt, the yellow-brown residue of egg mixed with caramelized onion. Usually, I'd have him take it off to soak and treat the stain right away, but I've learned you can't save everything. Beth has barely touched her food. She's been obsessed with diet and exercise ever since she got the full-ride scholarship from UW–Madison for track and field. I worry about her. I think she's doing too much, and I should say something, but how can I parent her after what I've done? My eyes go to Nicole, sitting on the left side of the table. She angrily eats her food, stabbing her fork through a chunk of ham. There's a chair between us because she's mad

at me, a buffer to remind me that I am not currently inside the envelope of her love. She's upset that I won't let her run off and hang out
with her *friends*. But they're not a good influence and she's too easily
influenced. If I can keep my children close, I can keep them safe. I look
back to Brian. Maybe I shouldn't keep the kids close. That means keeping them near him, the man I married . . . and the man I cannot trust.

"Can I be excused?" Beth asks.

Brian looks to me so that I can decide. Apparently now I get to
have a choice in something. I glance at her plate. The food has only
been pushed around to give the illusion she's eaten some of it. I consider telling her no and to eat more, that she needs fuel for her body to
stay strong, but I don't have the energy.

"Yeah, clean your dish though," I say.

She stands, thanks no one in particular, and then makes an abrupt exit.

There's a knock at the door and before I can get up, Beth sprints
toward it. She swings it open. Susan stands on the other side of the
screen. I get to my feet and close the distance between the table and the
entrance. A piece of my heart breaks off every time I lay eyes on her. I
don't think I have much of it left. But she's different this time. Her hair
is combed. There's a smidge of blush on her cheeks, and she's dressed in
jeans and a thick cable-knit sweater rather than sweats or pajamas. She
doesn't look angry or sad. She looks almost relieved. Emma Harper has
been missing for nearly five months. Perhaps she's finally shifted into a
new stage of grief.

"Hey, Susan," Brian greets her first.

I don't know how he's even able to look at her.

"Hi, Susan," I say, my gaze hovering right above her eyes.

Susan glances at the kids and then back at me. "Can I talk to you
and Brian in private?"

I swallow hard and exchange a worried look with my husband, but
he doesn't appear worried at all. *Does she know? Does she suspect us?*

We join her out on the porch, and I close the door so the kids can't
hear. I've tried to shield them from this but it's nearly impossible. It
happened in our own backyard, and so the tendrils of this ugly thing

I've been keeping at bay don't have to reach far. I notice I'm holding my breath, so I exhale through my nose slowly and calmly.

"What's going on?" I ask, still not able to look her in the eyes.

"They arrested him."

"Who?" Brian asks.

"Charles Gallagher."

My eyes go wide, and gravity takes hold of my jaw.

"He confessed. He said he killed Emma." Her voice cracks and tears streak her blush-colored cheeks, stealing the pigment on their way down. "He said he threw her away in a dumpster in Janesville, behind the furniture store. We'll never be able to lay her to rest, but at least I know the person that took her from us will finally get the justice he deserves." Her cries turn to sobs, and I pull her in for a hug.

This time I don't have to lie, telling her it'll be okay or that we'll find Emma. I don't say a word. I just let her cry.

She's right about one thing though.

Emma isn't coming back.

But this isn't justice served. In my peripheral view, I can see Brian staring off in the distance, as though he's searching for how he should feel. I wonder if he's asking himself the same question as I am . . . *What have we done?*

TWENTY-EIGHT
NICOLE

I splay the newspaper clippings out on the living room floor, so I can see them in their entirety. They're tinted yellow and some of the words have partially faded away, erased and forgotten, just like Christie Roberts. Many are updates, or lack thereof, from the sheriff's office, because they never had a single lead. Several clippings are classified ads her parents took out. They pleaded for the public to come forward. Most of those ads are to sell large-ticket items, like used cars or furniture. The Roberts wanted the most precious thing they ever had back.

"This doesn't mean Mom and Dad had anything to do with Christie's disappearance," Michael says, gesturing to the clippings. He paces the living room, rubbing his forehead as though he's fighting off a migraine.

"Why else would Mom keep these?" I glance up at my younger brother but he's not looking back, so I direct my attention to my sister. "What do you think, Beth?"

She's seated beside me, biting her thumbnail down to a nub, staring at the cut-up newspapers from decades before. She looks dazed, and I'm not sure she's even reading them.

"Christie ran away, or at least that's what everyone thought," she explains. "I don't know, maybe Mom was paranoid and believed Dad had something to do with it."

"Beth's probably right," Michael says.

"Or maybe Mom knew something no one else did." I tilt my head.

"Or she was paranoid, like Beth said. I mean she helped Dad get rid of Emma's body. She couldn't have been the same after that." Michael raises a brow.

"She wasn't," Beth says.

"How would you know?" I ask.

She lets out a sigh. "I watched another tape, one from November 1999. It was different from the others."

Michael's brows shove together. "How was it different?"

"Just the way she filmed it. It was like she was analyzing us, not capturing a family memory."

"Like she was paranoid," he says, and I can't tell if it's a question or not.

I get what Beth's saying. I noticed it too in Mom's journals. Her point of view changed after Emma's disappearance. She was removed, writing about *a* family rather than about *her* family, like a scientist watching lab rats try to navigate through a maze.

"Or like she knew more than anyone else," I argue.

"So, you think because Mom kept these newspaper clippings"—Michael gestures to the floor—"and because she filmed us differently, that means Dad had something to do with Christie's disappearance?"

"I'm not saying he did. I'm just saying Mom changed after Emma went missing, and the tapes she filmed after the fact are proof of that," Beth says.

"And Mom also kept everything on Emma Harper, and we know they had something to do with her death," I argue.

"You both really want to destroy Mom and Dad's memory, don't you?"

Beth folds her arms in front of her chest. "No, Michael. We just want to know what happened."

The truth won't change anything, but that doesn't mean it should never be exposed.

"And we agreed if we found something, we'd tell someone," I say.

When neither of us speak, Michael takes a closer look at the newspaper clippings detailing Christie Roberts's disappearance, carefully scanning over each one.

"The police said Christie was a runaway. It says so right here." He points to one of the articles.

"It says they *thought* she was."

"Well, they must have had a solid reason to think that," Michael says.

"Yeah, probably because of her parents. I would have run away, too, if I were her." Beth shrugs.

"What do you mean?" I ask.

Beth stares off, as though she's bringing up memories that had been stored away in the deepest corners of her brain. "Christie's parents were strange. They were overbearing, kept her sheltered, didn't let her go to school or anything. She was my age but always seemed much younger. I remember it being difficult to just talk to her. She took more than a beat to respond to anything, and she'd stare at you with those enormous brown eyes. It was unnerving because you couldn't tell what she was thinking."

I raise a brow. "But weren't you friends with her?"

"No, not really." Beth shakes her head. "Christie wanted to be my friend. I think she wanted any friend. She'd show up at our house and ask to hang out, or sometimes follow me when I was on a run. Mom told me to be nice to her, so I always was, but I didn't go out of my way to be her friend." She looks down guiltily at her lap and fiddles with her fingers.

I close my eyes for a moment, conjuring up an image of Christie back in 1999. She comes into view, faint on the back of my eyelids, grainy but alive. Her crooked half smile, like she couldn't decide which emotion to settle on. Her dark hair shiny from grease, not from some incredible product.

My eyes open, and I look to Beth, the figment of Christie disappearing back into the void. "I remember always seeing her walk laps around the Grove, over and over, rain or shine, taking pictures with that old camera looped around her neck."

Beth nods. "Yeah, she'd show me pictures she'd snapped when I was out for a run. I didn't even know she was taking photos of me, which was weird."

"That is weird," I say.

"I don't really remember her," Michael says. "Still, based on what you two can recall, it makes sense she was deemed a runaway. She was a hamster on a wheel going nowhere." He glances at Beth and then me. "But two girls disappearing within five months of one another, in a town of less than two hundred, is highly suspicious. Mom probably thought the same thing."

My eyes scan over the newspaper clippings again. So many of them mention the word *runaway*. Maybe Michael's right. It makes sense, after what Mom had done, she would become paranoid, looking for patterns that didn't exist. Just because our parents disposed of Emma's body doesn't mean they had anything to do with Christie's disappearance. And we still don't really know what happened to Emma before that camcorder started recording the night of June 15, 1999. Maybe Dad just stumbled upon Emma's body. Still, that doesn't explain why he wouldn't call the police. I pick up Emma Harper's case file from the couch cushion and plop it into my lap, flipping it open to where I left off.

"They had a suspect in custody for Emma's disappearance. He was charged with her murder," I say, reading from the report.

"Who?" Michael asks.

"Charles Gallagher," Beth says before I can find the answer myself.

He scrunches up his face. "Who?"

"That creep that lived at the end of our street," she explains.

"Oh yeah. I forgot about him. How was he even a suspect in the first place?" Michael asks.

"Lots of innocent people are suspects. That's just how the system works."

Beth's right about that. Charles Gallagher was an easy target. He was the town creep. I feel like every small town has one. A person no one else understands. He had poor social skills and no friends. He drank frequently, smoked like a chimney, and wore ill-fitting clothes. He never said much either. He lived in the brick house right across from the park.

His mom lived with him, or maybe he lived with her. No one really knew. His property was an eyesore, his home surrounded by old junk cars parked in the driveway and in his yard. People complained, but he said it was his house, and he could do whatever he wanted with it. There were rumors about him before Emma went missing. Some people said he had been in prison. If you asked what he served time for, everyone had a different answer. They also said he was prone to violent outbursts due to a head injury he sustained while serving in the military. I never knew if any of the rumors were true or not, but I avoided him all the same. Most everyone did.

I scan several pages of the case file before recapping my findings to Beth and Michael. "There was an anonymous tip that led the police to zero in on him," I explain. "Someone saw him talking to Emma at the park on the day she went missing. Then several others came forward to say they witnessed this interaction too. The police discovered shoe prints in his yard that matched a pair of sneakers she owned. Apparently, that was enough evidence to obtain a search warrant. The police found a Barbie playground ball, a pink jump rope, and a *Powerpuff Girls* zip-up hoodie in his home. They belonged to Emma."

"If I didn't know the truth, I'd say that's all pretty damning," Michael says.

"Not really." Beth shakes her head. "It's all circumstantial. Shoe prints? He lived across from the park. Kids trekked through his yard all the time. And everything found in his house could have been items that were left at the park."

"That's exactly what he said, initially," I say.

"Wait, what do you mean by *initially*?" Michael asks.

"Charles changed his story after being interrogated for sixteen hours straight without an attorney present. He ended up confessing to the kidnapping and murder of Emma. Said he disposed of her body in a dumpster behind a store in Janesville."

"Why don't I remember any of this?" Michael massages his temples with his pointer and middle fingers.

"Because Mom and Dad kept it hidden from us. Plus, it was 1999 and small-town news wasn't readily available like it is now. The only reason I knew anything was because Lucas told me everything he knew, but his parents kept a lot from him too," Beth says.

I flip to another page in the case file. "How could Mom and Dad sit back and watch this man's life be destroyed?"

"It was either his or theirs," Michael says.

Beth shoots a glare at him. "Yeah, but he was innocent."

"He confessed," he says.

"It's called a false confession. People do it under great duress," Beth argues.

"Or maybe he was telling the truth. Maybe his conscience finally got the best of him, and he let out everything in an act of catharsis." Michael's clearly playing devil's advocate. "We don't know what happened to Emma before that videotape, or after."

"Yeah, but Mom and Dad found her. That means she wasn't thrown away in a dumpster behind a store in Janesville and carted off to some landfill like Charles said. If you find a body, you call the police. It's pretty fucking simple," I huff.

"Sometimes the simplest things are the most complicated," Beth says, and I'm not sure what she means by that, but it doesn't feel like she's talking about Emma or our parents.

Michael raises a brow. "But why *did* he have Emma's belongings in his house?"

I scan the report in front of me. "He had toys and outerwear that belonged to a number of children in the neighborhood. Things they left behind while playing at the park. The police failed to disclose that in their report."

"And when was he arrested?" Michael asks.

I flip back to the beginning of the arrest report. "November 1, 1999."

"But those shoe prints in his yard wouldn't have still been there," Michael says.

"According to the case file, those shoe prints were discovered in the days after Emma went missing. Charles was asked about it and denied even seeing her that day and said it wasn't uncommon for kids to walk through his yard. The police concluded he wasn't a likely suspect, that is until an anonymous tip came in over four months later from someone claiming they saw Charles interact with Emma the day she vanished. After that, the police zeroed in on him," I explain.

"Let me get this straight, Charles was arrested for Emma's disappearance on November 1, and Christie went missing October 26." He looks to me not for confirmation on the date, but to confirm I'm listening to him. "So, he was out when she disappeared?"

I slowly nod.

"The timing is suspicious," Michael says.

"Not really." Beth shakes her head. "We know he didn't have anything to do with Emma."

"We don't know that," he says with a shrug.

Michael's face is concrete and stoic like he's trying to be a shield for our parents' memory, one that separates the now from the past. Beth has a look of determination mixed with indifference as though she wants to know the truth but also knows she can't handle it.

"And what about the break-in?" Beth asks.

I give Michael a strained look, hoping he'll keep his promise and won't tell her that it was a drug dealer I owed money to who broke into this house. If she knew, I'm not sure what she would do.

"What about it?" Michael says, almost flippantly. I know then he's going to keep his word.

"It couldn't have been random," she says.

"It could have been. Word had already gotten around that Mom had passed. Maybe someone saw it as an opportunity to burglarize the place. You can't really steal from the dead." He tilts his head, holding eye contact.

Beth twists up her lips and studies his face like she's deciding whether or not his explanation makes sense. I'm about to chime in, but Michael beats me to it.

"And what ever happened to Charles?" he asks, officially changing the subject.

I breathe a sigh of relief and flip through several more pages in the report. I remember something about the case falling apart, but I can't recall.

Before I find the answer in the file, Beth speaks first. "The case against him was dropped."

"How is that possible?" Michael squints.

"Yeah," I add. "Especially given his confession and the police finding Emma's belongings in his house and her shoe prints tracked through his yard."

Michael's eyes swing to the tape set on the VCR. "Plus, no one but us has ever seen that tape."

"Unless someone else saw it," Beth says.

I glance at the faded newspaper clippings that detail Christie Roberts's disappearance. The edges are straight and even. Mom cut each one out with precision like she planned on saving them for a lifetime. Or maybe she saved them for us.

TWENTY-NINE
LAURA

DECEMBER 2, 1999

The snow falls like it has no place to go, drifting aimlessly as though it's trying to float for as long as it possibly can. But it will eventually touch the ground. We all do.

Looking out the living room window, I spot Michael, Beth, and Brian traipsing around in the front yard, tossing snowballs at one another. They're dressed in winter jackets, snow pants, thick-knitted hats, and heavy gloves. Their cheeks and noses are rosy from the cold. Plumes of frosty air escape their mouths as they laugh and tease one another. Nicole sits off to the side, using my mop bucket to build herself an igloo. She didn't want to go out and play in the snow. But I told her to. When she asked why, I told her it was my house and my rules. Always the snark, Nicole had replied, *Fine, I'll build an igloo, and I'll live in it until the snow melts.* So, there she is—my difficult middle child, packing the mop bucket tight with snow and stacking the mold, one onto another. She's already erected five rows in a circle around the circumference of a small kiddie pool. I'm sure I'll have to drag her back inside at some point today to make sure she doesn't freeze to death trying to prove a point.

Eddie, Emma's father, appears at the top of the driveway dressed in blue jeans and a jean jacket. His hands are stuffed into his pockets, scrambling away from the cold. Hot air bursts out of his nostrils like he's a bull preparing to charge. Either he's out of breath or he's angry. He marches in Brian's direction. It's not until he's six feet away that Brian even realizes he's there. They exchange a few words before Eddie beckons Brian to follow him, and the two of them walk toward our house, stopping before they climb the stairs of the porch.

I can't hear them, but I can read my husband's lips. "What is it?" he asks.

Eddie speaks too quickly for me to pick up on what he's saying. His cheeks are flushed, and I don't think it's from the cold. Brian's eyes widen and his mouth falls open an inch or so. They nod and pat each other on the back before Eddie turns and makes his way up the driveway. Brian looks up at the window I'm standing at. I lift my chin and stare right back. His eyes tighten and he shakes his head—clearly disappointed in me.

I know they found Emma's bicycle.

I know that because I made sure they would.

THIRTY
MICHAEL

The Boar's Nest hasn't changed a bit. I figured it'd be the same. Small towns don't change. And if they do, it's gradual, like evolution, something you wouldn't notice in your lifetime. The Dodge Charger is still there. The only glory this town has ever seen. And it's really not. It's an illusion. A hollowed-out vehicle set on the roof of the only business still afloat. The same men are bellied up to the bar. Older. Grayer. Less room between the bar and their stomachs. And the same bartender is slinging drinks. She's not young and vibrant anymore. She's grown into her acceptance of an unexceptional and mundane life, her appearance following suit. Nicole and Beth enter first, taking a pair of seats at the bar. All necks crane in their direction . . . not because they're lookers but because they're something new to look at. I can tell by Beth's shoulders, which are practically pinned to her ears—she'd rather be anywhere but here. That makes two of us. I suggested coming here because I couldn't stand being in that house anymore. Too many memories. Plus, I had to pry my sisters away from their "investigation" which has just been a chain of maybes. Nothing concrete. It's all speculation, and it's distracting us from what we're here to do . . . settle Mom's estate.

Beth looks to me and says, "Beer?"

I nod. I don't want one, but I'll have one. It's how I feel about most things in life.

Nicole and I take a seat on either side of her. My eyes flick to the clock on the wall. I know the time is off by at least forty-five minutes. Behind. Not ahead. A place like this would never be ahead. No one here cares though—because for them, there's nothing to look forward to, so you may as well slow it down, savor the futile moments.

Pool balls rack and crack. A dart thuds into a board. The jukebox roars a Toby Keith song. And there's laughter and chatter . . . All small distractions from their small lives.

The bartender slides a beer in front of me and smiles. Between her skimpy clothes, her bleached blond hair, and her Fake Bake tan, it's obvious she's trying to appear younger than she is. It's not working though.

"Hey, Michael. It's good to see you." I recognize her now. We went to school together. She was two grades above me. In another life, she didn't know me. In this one, she does. But I don't know her. Funny how things change. I tell her the same back because it's the polite thing to do.

She asks me what I've been up to. I tell her that I'm in California now and ask her the same, expecting a short answer . . . maybe a word or two, *Same ole, same ole*. But she goes on and on, dragging out the most pointless of things. She has two guinea pigs. She told me their names, but I already forgot. She's in cosmetology school or was in it, I don't know. She recently took up some dance fitness class, Roomba or Zumba, or something like that. It's always the least interesting people that have the most to say, like their existence would cease if they didn't speak of it. I know I sound cruel. But how else do you survive a place like this and manage to get out? A place no one knows about unless you tell them. You get perspective. A townie whistles at the end of the bar for another drink, putting an end to this fruitless conversation. I should buy him a drink as a thank you.

"First round's on me," Beth says, holding her glass up.

I clink mine against hers and nod. First born, first round. Makes sense. But as the last, the youngest, I know what that means. I'll clean up the mess.

"I'll get the next," Nicole says, and I know I'll actually be paying for her round, but I don't mind. Even though she's my older sister, it hasn't felt that way in a long time. Age doesn't always mean maturity. Sometimes it just means they've spent more time on earth, and the only things to show for it are diminished bones and skin etched with deep ridges. Not wisdom. Not value, just time. Nicole pulls out her phone and buries her head into it, purposefully turning her body away from us. Whatever she's doing, she doesn't want us to see it.

"So, what do you think?" Beth gestures to the bar.

"It's how I remembered." It's a truth . . . just not a whole one, and I've learned that's where life exists, in between the wholes and the halves.

"I actually haven't been to the Boar's Nest in years," she says, scanning the bar.

I'm not sure why she tells me that. Maybe it's her way of separating herself from the other locals. She sips her beer while a beat of silence passes between us.

"Did you ever think you'd end up back here?" she asks. I can tell it's not the question she wants to ask. It's just the one she starts with.

I nod because I knew I would. There are only two types of roads in Allen's Grove: ones that lead out and dead ends.

"Never wanted to, but here I am," I add.

Beth slightly frowns into her glass.

"I'm sorry," I say, and I mean it. My intention is never to hurt her. But I already have, just by being here, a reminder of what could have been. It's one of the reasons I didn't want to come back. No one wants to be someone else's monster.

Beth's frown becomes a straight line, and she nods. She's not saying she forgives me. She's saying she'll let it go . . . for now.

"Cheers," Nicole says, rejoining the conversation. Her cell phone is stowed away again. She clinks a vodka soda against our beers. We all toast, strained smiles from me and Beth. It's the polite way to treat an addict. *Thank you for being here with us . . . still.*

Nicole slurps nearly half of her drink, and her lips relax as she releases the straw. I consider telling her to slow down, but I know she'd do the opposite, so I keep my mouth shut.

"What's the plan for tomorrow?" Nicole asks.

She's referring to Mom's funeral, if it can even be qualified as one. We haven't really talked about it, aside from listening to the instructions from the lawyer, that her ashes should be spread around our land. It feels so lackluster. Like emptying a dustpan into a garbage can.

"We'll walk the property and spread her ashes at sunset," Beth explains. "It was her favorite time of day, when the sun would slide past the horizon, creating a mosaic of colors. Mom said it was the only thing she could count on in life." She gulps her beer.

"That's pretty depressing," I say.

"Well, do you blame her?" Beth looks to me. "Knowing what we know now."

Nicole leans over the bar, so she can address both of us. "I'd like to read something I wrote at Mom's funeral."

I'm not sure if she's asking for permission or just telling us.

Beth nods. "That's fine. Also, Lucas and Susan are stopping by . . . just for a bit."

Nicole's eyes double in size. "What? Why?"

Beth shushes her. "Because he asked. And what was I supposed to say? 'That's not a good idea, because my mom and dad had something to do with your sister's disappearance, so it'll be awkward for us'?" Beth clenches her jaw so tight her teeth just might crumble into dust.

"Well, how are we supposed to act with them there?" Nicole huffs.

"Like you never saw that tape."

"And what about Christie Roberts?" She eyes Beth and then me.

"You agreed you'd give it a rest until after Mom's funeral," I remind her. "We've got a lot to do, and . . ." I lower my voice, craning my neck toward her, "pinning every unsolved missing person case on Mom and Dad isn't the best way to honor Mom's memory."

Nicole rolls her eyes. "I wasn't pinning it on them. I was just asking questions."

Beth chugs the rest of her beer and slams the glass against the bar top, signaling the end of the conversation. The bar lady notices almost immediately and offers her another one. This time Beth orders a double whiskey, specifying that she wants rail. I'm not sure if she orders that because it's all she can afford or because she's trying to punish herself.

"Hey," I call out, putting my hand up to get the bartender's attention. Her eyes flick to me. They're dull, clouded over. Her body's defensive mechanism to mask the reality of her surroundings.

"Yeah, Michael," she says in a cheery voice.

I wish I remembered her name, but I don't. She's an Edith, a Ruth, or a Maureen, something unremarkable and dated.

I scan the whiskey bottles set on the glass shelf behind her. It's a dive bar, so they don't have the best, but I pick out the best they have.

"Make it Elijah Craig instead, and put it on my tab."

If Beth is set on punishing herself tonight, at least I can make sure it tastes good.

The bartender grins. Generosity and money always garner a smile. "You got it," she says with a nod. "Anything else?"

I finish the rest of my beer and pass the glass to her. "Yeah, I'll have the same as her, and whatever you want, put it on my tab."

Her dull eyes seem to brighten, only for a second or so. It's all they have in them. She thanks me and starts pouring drinks.

"I was fine with rail," Beth groans.

"I know."

There's no point in arguing with her because I know she'll drink it . . . begrudgingly, but she will.

The entrance door opens with a high-pitched squeak, and a gust of cold air floats into the stale bar. I notice a change in Nicole. Her posture straightens like a marionette being yanked taut. She smooths out her hair and adjusts her oversized top. I follow her gaze. A police officer enters the bar. He's dressed in a waterproof shell jacket and a two-tone uniform, dark brown on top and light khaki on the bottom, complete with a tie and high-gloss oxford shoes. The patch on his shoulder tells me he's from the Walworth County Sheriff's Department. The gold badge pinned to his chest tells me he takes himself seriously. His chin isn't held high, so I know he's not here on official business. There's a flicker of recognition in his eyes when they land in our direction. He looks familiar, but like the bartender, I've forgotten him too. The officer strides toward us. He's taller than nearly all the patrons he passes by. Many exchange greetings with him. Others look away, slumping their shoulders like they're trying to appear as small as possible. I assume the ones shrinking into themselves have open warrants.

"Hey, Casey," Nicole greets him in a warm voice.

The officer nods and says, "Hey, Nicole."

Casey. Casey. My brain searches for familiarity. I catch a glimpse of his name tag. *Dunn*. That's it. Casey Dunn. He was good friends with Nicole in high school, and it looks like he's made something of himself.

"Hey, Beth," Casey says.

She swivels her barstool around, greets him, and brings the glass of Elijah Craig to her lips, taking a long sip.

Casey extends his hand to me. "Michael."

I shake it and say, "It's nice to see you."

His eyes scan over us as he expresses his condolences. It's that awkward song and dance of *thanks* and *yeah* and *it's such a shame.* No one ever knows what to say. We repeat what we've heard from movies or TV shows or, for some of us, we call on those experiences when death previously touched our lives.

"What brings you here?" Beth asks.

"Oh." His gaze briefly shift to Nicole. "Just stopped in for a drink."

He's lying but I don't call him out.

I flag the bartender down and order Casey a double whiskey. She pours it quickly and slides it to me with a smile.

"Here," I say to Casey, handing him the glass.

He stammers and thanks me, clutching it in his hand like it's a live grenade. He takes the smallest sip. His reaction and reluctance tell me he's still on duty. But then why is he here? Casey makes small talk, asking what I've been up to. I ask him the same, even though I can see exactly how his life has played out. The conversation is stilted and clumsy, like catching up with a stranger. Finally, he looks to Nicole and asks if he can speak with her outside.

That's why he's here. *Nicole*. And this is clearly the friend who "borrowed" Emma Harper's case file. The two of them head toward the entrance. He sets the nearly full glass of whiskey on a table he passes. I wonder what he's got for her now. Shaking my head, I swivel my stool to face the bar.

"What?" Beth asks, squinting at me.

"He's bad news."

"Who?"

"Casey." I sip my whiskey.

"Why do you say that?"

"Because what he's doing is illegal. You can't just take police case files and hand them out to anyone you want."

"No one's going to notice they're even missing." Beth shrugs.

"Someone might."

"I wouldn't think twice about it," she says. "We've got enough to worry about as it is."

"I guess." I take another sip and glance over at Beth. "Did you decide what you want to do with the house?"

"Not yet. Why?"

"I've been thinking more about it, and I'd like to buy it from you."

Her shoulders tense up, but she quickly relaxes them—not before I notice. She busies herself by rotating the glass in her hands. It's like she's giving herself time to come up with an excuse as to why she won't sell it to me. She said she wanted money, so why not take it from me?

I lean to the side and retrieve a piece of paper from the back pocket of my jeans. Unfolding it, I slide it across the bar in front of her.

"What's that?"

"It's a check for four hundred thousand dollars, well-above market value."

Beth doesn't take it. She just stares at it. Money talks . . . but only if you're listening. And I don't think she is.

Her brows shove together. "Why do you want the house?"

"Because it's where I'll be able to visit Mom, since she chose not to be buried in a cemetery."

"You didn't even visit her when she was alive."

"I know, and I regret that. But I can't change the past. Plus, Nicole needs a place to live too. I saw where she was staying. It's depressing and not safe. This will give her something more stable and keep her away from the people she's been hanging around."

Beth tilts her head. "Giving her a place to stay won't make her stay clean. Trust me."

"I know but it can't hurt."

"I'll think about it," she says, and she slides the check back toward me.

"What's there to think about? You won't get more than three hundred for it, so you should just take my offer."

"Not everything's about money, Michael."

My eyes tighten. "Then what's it about, Beth?" I ask, but I already know the answer. It's about spite.

"I don't know."

"I think you do."

She clenches her jaw and moves her mouth side to side as though she's deciding what to say. I'm sure she's chewing on the truth, determining whether to swallow it or spit it out.

"Say it, Beth." I'm pushing her because I know she's been doing nothing but lying since I got here.

"I don't want you to have it," she finally admits. Then takes a sip of the whiskey I paid for.

"Why?"

"Because you get everything, Michael. You always have. I just don't want you to get your way . . . for once."

"You think I've had it my way. Look at our family. Nicole's an addict. Dad abandoned us. Mom's dead. And you, you're barely a sister. I'm your little brother and rather than being happy for my success, you hate me for it." I shake my head.

A tear gathers at the rim of her eye, fattening up before it finally falls. Her bottom lip trembles, even though she tries to hold it steady.

She knows I'm right. It's the truth, and it's not my fault it's hard to swallow. I slide the check in front of her again. Her gaze falls on the five zeros. I know she's considering it. That's all I need, because if she considers it then I know she'll make the smart decision. Beth's not stupid. She's just miserable.

THIRTY-ONE
NICOLE

Casey rocks back on his heels and shoves his hands into his coat pockets. We're standing outside the bar, off to the left where his cruiser is parked. A couple of older, potbellied men puff cigarettes near the entrance, paying no mind to us. The air is cool, and the sky is dark, a thin veil of clouds blocking the stars out of sight. I like that it's overcast. Makes me feel like I'm not missing out on anything. The jukebox inside is turned up to full volume, causing the bar to vibrate and pound.

"Weird seeing your brother here," Casey says.

It's not a question or a statement. It's an observation.

"Yeah, it is. But he'll be gone soon, since Mom's funeral's tomorrow."

"Sorry," he says, pulling in his chin.

"Don't be."

My eyes flick back to where the men were smoking. There's only one of them there now, milking the last half inch of tobacco. He flicks the butt to the pavement and stomps it out before heading back into the bar.

"Where's the service being held?" Casey asks, grabbing my attention.

"Home. That's where she wanted it. She lived and died there, and that's where she wanted to stay. It'll be small."

He nods, and his eyes skim over my face. I wonder what he sees. The way I looked when we first met? Young and vibrant, with our whole lives ahead of us. Or does he see me as I am now? Someone who threw so much of her life away.

"Were you able to get the file?" I ask.

There's no sense in beating around the bush. I want to know what happened to Emma and Christie, and maybe it's for selfish reasons, but I don't care.

"Yeah," he stammers and turns away from me to open the passenger-side door of his cruiser. Casey rummages through a bag and pulls out two folders.

"This one is Christie Roberts's case file." I take it from him. It's thin compared to Emma's.

"Thanks," I say.

He holds out a second folder. It's even thinner than Christie's. "And there's this."

"What is it?" I ask, taking it from him.

"I cross-checked Emma Harper's case file, and it pulled a missing person report."

"For who?"

"Charles Gallagher."

THIRTY-TWO
LAURA

DECEMBER 16, 1999

The brick house on the corner sits quiet and dark. No Christmas tree with twinkling lights in any of the windows. The word *murderer* is scrawled across the two-car garage door, spray-painted in blood red. Cracked eggs are splatted on windows, yolks frozen against the panes. My shoes crunch over snow that's been packed down by trespassers and vandals. Clutched in my mitten-covered hands are a casserole dish and an assortment of baked goods. It's the least I can do after what Brian and I did. I still don't know why we got rid of Emma. When I bring it up, Brian tunes me out or just walks away. So, I started doing things that would make me feel an ounce better. Like this . . . bringing a hot dish and sweet treats to the man whose life we ruined.

The air is sharp and icy, pricking the sides of my throat as I breathe it in. A faint taste of blood enters my mouth as the capillaries seem to swell, bursting with the cold, then thawing on the exhale and trickling out of the fissures. At the door, I hesitate and notice the bell has been ripped clean off. He clearly doesn't want any visitors, and I don't blame him. I glance at the side street through the trees, the same one our house is on. Then I take a quick look at the park behind me that sits across from the main road, making sure no one is watching. I'm not sure how I'd explain bringing baked goods to Charles Gallagher.

I pound my fist against the door. It's a muffled knock thanks to my thick mitten. The wind whips against my face, stinging my skin. I knock again, this time harder. The drawn curtains on the front window flick and then settle into place. I know someone's home, but I don't know if they'll answer. Heavy footsteps grow louder as they clamor inside. A chain lock jingles. Three dead bolts click. The handle jerks. This type of protection is unusual for a small town, but not with what he's been through. Finally, the door swings open and on the other side stands Charles Gallagher.

I haven't seen him since the day Emma went missing, and he seems to have aged years in the past six months. He's still a tall, gangly thing but he wears a hardened face. Prison will do that to you, I suppose. He wasn't in long . . . only a month or so, but it was long enough. His dark hair is buzzed short. The same goes for his facial hair. A pair of thick glasses with silver frames rests on the bridge of his nose, and fresh pink scars stretch across his right cheek.

"What?" he asks. It's not a greeting, but I didn't expect one. He's been out of prison for ten days, and coming back to the Grove probably isn't much of an improvement. Although Charles was acquitted in a court of law, the court of public opinion said otherwise.

"Hi, Charles. I'm Laura. Laura Thomas. I live at the end of the street."

"Yeah," he says. His gaze dances all around me like he's readying himself for a fight-or-flight response.

I lift my hands a few inches, showing off the ceramic dish and stack of Tupperware containers. "I made too much, and I have extra casserole and baked goods." I don't want him to think I specifically made it for him, even though I did.

"And?"

"I thought you and your mother might enjoy them."

He eyes me and my Tupperware with suspicion and then scans the landscape behind me.

"Otherwise, they'll go to waste," I add, lifting a brow.

Charles squints as he studies my face. When he's finally made up his mind, he nods and beckons to follow him. I take a deep breath before crossing the threshold, reminding myself that he's not the dangerous one.

A tube television sits in the far corner of the living room, playing a rerun of *Garfield and Friends*. Charles glances at the screen, pausing for a moment to watch Garfield scarf down a pan of lasagna. He smiles faintly before continuing into the kitchen. I notice he walks with a limp now, and I'm not sure I should follow him, but I do. His house resembles what I've made of his life—a mess. A putrid scent of cat urine mixed with cigarettes permeates my nose. The sink is overflowing with dirty dishes, stacked a couple feet tall. Piles of old newspapers and ashtrays chock-full of stubbed-out Camel cigarettes clutter the kitchen table. Several cats meow from somewhere deep in the home but they don't make an appearance. Charles clears a small area on the table.

"You can set it there," he says.

I nod and place the containers down where he asked.

"Do you want a cup of coffee?"

"No, I'm fine."

He pulls open the fridge. It's nearly empty, aside from a case of Miller Lite and a dozen or so half-empty condiment bottles. "I've got beer too or tap water."

"I'm good," I say. "But you should refrigerate these two." I pull the casserole and another dish out from the stack of containers and extend them to him.

He eyes it suspiciously. "What is it?"

"This one's a cheese ball, and this is a tater tot casserole."

Charles collects the dishes and puts them in the fridge. He turns back toward me with knitted brows. "Why'd you bring me this stuff?"

I don't say, *Because I feel guilty for what you've been through.* I don't say, *Because this small gesture is more for me than it is for you.* Instead, I say, "Because I wanted to."

His face relaxes instantly, morphing from the near scowl of apprehension to a flat expression, as though he's feeling something new and isn't sure how to express it yet. I don't think anyone's ever done something for Charles because they wanted to.

"Charlie," a guttural voice calls from the other end of a dark hallway.

"Excuse me." He fills a glass with tap water and serves up several baked goods on a paper plate. Charles takes his time choosing, selecting a custard-filled red-and-green cupcake, smothered with cream cheese frosting; a fudge-covered Rice Krispie treat; and a Reese's Peanut Butter blossom cookie. As he walks out of the kitchen, he tells me he'll be back in a second.

A door creaks from somewhere in the house, and then there are muffled voices. I can't make out what they're saying, but I assume it's Charles speaking with his elderly mother. I haven't seen her in years. I don't think she leaves the house anymore, and she's not a person people would visit. She's like Charles in that sense, a pariah in a small town. She's an outcast because she is mean, whereas Charles is just odd, misunderstood. A black cat meows and presses his body against me, winding through my legs like a figure eight.

Charles reenters the kitchen carrying an armful of dirty cups and plates. "Sorry about that," he says as he sets them next to the sink where the tower of dirty dishes looms, a leaning tower of *grease-uh*. "My mother's not doing well. She's getting over a bout of pneumonia."

"I'm sorry," I say.

He nods, looking down at his feet briefly. I notice his big toe protruding out of a hole in his sock. "She really likes the cupcake," he adds. "That red-and-green one."

"I'm glad to hear that. It's a family recipe."

His gaze meets mine. "It's probably not a good idea that you're here."

"Do you want me to leave?"

"No." He shrugs. "I just mean with everything that's gone on. No one believes me. They all think I had something to do with that little girl." He shakes his head. "I would never . . ."

"I believe you," I say.

His eyes grow wide, and I finally notice the color of them. A mix of browns and greens that appear to change depending on the light. "Why do you believe me?"

I also can't answer this question truthfully. I want to. I want to tell someone what really happened because right now the truth feels like a parasite burrowed deep within my body, feeding on me, slowly weakening my will to live. I'm not sure how much more I can take of it.

"Because of the bicycle."

"Yeah . . . if it weren't for that bike showing up while I was locked up, I'd be facing life in prison. My lawyers said I didn't have a chance in hell. Lucky me." He sighs.

"If you didn't do it, why'd you confess?" I ask. I never understood it. Why admit to something you didn't do?

"I've asked myself the same question. But you try being interrogated for sixteen hours straight. Hungry, sleep-deprived, and just wanting it to be done. The more they talked about Emma and what they thought happened to her, the more I believed it wasn't just a story, but a memory of my own they were describing. Funny how quickly you can turn on yourself, mistake a lie for the truth. Then they told me if I confessed, it'd all be over. And I believed them." He leans against the counter.

"I'm sorry you went through that, Charles."

"Yeah, well, it's over now. At least the worst of it."

I scan the kitchen again. A telephone hangs on a wall covered in faded floral wallpaper. The coiled beige cord isn't connected to the receiver. It hangs freely, swaying left to right from the vent blowing hot air beneath it. An umbilical cord cut loose from its energy source.

"Is your phone broken?"

"No. But it rings off the hook with calls from people I have no interest in talking to. Reporters, pranksters, bill collectors, and those that wish death upon me."

"Have you considered moving? This town's not going to change their mind about you. You could leave and start fresh elsewhere."

"Can't. My money's all tied up in this house, and I've got my mother to look after. Ya know, before all this happened, no one in this town paid me any mind. I thought that was unbearable, feeling invisible, like I don't matter. But now I know that being detested is far worse than going unnoticed." Charles shakes his head and shuffles his feet. He looks to me. "You're the only one from town that's been kind to me."

I swallow hard and force a polite smile.

If only he knew . . .

THIRTY-THREE
BETH

The engine sputters once, twice before finally turning over. Michael clutches the handle above the passenger-side window like he's bracing for a bumpy ride. He offered to drive, but I insisted. I was the one with Mom in her final moments, so I should be the one who collects her and brings her home. Nicole sits in the back, thumbing through papers.

At the park, I turn left onto Highway X and head toward Delavan where the funeral home is located. It's two towns over. In the rearview mirror, I watch Nicole. Her eyes sweep left to right as she reads, pausing every now and then to take notes.

I know Casey gave her more police files at the bar last night, but she hasn't brought them up. Is she hiding something? And if so, why is she hiding it from us?

"What are you reading?" I ask.

Her eyes find mine in the mirror. "Nothing," she says.

Michael watches her via the vanity mirror fixed to his sun visor. "What was Casey doing at the bar last night?"

"Just hanging out." Nicole shrugs.

Michael and I exchange a look. Maybe he was right. Maybe Casey is a bad influence on her. He thinks he's helping Nicole with research, but really, she's spiraling. The case files are like the lyrics of a siren's song about the past, a place she can no longer live or visit.

"Oh yeah? Casey normally hangs out at the Boar's Nest while on duty?" Michael asks.

She lifts her head and squints.

"You shouldn't be involving him in this," I add.

"Casey doesn't know anything. He thinks he's helping me with research for a book," Nicole argues.

"He's going to get suspicious, especially since you keep asking him for more," I say.

"And what if someone notices those files are missing? One could easily be written off as an accident, multiple . . . not so much." Michael cocks his head.

Nicole's eyes darken. I try to keep my attention on the road, but I can't help but look at her, studying her facial expression. It's a defiant one, or maybe it's more indignant. The highway is clear in front, surrounded by corn fields on either side, so I'm not too worried about watching the road. It's only what's behind us that scares me.

"They won't," she argues.

"They might," I say. "Now, what else did he give you?"

She huffs and flips through the folders in her lap. "He brought me the case file on Christie Roberts's disappearance."

"Why?" Michael groans.

"Because I asked for it."

"No, I figured that much. Why did you want it? You still think Mom and Dad had something to do with her disappearance?" He turns in his seat to look at her.

"I don't know."

"What does the report say?" I ask, glancing back at the road.

"Exactly what we found in the newspaper clippings. The police thought she was a runaway, so there wasn't really any sort of an investigation."

"All right then." Michael readjusts himself and faces forward. "It's settled."

"No, it's not. We still don't know what happened to Emma, and Charles Gallagher went missing too," she says.

I find her eyes in the rearview mirror. "What do you mean *went missing?*"

Nicole holds up a thin folder. "Casey cross-checked cases connected to Emma Harper's disappearance, and pulled this one. His mother reported him missing on December 28, just a few weeks after he was acquitted and released."

"He probably just skipped town," I say, pulling off the interstate into Delavan. Compared to Allen's Grove, this place looks like a city. It has a Walmart, Starbucks, Kohl's, and a McDonald's, all the staples of a Midwest town.

"That's what the police thought, so they never looked into it. But the statement his mom gave casts a lot of doubt that Charles just left on his own accord."

"What'd she say?" Michael turns to look at her again. I can't tell if he's actually interested or just humoring Nicole.

I park the car on the street in front of Monroe Funeral Home and kill the engine.

"She said Charles walked over to the Boar's Nest for a drink the night of December 27, 1999. It was the first time he left his house since his release. The next morning she realized he had never come home. His working vehicles were all accounted for and none of his belongings were missing. She said there was no way he just up and left because he would never abandon her."

Nicole looks up from the paper, her eyes seeking some sort of response from Michael or me.

I glance over to the funeral home. It sports the facade of a real house with brick exterior on the first floor and white panel siding on the second. There's a front porch and an American flag is mounted to the railing. It flaps and twirls in the wind. If it weren't for the large Monroe Funeral Home sign affixed in the yard, I would have thought it belonged to a family, like every other house in this neighborhood. But it doesn't. It's meant to look like a home, to appeal to the living, so that the business of death feels personal, not cold and commercial.

"Neither of you think it's odd that Charles Gallagher went missing?" Nicole asks, pulling me from my thoughts.

"No," Michael says. "From the sound of it, the only person that cared about him was his mother. Can you even be considered missing if no one misses you?"

"Yes, Michael, you can," Nicole scoffs. "What do you think, Beth?"

I let out a sigh and push open the car door. "I think today isn't about Christie Roberts or Emma Harper or Charles Gallagher. Today's about Mom, and I'm going in to get her, so we can take her home."

I slam the door closed behind me and breathe in the scent of fall—the crisp, sharp air mixed with the decay and rot of withering plants, dry leaves, and trees hunkering down for the season. It has a musky-sweet smell to it. Just like death, it's all-consuming.

THIRTY-FOUR

NICOLE

The black long-sleeve top and pair of slacks I'm wearing are two sizes too big because they're not mine, they're Mom's. It feels strange to wear her clothes to her own funeral, but I didn't have any other options. I hold the urn close to my chest. She's inside of it, or at least what's left of her. Michael emerges from the hallway, looking polished and pulled together.

"Nice suit," I say.

He readjusts his cuff links and says, "Thanks."

"How much was it?"

Michael rolls his eyes and smooths the sleeves of his jacket.

As much as I resent him for having so much more than me, it hasn't been all bad having him home again. He buys the good liquor, he's kept the fridge full this week, and he protected me . . . just like he did when we were kids.

Beth's footsteps click down the hallway, growing louder. She's dressed in a black top, skirt, tights, and a pair of heeled boots that extend to her knee. Her clothes mold to her curves and most of them look new. Even her hair is swooped and clipped up. Her makeup is minimal but it's clear she took her time applying it. I can't remember the last time I saw her put any effort into her appearance. But I wonder if the effort is for Mom or for Lucas.

"You look nice," I say.

She nods and beelines to the bottle of scotch set on the counter-top. Beth splashes more than a shot into a coffee cup and slams the whole thing.

Michael looks to me with an expression that says, *What's going on with her?*

We're both concerned for Beth. She watched Mom die. That couldn't have been easy, and I think a part of her perished with Mom. She seems close to falling apart, splitting right down the middle. I'm already broken, so there's no need for them to worry about me. Shattering a fragment of a fragment means nothing once the structure is gone.

Beth straightens her skirt and glances at Michael and then me. She extends her hands, so I pass the urn to her.

"Ready?" she says, holding it against her chest. Beth's acting as though we're just running an errand rather than attending our moth-er's funeral service. But maybe it's helping her get through this.

Outside, we walk to the top of the property line where the old farm fence separates our land from the neighbor's cow pasture. The sun is starting its descent, a fireball crashing slowly into the horizon, streaking the sky with hues of orange and pink. I read online that it only takes around five minutes for the sun to set. It's fleeting, and I think that's why Mom had such an appreciation for it. We value the briefest mo-ments most because they're the ones that define us—a first kiss, a sudden death, an accident, a marriage proposal, a high . . .

"We're gathered here today to . . ." Beth starts.

I stifle a laugh, but it comes out fast and sudden like a sneeze.

"What?" she snaps.

"That's the start of a wedding ceremony, not a funeral," I say.

"Then you do it," she huffs.

A high-pitched squeak interrupts our bickering. Lucas pushes Susan in a wheelchair across the road, stopping at the top of the steep drive-way. One wheel screeches every few feet or so. Lucas waves his hand to signal to us. It's clear he won't be able to get her across the yard.

"We should go over there," Beth says.

All the color in her face has drained, leaving her looking pale and sickly. "Are you sure that's a good idea?" My eyes go to Lucas and Susan, thirty or so yards from us, and then back to Beth. "You don't look well."

She takes a couple of deep breaths. "I'm fine. I'll be fine. Lucas said they won't stay long, so let's just get this over with," Beth says, starting across the yard.

We follow behind.

"Hi, Lucas. Hi, Susan," Michael greets them as we approach. He shakes Lucas's hand. Then he kneels in front of Susan's wheelchair, holding her frail hand.

Susan looks exactly how I thought she would, like someone that life hasn't been fair to. Although she's wearing an oversized down jacket, it's obvious how feeble she is, weighing no more than a hundred pounds. Her sallow skin is etched with wrinkles and her eyes have lost their shine, like the person behind them is half here, half gone . . . or just wishing to be gone. I still can't believe what our parents did to her, especially my mom, since they were friends. I guess we do what we do to survive.

"Hi, Brian," Susan says, placing her hand on Michael's.

Beth and Lucas exchange a concerned look.

"Mom, that's Michael. Brian and Laura's youngest," Lucas corrects her.

Susan crumples her face in confusion. "Where is Brian then?"

My eyes go to the road, thinking this would be the perfect moment for him to arrive, veering into the driveway in his old black truck. But after our failed attempt to track him down, I've finally realized that I'll never see my dad again. Maybe I'm saying goodbye to him too today.

"He went to the store," Michael says, delivering a quick smile.

Her face flattens and she looks at her spindly wrist as though she's checking the time. "He's been gone a while," she says.

Michael nods and gets to his feet. "Yeah, he has."

"And Laura. Where's the birthday girl?"

Beth clutches the urn a little tighter. Lucas mouths, *Sorry*, to us and bends down to eye level with his mother. "Mom, we're here for Laura's funeral. She passed away. Do you remember me telling you that?"

Confusion gathers on Susan's face again. She furrows her brow in frustration. "No. That's not true. Laura and I were just talking the other day. She said she knew where Emma was, that she'd show me."

My eyes go wide. Michael coughs and clears his throat. Beth's eyes fill with tears. Her bottom lip trembles, and she sucks it in to bite it.

Did Mom really try to tell Susan what happened? Or is Susan's mind in 1999, back when Emma went missing?

"I'm going to take you home, Mom." Lucas holds eye contact while he slowly gets to his feet.

"Where's your sister at?" Susan asks, ornery now.

"She's out on a bike ride," Lucas says, exchanging a glance with each of us. He whispers, "I'm sorry. She was much better this morning."

"It's all right," I say.

"Don't worry about it," Michael adds.

Lucas reaches for Beth's hand and holds it while Michael and I retreat a few steps to give them a moment. He tells her he'll call later, thanks her for letting him stop by, and then drops her hand.

"Emma better be home before dinner," Susan says as Lucas starts to wheel her back up the driveway

Beth turns toward us, tears streaking her face.

"Do you think Mom really said something to Susan?" I ask.

"I don't know," she says through the tears, her voice cracking.

"What do we do?" I ask.

"Nothing. Even if Mom confessed to Susan, she's too far gone for anyone to believe her," Michael says in a hushed voice.

"But if Mom did tell her, maybe that's what she wanted . . ." I say.

"Stop," Beth interjects. She looks down at the urn and takes a deep breath, composing herself. "The only thing that I know Mom wanted was for her ashes to be spread around this property." She pulls the lid off, and Michael takes it from her. Her hand disappears inside of the container and emerges with a handful of ashes. Beth tosses them into the wind and says, "No matter what you've done, Mom, I still love you."

I slide my hand into the urn, collecting a scoop of ashes. I don't say anything before scattering them around me. I had planned to say something at Mom's service, but now that I'm here, I think those words are better left unsaid.

Michael hesitates when Beth extends the urn to him. He never liked the idea of cremation, so I'm sure flinging Mom's ashes around is even less appealing to him. She nudges the urn toward him again. Finally, he lets out a heavy sigh and dips his hand into it, holding up a palm full of ash.

"I can't believe this is what we're reduced to when we die—ashes." He turns his hand over. Some of the dust swirls in the air while the rest plummets to the ground.

"Sometimes we're reduced to much less when we're alive," I say.

Beth and Michael exchange a worried look. We walk the property, scattering her ashes and reminiscing on our favorite memories of Mom. The wind carries some of her away. The rest lands on the dewy grass, melding with the earth. By the time we're done, the sun is just a sliver, the horizon nearly swallowing it whole. Ashes to ashes, dust to dust, as the sun eventually sets on us all.

THIRTY-FIVE
LAURA

DECEMBER 27, 1999

The sound of the shower sputtering to life jolts me awake. It's pitch-black and quiet, save for the running water. The numbers on the alarm clock glow red with the time: 3:06 a.m. My hands search the other side of the bed, sliding along the twisted sheets and comforter. It's empty. Where's Brian? A streak of light glows beneath the bathroom door. Why would he be showering right now? I flick on the bedside lamp as I get to my feet and slip on my housecoat. I stare at the bathroom door for a moment, waiting for my eyes to adjust. When they do, I push it open. Brian stands on the other side of the fogged-up shower door. His head is tilted forward while the stream of water splats against the back of his neck, running down the sides of his face.

"Brian," I say.

His shoulders jump, and he slowly lifts his head. "Yeah, Laura."

"What are you doing?"

He hesitates before he responds, so I know whatever he says won't be the truth.

"I think I'm getting sick. I woke up sweating, thought it'd help to take a cold shower."

The steam fogging the mirror and shower door tells another story. I glance down at the floor, spotting his clothes crumpled in a pile. Bending down, I pick each one up and examine it.

"Laura," he says. "You can go back to bed. I'll be out in a minute."

I don't respond and continue inspecting the damp clothes. His winter jacket has several dark spots. I press my fingertips against one and pull away, noticing the red stain it leaves on my skin. Bringing my fingers to my nose, I sniff the smell of iron. I know exactly what it is, because only one thing smells like that.

"Laura," Brian says, poking his head out of the shower.

My gaze meets his, and he practically deflates.

"Are you hurt?" I ask.

He shakes his head and grabs a towel hanging from a hook on the wall. "It's not my blood." He dries himself off quickly.

I stare back at him, narrowing my eyes, but all I can see is a shadow. A looming black figure, floating through the steam toward me. "What did you do?"

"I didn't do anything," Brian says, wrapping the towel around his waist. "You did this."

"What?!" The word comes out as two syllables, the first sharp and angry, the second a forced whisper, realizing the time and that the kids are asleep. "How did *I* do this?"

Brian walks to the mirror and swipes his hand over it, clearing the condensation. He finger combs his hair while his reflected eyes lock onto me. "When you staged Emma Harper's bicycle at the Dead End."

I clench my jaw and fold my arms across my chest. "Yeah, so? I wasn't going to sit around and let an innocent man rot in prison for something he didn't do."

Brian turns to face me. He wears a look of frustration mixed with disappointment. "Well, you won't have to worry about that anymore . . . because Charles Gallagher is dead."

THIRTY-SIX
BETH

Mom's funeral was yesterday, and I think it'll always feel like it was only a day ago. That's how Dad's disappearance still feels: like it was yesterday. The moments that change us forever always feel recent, because we carry them with us whether we want to or not. I tape up a box marked *Donations* and set it in a stack with the others. The house is quiet, not peaceful, just quiet. Michael and Nicole left for Beloit about twenty minutes ago. She was getting shaky and needed her methadone treatment. If she went another day without it, I worry she'd relapse. I know she's been skipping days, trying to get clean faster, but it's only making things worse.

I get to my feet and survey the living room. It's all neatly packed away in boxes. We've gone through everything except the kitchen. I still have to decide on the furniture and the house. The more I've thought about it, the more I'm leaning toward selling it to Michael. He did offer well-above market value (I checked), and that money would be life-changing for me. I could pay off debt and visit my daughter in person instead of playing phone tag with her endlessly, always losing. And Nicole would have a place to live—although, I don't think it would make her any less of an addict. As much as I don't want Michael to get his way, I've realized that resenting him won't help me. Resentment only poisons the person who consumes it, not the one it's intended for. Michael and I are proof of that.

Knuckles rap against the front door. I get to my feet and make my way to it.

"Hey," I say, pushing the squeaky door open.

Lucas stands on the porch, holding a bouquet of yellow roses and wearing a faint smile. "These are for you."

I take the flowers from him and bring them to my nose, inhaling their bright scent.

"Thanks. Come in," I say, moving aside for him to enter.

He hesitates before crossing the threshold. Lucas hasn't been inside this house since he was eighteen. It must feel like stepping back in time. As I pull a vase from an open box and fill it with water, he kicks off his boots at the door. My eyes keep going to him while I unwrap the flowers and snip the ends.

Lucas walks into the kitchen and glances around, taking in his surroundings. The way his eyes bounce to every corner, to the ceiling, to the floor, it's like he's standing in a museum rather than my childhood home. I arrange the yellow roses in the vase and set them on the kitchen table. They seem out of place, at least to me. We lock eyes, and I wonder how I ever looked away from him to begin with. He looks a little rough, and I can tell he hasn't slept well. But he's still handsome to me. My fingers tingle as I imagine running them through his soft, scruffy facial hair, over his broad shoulders and down his firm pecs. I wonder if his fingers are tingling too, just at the thought of grazing them along my skin. Or am I the only one having these thoughts?

"How was the rest of the funeral?" he asks, delivering a sympathetic look. His hands grip the back of the kitchen chair in front of him.

"It was how she wanted it."

He slightly nods. "Sorry about my mom . . ."

"There's no need to apologize," I interrupt.

My eyes flick behind him to the VHS tape set on the VCR in the living room. It sits there, so unassuming. It's the only thing I didn't pack up. I just couldn't bring myself to. How do you pack up a secret like that? I force myself to look away, and my eyes land back on Lucas before he notices my split attention.

"Where are your siblings?"

"They went into town," I say, not offering any further explanation.

He nods, glancing around again, almost like he's looking for something. "It's kind of weird being in this house."

"I bet. It's been a while," I say as I walk into the living room and push around a few boxes. I don't know what to do with myself or how to act around him . . . especially with that VHS tape staring at me.

He follows me and stuffs his hands into the pockets of his jeans. "It feels like both yesterday and a lifetime ago." Lucas tilts his head. "It's funny how time works. They say it's linear but sometimes it feels like it's happening all at once. Ya know?"

"I know exactly what you mean," I say.

My eyes go to the tape again. If I played it for him, he'd be transported back to 1999 and finally, after all this time, he'd know exactly what happened to his sister. The past and present unfolding and happening all at once.

"Can I get a tour?" he asks, pulling me back to the now.

There's a small smile on his face, and I force myself to return it. "Sure. A lot has changed since you were last here."

"Really?"

"No," I tease. Our smiles grow just a half inch or so.

The tour is short, as the house isn't large by any means, and now we're standing in my bedroom, and it feels like we're sixteen again. The walls are bare now, and all that's left from my childhood is a bed, a dresser, and a desk. My suitcase sits open in the corner, which is what I've been living out of for a few months. Pencil markings on the door illustrate Lucas's and my heights. When we first started dating, we were basically the same height, but he shot up over a foot our sophomore year, and I stopped growing after that. My eyes go to the window and I remember all the times he snuck in and out of it. I wonder if that's what he's thinking about. He scans the room, not saying anything, but the corners of his mouth curve up, then straighten out before curving again. Waves of fond memories crashing against the shore of a much bleaker present day.

"Do you ever think about us?" he asks. His Adam's apple bobs as though he meant to swallow that question but uttered it instead.

"All the time," I say. I haven't told the truth in a while, and my words surprise me. I'm also not usually this forward. It's hard to be forward when you've been living life backward.

He inches closer to me, and we stare into each other's eyes, getting lost in them, finding our way back to one another. I used to think we were supposed to be together because he was the boy who lived across the street, but now I know geography had nothing to do with it. His hand brushes against my cheek, and it stirs every nerve in my body. I can feel him everywhere even though he's only touched one part of me.

"I missed you," I whisper, leaning my head into his hand.

"I missed you too, Beth," he whispers back.

There's nothing more to say. My heart races, pounding against my rib cage, and my mind calms for the first time in a long time when his lips meet mine. It's like I've found something I thought was lost forever. Our mouths open and close as our kiss becomes hungry. I bite his lower lip, and he moans. I remember the first time I did that to him. He responded the same way. His hands run all over my body, from my back to my breasts to beneath the waistline of my jeans. His fingers crawl past my pubic bone, eventually finding what they were looking for. I kiss him so hard that I have to pull away to come up for air.

His lips graze my ear and neck while his fingers rock inside me, leaving me panting and wanting more. Lucas pulls his hand from inside my jeans and kisses me again. His fingers curl under the hem of my shirt, and he tugs it off. I do the same to him, my nails running along his pecs and abs. We climb out of our jeans and fall onto the mattress. We could collide with pavement or loose gravel or even a floor covered in Legos, and I wouldn't care as long as it was him I was falling with.

———

I leave the bathroom and grab two beers from the kitchen before returning to my bedroom. Lucas slides his shirt back on and smiles at me as I stand in the doorway, watching him.

"Thirsty?" I ask, holding out a bottle of beer.

"Parched." He takes it and gulps, his eyes never leaving mine.

"Better?" I ask.

Lucas makes a refreshed sound and wipes his mouth with the back of his hand. "Better," he says.

I take a sip while Lucas meanders over to the window, looking out at the front yard. You can even see his house from it, just barely. I remember falling asleep staring out. Knowing he was close by always brought me comfort.

"Is this a one-time thing?" he asks, turning to face me.

"I hope not."

The corners of his mouth curve up, and his blue eyes seem to brighten to the shade of the sky behind him. "I hope it's not either."

I close the distance between us and lean into him, pressing my cheek against his chest. His heart beats slow and steady, but then it starts to race.

"There's something I never told you. It's about why I broke up with you our senior year," he says, looking down at me. His face has turned serious.

I take a step back so I can see all of him. "I thought it was because you were going off to college, and I wasn't."

He shakes his head. "I would have never ended it with you over distance."

My eyes start to sting, threatening a release of tears. "Then why did you?"

"It had to do with my dad."

"I know, Lucas. I know how hard it was on you when he died, and I wanted so badly to be there for you, but you shut me out."

"I didn't shut you out because I was grieving."

"I don't understand."

"My dad's death wasn't an accident," he says.

"Yes, it was. It was a hunting accident."

"No, he committed suicide."

I shake my head, but no words come out.

"He did, Beth. He even left a note behind. My mom just hid it, and the sheriff helped make sure the cause of death was listed as accidental for life insurance purposes. He felt bad for her, and I think a bit guilty after never finding the person responsible for Emma's disappearance." Lucas lets out a sigh and hangs his head.

"I'm really sorry, but I don't understand. What does that have to do with you breaking up with me?"

He furrows his brow. "I think my dad had something to do with Emma going missing."

"What? Why would you think that?"

Lucas takes a seat on the mattress. "Because of the letter he left behind."

"What'd it say?"

"It said he couldn't forgive himself for what he'd done."

My eyes are wide, flicking between Lucas and the door . . . the door that leads to the hallway, the hallway that leads to the living room, the living room that contains the VHS tape, and the VHS tape that holds the truth. How could he think his dad had anything to do with Emma's death? I mean, I remember Eddie being strict and a bit short-tempered when Lucas broke his rules, like being late for curfew or talking back. Maybe that was enough for him to think the worst of his dad.

"I worried that I was like him or could be like him." He looks up at me again. "So, I broke it off with you. I figured I was doing you a favor. Protecting you."

The tears that fall from my eyes are hot and heavy, full of sadness and anger.

"Maybe he wasn't referring to Emma," I say, taking a step toward Lucas.

"What else would it be about? Plus, he killed himself on the two-year anniversary of her disappearance."

I feel sick. My heart pounds so hard, I think it might crack a rib. Sweat gathers at my hairline, and my stomach flips and twirls. I force small breaths through my nose. Inhale. Hold for four. Exhale. But no matter how I breathe, years of regret and resentment are threatening to pour out of me. You can only hold so much in before it all comes gushing out. I race to the bathroom, making it to the toilet just in time before I throw up coffee, bile, and the few sips of beer I'd had. My entire body wretches. Then I feel a hand on my shoulder. He holds my hair and rubs my back, and I heave until I have nothing left inside of me. When I'm done, he leaves the bathroom so I can clean myself up.

I find Lucas in the living room, surveying the packed-up boxes . . . it's like he's looking for something. The VHS tape sits on top of the VCR. I wonder if he's noticed it.

I clear my throat to make my presence known. He stops inspecting my parents' belongings and whips his head in my direction, taking a step toward me. "Are you all right?" he asks.

I nod but look to the floor, unable to make eye contact. "Sorry," I say.

"Don't be. It's a hard truth to swallow. Trust me." He lets out a sigh.

It takes a few moments before I can finally look at him. It's difficult but I force myself. "I don't think it's the truth, Lucas."

He squints and tilts his head. Before he can say anything else and before I can talk myself out of telling him, I walk to the VCR and pick up the tape, flipping it over in my hand.

"What's that?" he asks.

"It's the truth of what really happened to Emma."

His eyes grow wide and his mouth parts slightly. It looks as though he's either going to scream or break down in tears, but I'm not sure which it will be.

"We found this tape when we were going through our parents' belongings. There's a short clip on here, only a minute or so in length. I don't think they ever meant to record it."

"What's on the tape, Beth?" A vein bulges on the side of his neck, and his bottom lip trembles.

"It's from June 15, 1999."

His eyes fill with tears and his mouth forms a hard line.

"Emma's on it. I don't know what happened to her, but I know my parents found her body down by the creek, and they got rid of it."

"What are you talking about, Beth?"

"Just . . . watch."

The tears fall fast and hard, streaming down his face and then clinging to his jawline.

He shakes his head but says, "Let me see it."

I look at the tape and nod. This might be a mistake, but I can't keep this from him, knowing that he's blamed his dad all these years and that my parents destroyed the future I should have had with Lucas.

Kneeling in front of the television, I slide the VHS tape into the VCR. It takes a moment before it clicks into place and then it makes a humming noise. Onscreen is our backyard at night. An owl hoots in the distance. The moon illuminates the tree line. The video camera scans the darkness. The branches of the trees look like hands and fingers stretching out in all directions. Lucas's breath hitches.

In the distance, my father calls out, "Laura." The camera swings to him and the screen fills with black-and-white static. I squint and take a step closer, waiting for the picture to come back onscreen. I know what happens next. My dad appears covered in blood. But it's just static. I glance over at Lucas. His eyes are narrowed but still glued to the TV screen.

Picking up the remote, I fast-forward. The tape stops and auto-ejects. I pop it back in and rewind it to the start of the dark tree line. It plays out again and as soon as my dad calls for my mom, the screen turns to static again.

"Is this some kind of sick joke?" Lucas seethes. The veins throb in his neck.

"What? No!" I eject the tape and look it over. The label reads *Summer '99*. This is the tape. Emma was on this tape. "I swear, Lucas, it was here. Emma was on this tape. She was dead. My parents got rid of her body. They kept it from everyone." My words come out in a desperate panic.

He shuffles a few steps back, shaking his head. "You're losing it, Beth. You're really losing it."

"No, I'm not, Lucas," I cry out. "I'm telling you it was on this tape. I don't know what happened to it, but it was here, I saw it."

I glance at the tape again. It's over twenty years old, and I know they wear out. But I saw it a couple of days ago; how could it just wear out? Or maybe . . . it was the break-in. Maybe the only thing they took was this clip. Erased it somehow. Or the tape was damaged when I watched it over and over again. Or Nicole or Michael? They didn't want their *precious* reputations ruined. Before I can explain any of this, Lucas is already backing out of the living room, eyeing me like I've lost my mind, just like everyone else in his life.

"This was a mistake," he says.

My face crumbles, and the tape slips from my hands, crashing to the floor.

"No, it wasn't." I try to close the distance between us. "I love you, Lucas."

He backs away from me like he's scared of what I might do, or maybe what he might do.

"I'll always love you, Beth, but I was foolish to think we could just pick up where we left off. You're not well, and I'm not well either."

"We can get through this together this time," I plead.

Lucas doesn't argue with me. He just shakes his head, turns on his foot, and leaves the house. Saying nothing is the worst way to end everything. No chance to plea. No chance to explain that I am trying to do the right thing and give him closure. He's just . . . gone. My eyes go back to the VHS tape, lying on the floor of the living room. I saw it. Didn't I? I drop to my knees, letting out a howl of a cry. The pain of losing him when I thought I had him back is nearly unbearable. We can only endure so much before we can't anymore.

THIRTY-SEVEN
MICHAEL

"What the hell?" I yell as I pull into the driveway.

Nicole lifts her head from her notebook. "Oh my God! What is she doing?"

A fire is ablaze in the front yard. Flames dance and flicker atop a pile of cardboard boxes. Beth stands beside the inferno squirting a container of lighter fluid into the roaring heat. The fire leaps with joy at the new fuel, rising to over six feet in height. She picks up another box and tosses it with the others. Embers shoot into the air and the fire continues to dance. I throw the car into Park at the top of the driveway and jump out of the vehicle, racing toward Beth. Nicole does the same, screaming her name. Beth ignores us or doesn't even register that we're here. She throws another box onto the fire. It's labeled *Elizabeth*. She picks up a jerry can of gasoline lying in the grass beside her and throws it on top of the flames.

I increase my speed, running as fast as I can. "Beth!" I scream.

She never looks in my direction. She just stares at the fire as it licks the can of petroleum. When I finally reach Beth, I tackle her off her feet, carrying her away from the blaze as far as I can before slamming us both to the ground. The jerry can explodes. The flames grow to twenty feet, and debris and embers spread in all directions. I use my body to shield Beth's. I can feel the heat in a wave on the back of my exposed arms and neck, the hairs singeing off. When the debris stops falling and the flames fade, I roll off of her. She lies on her back, staring up at the blue sky. Tears pour from her eyes in a steady stream, spilling down the side of her face and into her hair.

"Beth!" I yell, shaking her shoulders. "Beth!"

"Is she okay?" Nicole stands over us.

I shake her again, harder this time. She finally snaps out of it. Her eyes dart to me, then to Nicole and then back to me.

"What the hell were you doing? Are you trying to kill yourself?" I say, getting to my feet and brushing off dirt and grass clippings from my clothing.

"If I am, I'm not doing a very good job," Beth scoffs as she sits up.

"Why are you destroying all of Mom and Dad's stuff?" Nicole screams. She looks at the burning boxes. Some are labeled *Donate* or *Sell*. Her eyes twitch like she can't decide whether to be angry at Beth or feel sorry for her.

Beth wobbles as she slowly stands. It's like the ground is shaking beneath her. "It's not theirs anymore. They're gone."

"Yeah, so? That doesn't mean you just get to burn it." Nicole throws her hands on her hips. "What was the point of sorting through everything this past week if you were just going to light it all on fire?"

"There's no point to anything."

"Why are you acting like this?" Nicole yells.

"Like what?" She squints. "Like there aren't consequences to my actions. Like I can do whatever the hell I want. I figured I'd try life your way for a while."

Nicole shakes her head. "You're such a bitch."

"At least I'm something." She scowls and then a smug look crawls across her face. "Oh, and by the way, I'm selling the house. I'm selling everything. There's nothing left for me here," Beth says, looking right through us like she's moved on and we're already a part of her past.

"That's fine. Go ahead and sell it all," Nicole shouts.

I clear my throat and pull my shoulders back. "I'll have my financial adviser send over the paperwork tomorrow. You don't have to worry about anything, Beth. I'll take care of it all."

Her eyes darken. She's no longer looking through me, she's glaring at me.

"No." It's resounding. "I'd rather burn this place to the ground than ever sell it to you." She raises her chin.

Anger simmers inside of me, threatening to boil over. I can't take any more of this. "Fine. Keep the stupid house. You can live in it and die in it just like Mom, for all I care."

"Michael!" Nicole chides.

My eyes become slits. "I came back here to help, but I should have known you're not salvageable—neither of you are." I look to Nicole, my older sister who'd rather shoot up than shoot the shit. "I'll see you at the next funeral," I say, turning on my heel and heading toward my car.

"I'm sure it'll be one of yours," I call over my shoulder.

THIRTY-EIGHT
LAURA

DECEMBER 27, 1999

Brian takes a seat on the mattress beside me. His hair is still wet from his shower. Beads of water drip from his locks, slithering down his neck. His hands shake, so he places them firmly on his thighs and rubs them up and down the length of his femur. The bedside lamp provides a golden glow but not enough to fully light the room. It leaves his face in the shadows.

"What do you mean Charles is dead?" I ask, staring straight at the tube television set on the dresser in front of the bed. There's nothing on the screen. I should be looking at Brian for a tell of another of his lies, but I don't need to. I'll hear it in his voice. He's never been good at lying.

"I mean he's dead."

"How?" I ask. Apparently, I'm going to have to pull every single detail out of him. We used to never keep anything from one another, but now it seems we keep everything.

He lowers his head. "Eddie killed him."

My breathing immediately changes. It's deeper, coming from my gut rather than just my lungs.

"What? How? What happened?" The words come out sharp.

Brian sighs heavily. "We were at the Boar's Nest, Eddie and I, and then Charles showed up. He kept to himself, but Eddie couldn't take his eyes off of him."

"Why didn't you leave then?"

"I tried to convince Eddie to leave with me. I didn't want any more trouble, but he wanted to stay and have a good time. Then, he started pounding shots, and the more he drank, the less he paid any mind to Charles. So, I thought everything was fine."

"But it wasn't, was it?" I say.

Brian shakes his head. "No. At some point, Eddie said he had to use the bathroom. It was shortly after Charles left. But he never came back. I went to check on him, thinking he got sick, but he was gone. Figured Eddie headed home, so I closed out and decided to do the same." Brian lets out a deep breath and rubs the back of his neck.

"Then what?"

"When I was crossing through the park, I heard a muffled cry, so I followed the sound of it, and I found Eddie. He was curled up beside a tree, covered in blood, sobbing—and a few feet from him, Charles was lying in the snow, bloodied and beaten." Brian chokes back tears.

"Did you call the police?"

He whips his head in my direction, but I don't look at him. I just keep staring at the black screen. "Of course not."

"Jesus, Brian. Don't give me 'Of course not.' Why wouldn't you?"

"You think I'm going to call the cops on Eddie?"

"He killed a man."

"Yeah, because he was convinced Charles had something to do with his daughter's disappearance."

"Charles would have never been involved if it weren't for you and your anonymous tip." I narrow my eyes.

A look of surprise stretches across his face, but he doesn't argue, so I know it's true. He called it in just so they'd stop looking. Charles was an easy target. There was already the question of her shoe prints being in his yard. Plus, no one in town cared about him. So, of course others went along with it, echoing Brian's anonymous lie. The Grove wanted justice for Emma, and they didn't care where they got it.

"I'm sorry," he whispers. "I just wanted to protect us." His voice cracks and he hangs his head in shame.

"You've done everything but."

"That's not true, Laura. I am protecting us."

"Where's Charles now? I mean, his body," I ask.

"I took care of it."

"What do you mean *you took care of it*? How?"

"You know how."

I massage my temples with my pointer and middle fingers, rubbing them in small circles. I don't have a headache yet, but I will by the end of this conversation.

"And what about Eddie?"

"I got him cleaned up, walked him home, and told him to not tell anyone about what happened, not even Susan or Lucas," Brian says. "I said if anyone asks, he and I walked home together at twelve thirty a.m."

"You should have never phoned in that tip."

"And you should have never planted Emma's bicycle."

"Don't you dare put this on me. You're the one that refused to call the police about Emma," I spit. "I still ask myself every day why I went along with what we did. Why I let my love and loyalty to you blind me to what we were doing, silence me from asking questions. So don't you start to question me in all of this. Why are we even in this mess? Why didn't you call for help?"

"I told you I couldn't. I need time."

"Time's up, Brian. If you don't tell me everything—I mean every single fucking detail about what happened to Emma Harper—I'll go to the police myself. I don't care what happens to us. I can't live like this anymore." I turn my head to face him.

He lets out a deep breath and cranes his neck, meeting my gaze.

"You really wanna know, Laura?"

"No. I don't want to. I have to. And if you had anything to do with Christie Roberts's disappearance, I want to know that too."

Brian lowers his chin, accepting defeat. "Fine," he says, taking a deep breath, but this time he exhales the truth.

I sit there silently listening to my husband as he tells me what happened to Emma Harper and everything that occurred as a result of what we did. By the time he's finished speaking, I hate him and I hate myself, but I don't blame him . . . because I would have done the exact same thing.

THIRTY-NINE
NICOLE

The tires on Michael's rental car screech as he peels out of the driveway, hurling down the road at forty-plus miles per hour. He didn't even grab his belongings. He just left. Beth stomps off in the opposite direction, toward the house. The front door slams with a *bang*, punctuating her rage. The fire is still ablaze, burning through the boxes. With no one feeding it, it'll be out within the hour, just a pile of embers and ash. It's true what they say: nothing lasts forever.

A light breeze tickles my bare arm. It hasn't felt anything but the cast that encased it for the past four weeks. The doctor finally removed it today. He said my arm was strong enough to not need the extra support. That might be true for my arm, but I'm not so sure it's true for me.

Inside the house, I call Beth's name. I can't remember the last time I've seen her so upset. Maybe when Dad went missing. Maybe when she blew out her knee. Or maybe with me. The glass sliding door to the deck is slightly ajar. The wind whips through the crack, whistling. I go to close it and see Beth's head bobbing up and down as she stomps across the hillside, heading toward the valley. One hand is a balled-up fist by her side while the other clutches a spiral notebook. It looks like one of Mom's journals. I wonder if she's also going to incinerate that. I consider going after her but figure she wants to be alone. I can put out any fires she might start, but I can't extinguish the one burning inside of her. When the valley swallows Beth, my eyes go to the bare trees. They've been stripped of nearly all their leaves, their most fragile organs, expelled to conserve energy in order to endure the winter season. Sometimes you have to lose parts of yourself just to survive.

The sky has darkened to a steel gray. In the distance, thick, bulbous clouds pile on top of one another, brewing a storm as they head in our direction. *How fitting.* Stacks of boxes still fill the living room, even though Beth burned at least a dozen of them. I drift down the hallway toward my bedroom. I don't know what to do with myself now. The sealed white envelope sits propped against my bedside lamp. *Nicole* is scrawled across it in my mother's handwriting. I haven't opened it yet. I remember the instructions the lawyer provided when he handed us each an envelope: *Your mother requests you don't open until after the funeral.* That was yesterday. I pick it up and turn it over. A piece of Scotch tape holds the flap down, sealing the words Mom left for me. My fingers pick at the sticky adhesive. What did she want to tell me?

Lifting the flap, I pull out a folded piece of computer paper. It looks like a piece of scrap because about a third of its length is missing. I wonder why she didn't use a full sheet. Did she not have much to say? One side is blank, but the other has two lines of her handwriting. My eyes scan the words. There's not many of them. But I read them over and over anyway, ingesting every letter. A teardrop splashes onto the paper, making the word *deserved* bleed black ink. Another tear lands on the word *wanted*. My breaths become rapid and frenzied, expiring from my nose in short, quick bursts. My skin warms as the blood underneath begins to boil. The letter slips from my fingers and slowly floats to the floor. I mouth my mother's parting words once more . . .

You're not the child I wanted, but you're the one I deserved.
—Regretfully, your mother

FORTY

BETH

The rain doesn't fall today. It crashes, hurls, bombards, punishes. It's like the sky is angry, making a show of its displeasure. My grip tightens around the wooden handle of a shovel as I drag it behind me, trudging through the long grass. Clutched in my other hand is one of my mother's rolled-up notebooks, opened to an entry dated August 15, 1999, two months after Emma went missing. It was the last line that stuck out to me. She wrote, *I've learned there's a lot of things you can bury, but the past isn't one of them.* Emma Harper was never found, and I think that's because she never left this land.

I can hear the creek up ahead, babbling like it's trying to talk, trying to tell secrets its mouth swallowed two decades before. Without that VHS tape, I have nothing to prove to Lucas that I'm telling the truth. And without Lucas, I have nothing.

The rain softens and muddies the ground, making it easier for the blade of my shovel to pierce. It's as though it wants me to unearth the past my parents buried. I start underneath the bridge where Highway X runs over the creek. This is where she was in the video. Lying underneath the overpass. The muscles in my arms explode as I dig, scooping up heaping piles of dirt and tossing them aside. *She has to be here,* I repeat to myself each time the blade penetrates the soil.

I pause only to catch my breath, shake out my arms, and tie back my soaked hair when it clings to my face. The rain falls harder and thunder roars in the distance. Lightning stretches across the blackened sky. I stop for a moment and lean against my shovel, surveying my progress. Several small holes, each a few feet deep, are scattered beneath the bridge. But there's no sign of her. I steal a couple of deep breaths, readying myself, and go at each hole again, digging as quickly as I can. When my muscles are fatigued, I collapse to my knees. Mud clings to my jeans and shoes, weighing me down even further. My lungs gasp for air. It feels like I'm breathing in shards of glass, and I'm not sure how much more I can take. I let out a wail of a scream. It echoes against the concrete overpass but is quickly drowned out by a loud burst of thunder, the sky not wanting to be outdone. The creek rises, slowly filling the freshly dug hole closest to its shallow bank. I remember how high the creek can get in the spring. All of this is under water for a few months of the year. If Emma were buried this close to the creek, the earth would have spit her up a long time ago.

My eyes follow the shoreline all the way to the barbed wire fence that separates this property from farmland. There are thick woods on the right side, with overgrown weeds, swollen bushes, and less mature trees that twist into one another, fighting for resources. There's the path that leads to the field of wild grass and the valley beyond that. Maybe she's there. I get to my feet and start in the direction of the hillside, dragging the shovel behind me. If I don't find Emma, no one ever will. Just before I reach the wild grass, the chime of a bell stops me in my tracks. The wind whips and there's that chime again. I hold my breath to hear it better, to figure out where it's coming from. It rings from somewhere deep in the twisted woods.

Pushing past low-hanging branches, I climb over fallen trees, step around burdocks and thistles. I use the shovel to hack through a wall of lush weeds that have grown into a dead bush. Their stems, nodes, and veiny leaves entangle the woody shrub, choking out its existence. I finally break through the invasive species. The gap opens to a small clearing. The bell rattles again. It's attached to a collar meant for a cat.

The collar hangs from a wooden cross staked into the ground. Written in Sharpie on the crosspiece is the name *Mooch*. The handwriting is childlike, and the letters have faded to a light gray. I recognize the handwriting. It's mine. Mooch was my cat. She died when I was eight. Another cross stands a few feet away. The name *Timmy* is written across it, our first family dog. Another cross bears the name *Sasha*, another dog.

The shovel slips from my fingers, thudding against the ground. I fall to my knees and weep for the past. When there are no more tears left to cry, I pick my head back up and scan the clearing. Raindrops slither through the snaking branches above. A bolt of lightning briefly illuminates the sky. The thunder booms and rumbles. I let out a heavy sigh and get to my feet. My eyes go to the crosses, and I realize there are more of them, six to be exact. Two rows of three sit on either side of the clearing. Timmy, Sasha, Mooch, Butterfly, Goofy, and Garfield. I inch closer to the opposite end of the clearing where the other three crosses stand. Butterfly, Goofy, and Garfield.

"Butterfly," I say out loud, but the name feels foreign, not one I've ever called out. I don't remember having a pet named Butterfly. Maybe Mom and Dad did after I moved out. But I would remember that.

The shovel spikes through the dirt in front of the cross labeled *Butterfly*. I dig until my muscles are weak, and then I push past the weakness and just keep digging. The hole grows deeper and wider until finally the spade hits a hard object. I drop to my knees and use my hands to scoop and scrape away the soil, unearthing whatever it is that's been buried here. When it comes into view, I gasp for air, falling backward, choking, unable to breathe. It's a skeleton. But it's not an animal.

FORTY-ONE

NICOLE

I slam on the brakes; the tires skid across the wet concrete as I throw my mom's station wagon into Park in front of U.S. Bank. Well, technically, it's my station wagon now. I don't remember the drive here. I don't remember seeing a road or other cars or street signs. It was like I was underwater the whole time, my senses drowned out. I glance at myself in the rearview mirror. Blood vessels have ruptured around my eyes, leaving a spattering of tiny purple and red dots. It could have been from holding in a scream until it felt like my head was going to explode. My mascara is smeared and streaked down my cheeks. I wipe it away and try to compose myself, smoothing out my hair and dabbing my eyes.

The rain drums against the windshield. I unclench my hand, revealing a small silver key surrounded by a palm of bloody gouges. The air stings my skin that's been frayed from squeezing it so tightly. I take a couple of deep breaths. The lockbox Mom left for Beth is in this bank, and I'm sure it must contain some money or at least something of value I can sell. My hands shake and my collapsed vein almost seems to bounce at the mere thought of a high. The little prick of the skin, the red cloud, the rush. The feeling of a full body massage from the inside out. All of my problems gone in an instant. And Mom's words forgotten. It's exactly what I need.

I put on a pair of sunglasses and step out of the vehicle, racing for the door to escape the rain. Inside the bank, I'm greeted by an older woman wearing a name tag that says *Mel*. Her eyes skim over me, tightening and relaxing like she's made her judgment. She asks how she can help and purses her thin lips.

I retrieve a piece of paper from my bag and slide it under the glass window that separates me from her. "I'd like to access a safe-deposit box."

The woman brings the paper to her line of sight and examines it. "And you're Laura Thomas."

"No, I'm her daughter. She passed away this week."

Mel tilts her head and delivers a sympathetic look. "I'm very sorry for your loss."

"Thanks," I say.

"Do you have a death certificate?"

I shake my head.

The bank teller glances at the paper again before typing on her computer. "Let me see what I can do." Her eyes scan left to right on her screen. "It says here that Elizabeth Thomas is authorized to access the lockbox. I assume that's you."

"That's right." I nod.

"All right, I'll just need to see an ID." She delivers a faint smile.

I start to dig through my bag, pretending to look for something I know I don't have. My hands shake as I flip through notebooks and journals.

"I must have forgotten it at the house," I say, slumping my shoulders.

Mel pulls her chin in. "I'm very sorry. I can't do anything without proper ID."

"Please," I beg.

"I can't. I'm sorry."

I pull my sunglasses off for only a moment to wipe the tears away. The woman offers an even more sympathetic look. It's clear she feels bad. Loss is a shared experience, and it's why we give to others when they are going through it. Casseroles, money, flowers, even a break. She looks over her shoulder toward an open door at the other end of the bank. Voices murmur inside the room. Her eyes dart to me.

"Do you have the lockbox key?"

I pull it from my pocket and hold it up.

"Okay. If anyone asks, you showed ID," she says with a small smile.
I nod.

Mel escorts me through the back, her heels clicking along the tile
floor. It leads to a large vault door which requires several keys and a code
to open. Behind it is a room lined with metal boxes, stacked floor to
ceiling. She walks to one labeled *1407* and inserts a key.

Looking over her shoulder, she says, "Yours goes here."

I slide mine into the keyhole and we turn them at the same time.

A little door pops open. Mel pulls out a long metal box and places it
on the table in the center of the room. "I'll give you a moment," she says.

I thank her, and she exits, leaving me alone with the items my mother
left behind . . . ones that will help set me free.

I pause, letting out a deep breath before opening the safe-deposit
box. There are no stacks of money, no rare pieces of jewelry, no valu-
ables I could pawn off. There's just a sealed manila envelope with the
words *The Truth* scrawled across it in my mother's handwriting. I pick
it up, running my fingers over it. There's more than a letter in here.
It's bumpy in some areas. Undoing the metal clip, I open the flap and
dump the contents of the envelope back into the box. A small ring with
a black gemstone set in the center clatters against the metal tin. I pick it
up, running my fingertip over the oval-shaped stone. The color changes
from black to blue. It's a mood ring, a relic from the '90s. I set it down
and shake the envelope again. An old receipt and a piece of torn clothing
fall to the table. Not everything spills out, so I reach inside, removing
a First Place blue ribbon and place it next to the ring. For some reason,
I feel like they go together.

I examine the receipt first. It's for a money order for five thousand
dollars. I recognize the name it was made out to, and my father's signature at the bottom of it. My fingers go to the frayed, ripped fabric. It
looks like it used to be black but has faded to dark gray. I turn it over
and stitched to the other side is a name. I recognize that name too. My
hand dips back into the envelope, retrieving a letter.

Carefully, I unfold it, already knowing the words inside are going to separate my life in two: before I knew the truth, and the aftermath.

I read the letter, gasping at every startling admission. It's unbelievable, so much so, it feels like I'm reading a work of fiction but it's not. It's the truth . . . an ugly one at that.

I reach the final line:

I've taken these secrets to the grave, but that's as far as I can take them.

                                        Laura Thomas

FORTY-TWO
BETH

I don't stop shoveling until the plots for Butterfly, Goofy, and Garfield are all dug up. And when I do, I collapse, staring straight up at the tangled branches, the dark sky above them. The wet mud isn't the dirtiest thing I'm covered in—it's the deceit, the grief, the shame. Rain slithers through the natural-formed canopy, splashing onto my sweaty skin. I know it's thundering because I can feel the vibration in the soil, but I can't hear it. I can't hear anything except my own heart pounding inside my chest. Every thump feels like a warning—run, leave, tell someone, do something. But I just lie there, gasping for air, trying to understand how this could have happened . . . all of it.

I think I might be crying too. It's hard to tell. It's like I'm numb but I can also feel everything. My fingers ache from gripping the shovel. The palms of my hands are covered in blisters, already torn open. A sob lingers in my throat, stretching out the walls of my esophagus as it builds. I swallow hard, trying to force it down, but it's not going anywhere. Rolling onto my side, I glance into the freshly dug holes.

It didn't take long to figure out Butterfly's identity. Susan used to call Emma that because she was bright and always fluttered around. Her skeleton is small and frail. It's all that's left, as her body has decomposed and her clothes have disintegrated.

I'm not sure who Garfield is, and I don't recognize the nickname. I just know it's an adult who's been dead long enough for there to be nothing remaining but a skeleton as well.

I weep for Goofy. It was what Mom used to call Dad because he could never keep a straight face, even when he was mad. I know it's him because of the gold wedding band hanging loosely from the bones of his ring finger.

My mother's warning comes back to me, but now I understand what she was saying, at least part of it.

Your father. He didn't disappear.

A familiar voice shouts my name but it's like I'm hearing it underwater, a muffled call. I sit up and wipe my face. The tears, rain, and dirt smear together. I try to calm myself, so I can slow my heartbeat enough to get to my feet without falling over. I hear my name again. Louder this time.

"I'm here," I cry out as I peel myself out of the sticky mud.

Twigs snap. Shoes clomp through wet grass. Overgrown weeds softly rustle as they're pushed into one another.

"Hey," I hear again.

The wind whips and whistles through the branches, carrying my mother's final words to me one last time. It whispers, "Don't trust . . ."

FORTY-THREE

NICOLE

On the highway, I swerve around a semitruck driving ten below the speed limit. He flips me off as I pass him. Usually, I'd return the gesture, but I've got one hand gripping the steering wheel and the other is desperately trying to dial. I hadn't saved any numbers into my new phone, so I'm going off memory, typing each digit in. It goes straight to voice mail. I call again and again, and every time it goes straight to voice mail. Frustrated, I toss the phone onto the passenger seat and grasp the steering wheel with both hands. My foot presses harder on the gas pedal, taking the station wagon from seventy up to eighty. The climb in speed is slow as the engine chugs, struggling to go faster.

The world passes by me in a blur, not because of how fast I'm traveling but because I've only just learned that everything I've ever known has been a lie. And I'm not sure I'll ever be able to come to terms with that. I reach for my phone again and bring up the Call screen, dialing a new number. The line connects immediately.

"911, what's your emergency?" the dispatcher asks.

"I need police to W9164 Hustis Street in Allen's Grove, Wisconsin."

"Ma'am, please slow down. What's your name?"

"Nicole. Nicole Thomas."

"And you're requesting police? Can you tell me what's going on?"

"There are bodies buried. Three of them."

"Do you need paramedics," she asks. Her fingers tap against a keyboard.

"No, they're already dead."

"And you said the address is W9164 Hustis Street, Allen's Grove, Wisconsin?" she confirms.

"Yes," I say.

The house comes into view just as I crest the hill of Highway X that leads right through the Grove. Our property is on the right, the house sitting at the highest point.

"You said you found three bodies?" the dispatcher asks, but the question doesn't register. "Ms. Thomas, are you still there?"

"Yes."

"I've dispatched police, and they're on their way. Is the address where you found the bodies a commercial building or a house? Does it belong to you?"

"It's home," I say.

FORTY-FOUR
BETH

Before he can break through the wall of overgrown weeds, I'm already slipping through it. Startled, he jumps and looks me up and down, taking in my disheveled appearance. I keep my distance, putting six feet between us. The rain still falls but lightly now.

"What are you doing here?" I ask.

Lucas glances down at his boots and then back at me. "I came to find you."

"Why?" I take the smallest step back, putting another foot between us.

A rock lays by my shoe, large enough to do some damage, but light enough for me to pick up. My gaze goes to Lucas again. I study his face. Did he know already? Is that why he seemed to be snooping around the house, looking for something? Is that why he stormed off? Was I close to figuring it out, and he needed to break me?

"What's going on? Is something wrong?"

I'm not sure what to say because I don't know if I can trust him, so I just stare back.

"You look like you've seen a ghost, Beth," he says, taking a small step toward me. I nearly flinch.

I glance at the tangled web of overgrowth behind me. The truth is in there, the entire mess of twenty-plus years, reduced to three holes in the mud. I can prove I wasn't lying to him, even if it means tarnishing my own parents. I can give him closure, answers . . .

Don't trust . . .

Maybe he already has the answers. Maybe he already has closure, and he's here now to ensure that closure stays buried.

"Lucas . . . how did you know I was down here?"

"I took the trash out, and then I was standing at the top of your driveway, deciding whether or not to come talk to you. I felt bad about the way we left things. I heard you scream, and I came running."

I just stare. There are too many emotions and questions swirling around my brain to think clearly. I don't remember screaming. But maybe I did. I can't even remember digging up the graves anymore.

"Beth? Are you hurt?" Lucas asks, taking another step toward me.

I shake my head and take an equal step back.

"Then why were you screaming?"

"Was I?"

He gives me a peculiar look. "Yeah, but why?"

"Because I found something."

"What? What did you find?"

His blue eyes pull me in like the ocean's tide. I can't resist him, even if I'm not sure I can trust him. "Emma," I say.

His mouth falls open, and his eyes go so wide that I think they might split at the corners.

Before he can speak or react or call me a liar, I say, "And my dad."

"What? Your dad left town years ago."

"No, he didn't, Lucas." My bottom lip quivers. "He's been here this whole time."

"I don't understand what you're saying."

"They're dead. They're buried in holes in the fucking ground behind me! What don't you get?"

"How?" He shakes his head in disbelief as tears spill from his eyes. "And who put them there?"

"I told you my parents had something to do with Emma's disappearance. They must have been the ones that buried her in there." I point to the wall of tangled weeds that have concealed my parents' dark secret all these years. "But I don't know who buried my dad or the person in the grave next to his."

Tears fall in a never-ending stream. I'm shaking, and I can barely see. My heart beats so fast, it feels like it's not beating at all. It's just a continuous hum.

The color drains from Lucas's face as he registers what I'm saying. "There're three bodies?"

"It's just bones, but yeah, there're three of them."

"Beth . . . did your parents kill my sister?" His voice cracks. The sadness is gone from his face, giving way to only anger. The red streaks from his tear tracks have melted, filling every bloodshot branch and tendril as they crack and fissure across the whites of his eyes.

"I don't know, Lucas."

He balls up his fists and a thick vein throbs in his neck. I take another small step back, worried at how angry he is and scared that he might erupt at any moment, a dormant volcano ready to let loose after decades of inactivity. Lucas looks at me with narrowed, accusatory eyes. "Do you *think* they killed my sister?"

"I don't know." I tell him I'm sorry because I don't know what else to say.

Questions flood my brain, trying to make sense of it all. Why would they kill Emma? No, they couldn't have. Not Mom or Dad. But if they didn't kill her, why would they get rid of her body rather than call the police? Why would they risk going to prison? Why cause so much pain and mistrust and sorrow, especially when they had young chil . . . Oh my God! I let out a gasp as realization sets in and the pieces start falling into place.

Lucas looks at me with wild, tearful eyes. "What is it?"

"Don't trust . . ." I say.

He takes another step forward. "What? Don't trust what?"

"Not what . . . who." I hang my head, shaking it back and forth in disbelief.

"Who shouldn't you trust, Beth?" he asks.

The sound of metal hitting bone twangs with a dull thud, immediately muffled out of existence by the rain and wind. My head snaps up just as Lucas falls to the ground, blood gushing from where the shovel connected with his skull. I want to run to him but I can't. I want to run away but I can't do that either. Neither fight nor flight has kicked in. I'm frozen in fear and disbelief, completely immobilized.

"You should have just left the past in the past, Beth," Michael says, gripping the handle of the bloody shovel.

I stumble backward several steps, putting more distance between him and me. Lucas lies still in the tall grass. I focus for a moment on his back and watch his lungs slightly expand and contract. He's breathing. He's still alive.

"What have you done, Michael?"

He tosses the shovel at my feet and pulls a gun from his pocket, pointing it directly at me, "Pick it up and let's go. Back into the thick of it." Michael flicks the gun, gesturing for me to move.

"Please, don't do anything . . ."

"Crazy? Jesus, Beth, I'm not gonna hurt you. I could have done that a million times already if I really wanted. Now walk."

I turn and look back into the dense mess of branches, dead vines, bushes, and trees. All these years, right in plain sight, this vegetation encased my mom's deepest secrets, the roots contaminated, feeding off the decaying bodies of the past. Am I about to join them? I crouch down and crawl through the opening, swallowed into a womb of death.

"That's far enough. Now turn around," he says, passing through the clearing and standing upright.

My eyes go to the graves and the remains inside of them. "This is why you wanted the house so badly, isn't it?"

"Ding. Ding. Ding. If someone would have just let me give her a ton of money for this dumpy piece of shit house, we would all be on our merry way, but nope. You just couldn't do that, Beth."

"You can have the house," I say.

"It's too late for that. Who else knows about this?"

"Just me."

"Where's Nicole?" He scans the area and listens for movement through the storm.

"I don't know."

"Mom's station wagon wasn't parked out front when I pulled in. Did she leave?"

"She must have."

"Probably opened that letter from Mom and went and got a fix. Shit, when I read it, I thought about shooting up heroin, and I don't even do drugs, so I can't imagine what it did to her." He smirks.

"What are you talking about?"

"I may have switched mine with hers," he says with a shrug. "Mom had much nicer things to say to Nicole than she did to me, which was surprising since one of us is a drug addict and the other is a successful tech entrepreneur."

"Yeah, and one of you is a murderer. So, I bet for Mom, that canceled out your success."

"I'm not a murderer," he says in a serious tone while standing stone-faced.

I gesture to the holes. "Then why are you pointing a gun at me while hovering over three unmarked graves?"

His eyes shift to the holes, and he sighs, lowering the gun to his side. But I notice his finger is still on the trigger.

"Did you kill Emma?" I ask.

"No . . . it was an accident."

"How? If it were an accident, Mom and Dad wouldn't have buried her. They would have called the police."

"Maybe. Maybe not." He shrugs. "It's hard to know what someone will do in a stressful situation."

"What happened?" I press.

He pulls his lips in. "Does it matter? She's dead, has been for a really long time."

"It matters to me."

"Like I said, it was an accident." His nostrils flare.

"How?"

"We were playing down by the creek, skipping rocks, just goofing around. We climbed the hillside to the bridge, so we could skip rocks from up high. Emma leaned over the guardrail and pretended she was in that *Titanic* movie, arms out, declaring she was the queen of the world." There's a sheen to his eyes, but he speaks with no emotion like he's reading from a cue card, a rehearsed speech. "I thought it'd be funny to scare Emma, so I ran at her like I was going to push her off. I wasn't going to, but she turned just in time to see me running and got startled. She leapt back and fell." Michael lets out a sigh and blinks five or six times as though there's distance between himself and his story. "She missed the creek by a foot, hitting the bank instead. Her head must have caught a rock because there was blood everywhere." His jaw tightens. "I tried to wake her, but she wouldn't move. I was just a child. I didn't know what to do, so I covered her with brush like we were playing a game of hide-and-seek."

"What about Dad?"

"I told him what happened later that night after everyone got back from searching for Emma. He cried and he held me and he said he would take care of it."

I'm not sure I believe him, but I'll pretend I do because his finger is still on the trigger.

"But why is Dad lying in one of those graves?"

He looks at the holes again and then back at me. "How do you know it's him?"

"Because he's wearing his wedding ring."

Michael nods and his mouth forms a hard line. "I don't know what happened to Dad."

"Did you know he was buried here?"

"No."

I don't believe him. He just learned that our dad is dead and buried in that hole and he's not shocked or sad or devastated. He had to have known. I want to scream, but I need to stay calm. I need to keep him talking because he might be the only person alive that knows the truth of how these three bodies ended up buried on our parents' property.

"Why didn't you ever come home after Dad disappeared?"

"Because it wasn't home to me anymore," he says with a shrug.

Another lie. His hand grips the gun a little tighter.

"Who's in the third grave?" I ask.

"Your guess is as good as mine. I only knew about Emma's."

"And Dad's," I correct.

Michael lets out a heavy sigh and shakes his head. "The guilt put him in that hole more than I did."

"What do you mean?"

"Dad never forgave me for what happened to Emma, and he never forgave himself for his part in it."

"Can you blame him?"

"Yeah, I can," he yells suddenly. "It was an accident, and I was a kid. He could have gone to the authorities, but he chose not to."

The memory of Dad pushing me off my bike and out of the way of an oncoming car floods my mind. His head cracked against the windshield as he took the hit that would have probably killed me. Only my small knees were scuffed up, thanks to him. That was the kind of man he was. He would do anything to protect his children. Dad didn't go to the police to report Emma's death because he didn't think he had a choice. It couldn't have been an accident.

"What happened to Dad, Michael?" A tear rolls down my cheek as I remember all that time I spent searching for him. I destroyed my life trying to find him, and he was dead all along, buried in the backyard of my childhood home.

"Like I said, he never forgave me or himself." There's anger and resentment in his voice. "I came home seven years ago. The girl I was dating had passed away unexpectedly, and I wanted my mom and dad. I was depressed and broken and alone. Doesn't matter how old you get, sometimes you just need your parents."

I lift a brow. "Did you kill her, your girlfriend?"

"Fuck you, Beth," he spits. "You're just like Dad. That's exactly what he thought, and he wouldn't believe otherwise. He kept asking question after question while I was grieving, or at least trying to. I could see it on his face. He thought I was some psycho killer." Michael shakes his head and scoffs. "It was obvious he regretted protecting me. He thought he'd made a mistake."

"You can't be sure he thought that," I say.

"You're right. I wasn't sure. Until I was."

"What do you mean?"

"Dad went off on me. Screaming, 'How many more holes do I have to dig back here, Michael? My marriage is already buried in there, as are our souls. We are nothing because of you!' and on and on. He had every right to be mad and yell, but he should have been doing that in a mirror. He made his own decisions. But then he lunged at me, wrapped his hands around my neck, and squeezed as hard as he could. He was trying to kill me, and . . . it was self-defense."

I keep my eyes on Michael, watching carefully for any sudden movement. He's not looking at me anymore. He's staring off into the woods, almost in a trance, like he's reliving that memory.

"What about Mom?"

His gaze meets mine. "What about her?"

"Did she know what you did to Dad?"

"She helped me bury him."

Something in me breaks. Maybe it's my soul. Mom knew? How could she go along with something like that? How could she watch me lose my family while trying to find him? How could she sit back and watch Nicole destroy herself with drugs? Why would she ever let us believe that Dad was out there? Let us hope that one day he would return and walk right back into our lives?

"Why would she do that?" I ask.

"Because it's what Dad would have wanted."

"Dad wouldn't have wanted any of this. Look what it's done to our family."

I narrow my eyes at him, realization dawning. He didn't reappear after seven years to lay Mom to rest. He's here to make sure the past stays buried. "How the hell did I get an email from Dad this week if he's lying in that hole, Michael?"

"Oh, come on, Beth. That's an easy one. You know how good I am with computers."

"But why? Why bother going through the trouble?"

"You mean, send Nicole on a wild goose chase to keep her busy, get you two fighting so you ignore everything else, and then I buy the house and make sure it all stays buried . . . simple. Same reason I erased the tape. Same reason I tore pages out of Mom's journals."

"And the break-in?"

"That was Nicole's drug dealer." He rolls his eyes and shakes his head. "You two are so easy to just nudge right off the deep end. I'd call it pathetic if it wasn't so convenient. Like little wind-up dolls marching in circles. You should have just listened to me, Beth. You should have sold me the house, taken the money, and left this place, because now . . ." Michael's gaze falls to the graves. "You never will."

While he's lost in thought and distracted, I grab my shoe and throw it at him. A mass of wet mud flings off the heel, splatting across his face.

"Ah, what the fuck?" he yells, scraping the sludge from his eyes.

I lunge for the gun clutched in his hand. His elbow connects with my face, crunching the bones in my nose, and sends me tumbling backward. I nearly fall into Garfield's grave. Getting to my feet, I charge at Michael again, taking him by surprise as he's still trying to get the mud out of his eyes. He gasps for air when I hit him in the side with my shoulder.

"Goddamn it, Beth," he wheezes as his body collides with a tree.

I bring my knee up, thrusting it into his groin. He crumbles and sinks to the ground. I twist the gun as hard as I can, prying his fingers from it. But then I feel a sharp pain in my lower back. It knocks the wind out of me. He slams his fist into my kidney again. This time I release the gun and collapse to my knees, sucking for air and wheezing through the pain.

"Beth!?" I hear Nicole's voice in the distance.

"Nicole!" I scream with what breath I have left. "I'm down . . ." Michael's free hand covers my mouth, smearing mud into my nostrils, pushing it through my teeth, trying to choke me into silence.

"You'll only get her hurt too," he seethes.

"Beth!" she calls out again.

I consider prying his hand from my mouth and screaming for Nicole, but he's right. He'll just hurt both of us. Instead, I open my mouth and use my hand to push one of Michael's fingers into it. Then, I bite down as hard as I can, until a new liquid besides mud and water begins slosh-ing around my mouth.

Michael screams and clocks me right in the face with the gun. A stream of warm liquid gushes from my nose and lip. My mouth involuntarily opens as I shriek in agony. He pulls his mangled finger free from my teeth. I spit out my blood and Michael's, trying to plead, but no words come out.

"I don't know why I even thought I could have a civil conversation with you, Beth." He stands over me with the gun cocked, pointing it right at my head.

I put my hands in front of my face, shielding what I know I can't stop, and look over at the unearthed soil that I'll soon call home.

The dull thud of metal on bone twangs again, and I glance up to see Michael clutching his arm. Blood spills from a fresh wound, and Nicole stands behind him with a shovel in hand. She raises it again, but her arms shake and her movement is too slow this time.

Michael drives his elbow back hard and fast, connecting with her mouth. Her lip splits open and blood pours from it like a faucet. She stum-bles, tripping over a fallen branch, her head smacking against the ground.

I'm on my feet, taking two steps and diving toward the shovel. Mi-chael notices my movement and lunges to beat me to it. Nicole lifts her leg and trips him midstride, causing him to crash face-first into the mud. I grab the shovel, raise it over my head, and swing. Just before the blade hits his skull, he rolls out of the way. The shovel punctures the ground.

Sirens roar in the distance, and Michael's eyes go wide as panic sets in. The only way out is death, either his or ours. And he knows this.

He raises the gun again, pointing it at me. But Nicole leaps forward, grabbing onto it with both hands. I follow suit, and now the three of us are grappling over the pistol. Tugging back and forth like we're children again, fighting over our favorite toy.

The sirens grow louder and louder, slowly drowning out our grunts and curses and cries and pleas. Nothing but sirens . . . until the gun-shot rings out.

FORTY-FIVE

NICOLE

Red and blue beams dance all through the overgrowth. A sparkling light show reflecting off the raindrops still clinging to branches and leaves. There's lots of shouting, but it all sounds far away, like the volume has been turned down on my life. Casey stands beside me. His hand is between my shoulder blades, rubbing, massaging. He's talking, but I can't hear what he's saying.

My attention is fixed on the gurney being carried across the yard by two paramedics. They load it into an ambulance.

Lucas is seated at the back of another ambulance. One paramedic is wrapping bandages around his head while another is checking his eyes with a flashlight.

"Lucas is going to be okay," Beth says over my shoulder. For some reason her voice cuts through all the fog and registers.

"He is?" I ask.

"Yeah, but they're going to bring him in for an MRI to make sure there's no bleeding or swelling in the brain."

"What about you, Beth?" Casey asks. His thick brows draw together with concern. "Did the paramedics check on you?"

"Briefly."

"You should go to the hospital and have a doctor look you over, the both of you." His eyes shift between Beth and me.

She's soaking wet from the rain, covered in mud. Her skin is a mix of black and blue and dried blood clings to her face. I'm sure I look the same.

We nod and tell him we will.

With the gurney loaded, one paramedic jumps in the back and the other races around the ambulance to the driver's seat.

"How's Michael?" Beth asks.

Casey purses his lips as though he's not sure if he should answer. The doors of the ambulance close with a thud. The lights flick on, and the sirens roar as it speeds up the driveway.

"They don't know yet," he finally lands on. "He's lost a lot of blood and hasn't regained consciousness. They'll have to bring him in for emergency surgery in order to find out the extent of his injuries. Gunshots to the stomach are tricky."

Beth and I exchange a look of fortitude. We did what we had to do. But I think it was me who fired the shot. I can't be sure. It all happened so fast. But it all happened so slowly too. Moments that change us don't play by the rules of time. They're everywhere all at once.

"What are they going to do about the three graves?" Beth asks. She turns her head, looking down at the valley where dozens of cops roam the property.

"They'll excavate the bodies, bring them in for identification, and open an investigation," Casey explains.

"Detective Dunn," an officer calls from the top of the hill.

"Yeah," Casey says.

"Captain needs ya."

Casey nods and tells us he'll be back shortly. He joins the other officer and heads down the valley.

I tilt my head and look to Beth. "Are you okay?"

"I will be," she says. "Thanks to you."

"I didn't do anything."

"Yes, you did, Nicole. You saved my life."

"You would have done the same for me. That's what sisters do. They save each other."

She wraps her arms around my body and hugs me. It's one of those embraces that heals a part of you. One that serves as a reminder that love truly can conquer all.

"Love you." The words come out so quietly, I almost hope she doesn't hear them.

"Love you too, Nicole," she whispers back.

Tears well from deep inside me, a place I haven't cried from in a long time. They spill out and course down my cheeks. They're tears of relief. Beth pulls away, looking me in the eyes. She's crying just as much as I am. She looks so much like Mom did at her age.

She slides an envelope from her pocket and holds it out. "I found this."

I hesitate for a moment before taking it from her. On the front, written in my mother's handwriting, is the name *Michael*.

"What is it?"

"It's the letter Mom wrote for you. Michael switched his out for yours."

My bottom lip trembles and I feel my throat closing. I pull the letter from the envelope. It only takes a few words for me to know Beth is right. This is the letter Mom wrote for me. The tears continue to build and fall. I fold the letter.

"You aren't going to read it?" Beth asks.

"Not yet. This isn't the right moment."

She places a hand on my shoulder and squeezes. "I get it."

"I have something for you too." I reach into my pocket and hand Beth the key for the safe-deposit box.

Her brows shove together as she flips it over in her hand. "Did you open it?"

"Yeah."

"What was inside?"

"Hold on," I say, putting a finger up. I walk to my car parked in the driveway and grab the manila envelope from the front seat. I'll let Beth read Mom's letter before I turn it over to the police.

My hand trembles as I extend it to her. It's withdrawals, my body craving a drug. It used to scare me when my body quaked because I wasn't strong enough to stave them off without giving in. But I'm not scared anymore. I'm stronger than I ever gave myself credit for, and I know chasing the high is the equivalent of running in place. With each stride, dirt gets kicked up and all that happens is you end up digging a hole beneath you. If you dig long enough, you'll eventually get buried in it.

Beth hesitates for a moment before taking the envelope from me. She doesn't say anything about my trembling hand. The flap is already open, ready for her to look inside and get a glimpse of the past.

"What is it?" she asks, briefly looking at me.

"It's everything Mom wanted us to know."

"And what's that?"

"The truth," I say.

FORTY-SIX

LAURA

To those I've lied to,

My job as a mother was to protect my children . . . but I think I took it too far. My husband and I both did. We wanted the world for our kids, and we were willing to destroy it, just so they could have it. I've lived with this for over twenty years, and I know I'll die with it too, but I won't take it to my next life. In death, I want to be free of it. This is the truth of what happened to Emma Harper, Christie Roberts, Charles Gallagher, and my husband, Brian Thomas. This is the truth of what we did.

On the evening of June 15, 1999, my husband, Brian, told me Emma Harper was dead, and we needed to get rid of her body. He didn't tell me why. He didn't tell me what happened. He just told me it needed to be done. Somehow, I went along with it. It's strange how quickly we can do the things we thought we never would. It only takes a second to make the wrong decision. After we buried her, I knew it wouldn't be the end of it, but I thought the hardest part was behind us. It wasn't. Seeing Emma's parents, Susan and Eddie, go through the grief of not knowing where their child was, that was far worse.

In order to know what happened to Emma, we have to skip ahead to Charles. Brian called in the anonymous tip. I was overcome with guilt that he was suffering because of us, so I planted Emma's bicycle. Despite

Charles's acquittal, Eddie was convinced he had something to do with Emma's disappearance. He killed Charles in a fit of drunken rage after leaving the Boar's Nest on December 27, 1999. The night Charles was murdered, I learned the truth of Christie Roberts's disappearance and what happened in Emma Harper's final moments. Eddie couldn't let it go. So, he took matters into his own hands. He beat Charles to death in the Allen's Grove park. Brian cleaned up the mess and made sure Eddie wouldn't go down for it. How could he not? It was our fault that Charles was dead and that Eddie was now a murderer. Grief makes you do things you normally wouldn't do, the kind of things that splinter your soul.

What happened to Emma in her final moments? You'd have to ask my son, Michael, about that, but I know he would lie to you, just like he did to Brian. Michael told Brian it was an accident. That he and Emma were playing down by the creek, just being kids. That she'd fallen from the bridge when he startled her. He told us he panicked and didn't know what to do, so he dragged and hid her body under the bridge, covering her with branches and long grass. Then he went back up to the house and showered like nothing had happened.

I remember making dinner that night. I prepared pork chops, mashed potatoes, and corn on the cob. Brian and I even split a bottle of sauvignon blanc to celebrate how well Groovin' in the Grove had gone. He and I clinked our glasses, sipped on the crisp zesty wine, and took our seats at opposite ends of the table, completely smitten with one another. Michael sat to my right. Beth and Nicole sat to my left. I smiled at each of them, and I remember asking myself how I got so lucky. I really took in the moment, not realizing I'd never have one like it again. Nothing seemed out of the ordinary. We were just a happy family enjoying a home-cooked meal together. After learning the truth, that's what disturbed me most of all—that <u>nothing seemed out of the ordinary.</u>

It wasn't until much later that evening, after we had been informed Emma was missing and after we'd spent the night looking for her, that Michael finally confessed to Brian what had happened. I think Brian knew Michael wasn't being honest or—at the very least, deep down in his gut—he knew. That little pang of doubt is why Brian was convinced he couldn't call the police.

Brian didn't learn the truth of what had actually happened to Emma until Christie Roberts knocked on our door a couple months later. She showed Brian a roll of developed film, tucked in an envelope from the Kmart photo department. Inside was a stack of 4x6 photos. Brian said if you viewed them in quick succession, it looked like one of those old flip-books, the images animating a dark truth and uncovering the lie our son had told. She hadn't fallen on her own. Michael had shoved her right off the bridge. We don't know if Michael meant to push her so hard. You can't tell from a picture. But he did splash water onto the blood that poured from her skull, making sure it seeped into the dirt. Then he dragged her body under the bridge, covering her with vegetation. He never even checked for a pulse or to see if she was breathing. Fifty photos captured all of it.

Christie didn't say anything, didn't tell anyone what she had seen. I don't know why. Maybe she was scared, or maybe it was because she had something else in mind. She didn't take the photos to the police. She took them to Brian and made him an offer. She said he could have them if he paid her five thousand dollars and helped her get out of town. For her, her freedom was more important than the truth. It took Brian a while to scrounge up the money, because we didn't have much as it was. He sold most of his guns, picked up extra shifts at work, emptied out a chunk of his 401(k). He was smart about it because I didn't even notice. Then he paid her off, helped her get a fake ID, and put her on a train heading south from Harvard, Illinois. I do remember Brian being tired and run-down. I figured the guilt was eating him away too, but then Christie went missing, and I knew he had something to do with it. I thought she was dead, just like Emma, but last I checked, she was living in the South under the new name Brian helped her obtain. She's married with two kids, experiencing a life she never would have if Michael hadn't taken Emma's. Christie is the only one that got a happy ending out of all of this. They say it's the truth that will set you free, but they never specify whether telling the truth or knowing the truth will give you your freedom.

It's obvious we were never the same again after the summer of 1999. It changed our perspective on everything. We no longer tried to protect our children from the world. Instead, we tried to protect the world from Michael. Since the decision was made to hide what he had done, we knew it was on us to make sure he never did it again. We wanted to fix him, rehabilitate him without the law involved. After all, he was just a little boy, and he was our little boy. I had read about children who did very bad things but grew up to be perfectly normal adults. Brian and I wholeheartedly believed Michael could be one of them. So, we kept him busy, enrolled him in coding classes, bought him a computer, and sent him to summer camps, all in an effort to direct his energy toward something else. Brian kept a close eye on him at all times, monitoring everything he did. We smothered him with love and attention, most likely neglecting our daughters in the process. But we had to. We needed to make sure what he did to Emma was a one-off. We needed to protect our other two children. It was our responsibility because we'd covered it up. When Michael made good grades, graduated high school, and was accepted into a great college on a full-ride scholarship, we thought we had done the right thing.

But then he showed up at our doorstep in 2015 completely grief-stricken. He had driven thirty-one hours straight. He said his girlfriend had died in a freak accident and that he needed his parents. He said he took time off from work to process the loss, and that he wanted to grieve at home with us. We hugged him while he cried and fell apart in our arms. I remember exchanging a quick look with Brian while we held our broken boy, and I saw it in his eyes. _Regret._ _Remorse._ _Shame._ _Defeat._ He believed Michael had killed again. He believed we had failed as parents.

The next day, the two of them got into an argument. Brian kept asking him questions, rapid-fire, one after another about his girlfriend and her death. It was more like an interrogation. Michael grew angrier and angrier, but he answered each one. I tried to get them to cool off, told Brian to take it easy on him, that it could have been an accident. But I think between the guilt Brian had lived with for the previous sixteen years and knowing Michael had lied to him about what happened to Emma Harper, he could never believe him again. He told Michael he had learned the truth about Emma's death. Michael denied it all. They screamed at one another, hurling insults back and forth, saying the most hurtful things they possibly could. I was in the kitchen cooking dinner when the fight turned physical. The yelling stopped. There was a crash in the back bedroom, a struggle, a thud. I turned off the burners on the stove and stomped down the hallway to break it up. But when I got there, there was nothing left to break up.

Brian was lying on the floor, blood seeping from a crack in his skull. Michael stood over him with wide eyes. His neck was a mix of colors: deep purple spreading across his throat, beet red near his jawline, and white circle markings from where Brian's fingers had pressed into his skin. Clutched in Michael's hand was a trophy he'd won at a science camp. His father's blood coated the large wooden base.

I've never cried so hard in my life. I broke a rib while sobbing. Michael said he thought Brian was going to kill him. He said he couldn't breathe, and he wasn't thinking when he struck him in the head. He said he was sorry. That he wished he could take it back. He claimed it was an accident. Then he said it was self-defense. I didn't know what to do. But I knew what Brian would want me to do. He spent his whole life trying to protect his children. Death wouldn't change that priority. So, I told Michael this was it . . . this was the last time we were going to protect him. We buried Brian's body next to Emma's. It's why I chose to be cremated and have my ashes spread around the property. I knew it was the only way I could lie with my husband in death. I gave Michael the keys to Brian's truck and told him to drive it to Texas and leave it somewhere near the Mexican border. I told him to only use cash, to keep his face covered, and to go back to California when he was done. I told him to pretend that he was never home. Only Brian and I had seen him anyway. I put Michael's car in storage and sold it a year later. Brian had left a note on the kitchen table a week before after we'd gotten into an argument over something silly, I can't remember now.

It said, _Laura, I'm sorry. Love, Brian._

When I filed a missing person report the next morning, I used the note from our squabble as evidence that he may have abandoned me. I said he had been suffering from depression but had refused to go and talk to someone about it. I played the role of the concerned wife, but I wasn't concerned. I was grieving. They started an investigation, looking into me first. Because it's always the wife. However, when they discovered his vehicle parked near the border, they stopped the search. After all, it's not a crime to run out on your family.

The last time I saw Michael was the day he left in Brian's truck. I hugged my boy. I told him I loved him, and I told him I never wanted to see him again. He cried. The tears came fast and heavy, streaming down his crumpled face. But I just stared back at him, stoic and emotionless. I had no desire to console my child or dry his tears or tell him everything would be all right. Every motherly instinct within me had evaporated. The maternal bond severed forever. They say the love you have for a child is unconditional. I don't believe that anymore. There are conditions. And the condition I had for Michael was that I would love him forever and always . . . but only at a distance from that day forward.

I know Brian and I didn't do the right thing on the night of June 15, 1999. We buried a truth that wasn't ours to bury. And I've hated myself ever since. Sometimes you become the monster and sometimes the monster becomes you. Our intentions were just that . . . intentions, and I'm sorry for ever having them. I'm sorry for what I've done, for what we've done. I've taken these secrets to the grave, but that's as far as I can take them.

Laura Thomas

FORTY-SEVEN
BETH

THREE YEARS LATER

The butter spurts and hisses as I crack an egg into the skillet and then another and another. Hash browns cook in one pan, sausage in a smaller one. The smell is divine, and this cozy combination is my favorite way to start a morning with my family. I look to my right and smile, watching Marissa methodically turn the hash browns to get them crispy. My daughter wears a look of determination. Everything she does is done to perfection, a trait she picked up in the military.

"How's it going over there, sous-chef?"

"Fine, these just take forever to cook," she says, flipping them over again.

"Potatoes always do. If you crank the heat up to nine or ten and add some more butter, the fat and oil will help crisp them faster."

Marissa nods, turns the burner up, and adds a glob of butter.

She won't ever know how much just standing next to her in the kitchen means to me. Well, maybe she will one day—when she has children of her own. She and I have healed these past three years, really worked on fixing our relationship. Much like the eggs I just cracked into the skillet, sometimes something needs to be broken before it can be repaired, and I mean *truly* broken. A cup that has some cracks in it but still holds water, you don't work on fixing it; instead it goes to the back of the cabinet. But a shattered cup needs to be mended to work again. Being pushed beyond my limits, having a mental breakdown, losing everyone and everything . . . I was shattered. What happened with my family—my mother and father and brother—meant losing the family I had, but it helped me gain the family I wanted and needed.

"I'm gonna get ya. I'm gonna get ya!" Lucas says in a singsong voice as he chases our three-year-old son around the kitchen table. His name is Jack, and he's a ball of energy. We adopted him four months ago. He's made our family whole. Lucas has been nothing short of a wonderful father, someone he never thought he could be but someone I knew he was meant to be.

"Gotcha!"

High-pitched squeals and laughs ring out as Lucas tickles Jack, blowing raspberries on his belly. His laughter is the most perfect sound in the world.

We don't live in the Grove anymore. It carried too much baggage, too many memories that are best left buried—actually buried. We didn't move far, just a few towns over, but that change made all the difference. We don't have to see those familiar streets, with reminders of what happened, or run into people we don't want to talk to, who know about our past. It was a fresh start. Lucas and I married eighteen months ago. It was eighteen years overdue in my opinion. It was nothing extravagant, just a courthouse wedding, something intimate and small. Nicole was our witness. She and I have helped one another heal in ways neither of us thought possible. All these years, the secret that kept us apart was actually the one that united us. Before, we were bound through pain, with bindings that cut and constricted. But now, we are bound by love, hope, and our desire to live better lives and be a better family, together.

Michael didn't die that day. He was in the hospital for a long time. He had countless surgeries. His recovery was grueling and painful. But he did survive, and I think that was the worst thing for him. A boy that was so proud to have outgrown the Grove is now confined to a six-by-six cell, only thirty miles from his hometown. It's like he never really got out. He won't be up for parole until 2050, and by that time he'll be in his sixties. I've sent him more than thirty letters over the past three years. He's never written back, and I'm okay with that. I think he doesn't write out of shame, not out of hate. I don't hate him either. I just feel sorry for my little brother. He'll always be that to me.

"Lucas, can you get Jack's high chair set up in the living room?"

"Sure thing, my love." Lucas kisses me on the forehead and covertly squeezes my butt. My heart races and my cheeks flush. I've had that same reaction to him since I was young, and I don't think that will ever go away.

"Cook, potatoes, cook," Marissa says to her pan of hash browns like she's a lieutenant in the culinary division.

"They're looking good," I say, serving the fried eggs and seared sausages onto several plates.

"She's going to be on soon," Marissa says, almost in a panic.

I take the spatula from her. "Go ahead and get the TV ready. I'll finish the hash browns."

"Thanks, Mom," she says as she races toward the living room.

Steam rises off our delicious, artery-clogging, dopamine-releasing delights as we hunker down and wait for the segment. All of a sudden, onscreen, there she is, my sister. Tears fill my eyes, and a smile spreads across my face.

"Good morning, America. I'm Rebecca Sanford, and today, I'm pleased to have a special guest with us. Nicole Thomas is the bestselling author of the memoir *Home Is Where the Bodies Are*, where she recounts her harrowing and horrific experience of a family bogged down by the sins of some of its members. Nicole, thank you very much for being here today."

We're glued to the screen, anxious to hear what comes next. Lucas, Marissa, and I all read her book—not that we needed to, we knew every word that would be in it. When she came to ask me how I felt about her sharing our story with the world, I was more than happy to let her have that catharsis. Plus, I knew she'd tell it well. Nicole hasn't relapsed again. She's stayed strong and become a writer like she always wanted to be. She and Casey are dating too. I wish Mom could see her. See us. She'd be so proud.

As I scan the room and watch my daughter smiling, delighted for her aunt, and my husband bouncing our son on his knee, I can't help but reflect on what our parents did. They weren't bad people. They were good, and they loved with every ounce of their being. They wanted the best for their kids. All parents want that. But they made poor decisions in an effort to protect their children. They were human, and they were flawed. Sometimes we do the wrong thing for all the right reasons. I don't blame my parents or hate them for what they did. Because as I look at my own children, I know I would do the exact same thing for them.

FORTY-EIGHT

NICOLE

The lights on set are brighter than I thought they'd be, but then again, light has never shined very bright on me before. My skin warms underneath them. I pull at my skirt, readjusting and straightening it before I take a seat. A man stands between two oversized cameras, pointed directly at me. He holds his hand up and starts a countdown, indicating when we'll be live again. Rebecca, one of the *Good Morning America* cohosts, sits kitty-corner to me, dressed in a tailored pencil skirt and matching blazer. Her shiny blond hair stops right at her shoulders, and she's perfectly polished from head to toe. She's stunning. Even her knees look amazing. A makeup artist dabs a brush dusted with powder along Rebecca's T-zone while she reviews her cue cards. The artist offers me a touch-up as well, but I decline.

"You ready?" the cohost asks, flashing a pearly white smile at me.

I nod.

"Remember, we're just having a conversation. Don't be nervous," she says.

"I'm not."

I spent my whole life being nervous up until I realized that life happens in between the beats of our own heart, and if it thumps too fast, there's no space for us to live.

The man between the cameras calls out, "And we're live in five, four . . ." and silently his fingers mark three, two, and then he points at Rebecca, who introduces me, smiling as she speaks. She says, "Nicole, thank you very much for being here today."

"Thank you for having me, Rebecca."

"Of course. So, tell us a little more about your novel."

"Yeah, sure." I want to correct her, explain that it's not a novel, but I don't. "*Home Is Where the Bodies Are* is about life, my life to be exact. But I think we all endure similar experiences, in a way, maybe not the same ones I have, but there are universal themes. It's about death, grief, regret, the things we need in life, and the things life needs from us. It's about love with and without conditions. It's about addiction and healing. But most of all, it's about family. What it means to be one, what it means to have one, and what it means to lose one."

"Well, I read it and loved it. It's riveting."

I politely smile back at her. It's only riveting if you haven't lived it.

"So, three years ago, you found out your parents covered up a murder that your brother committed back in 1999. How did that feel?" she asks.

This is exactly why I should have bit the bullet and paid for a publicist . . . to ensure questions like this weren't asked. I let out the smallest sigh to make sure it's not picked up on the microphone clipped to my blazer.

"It felt like my whole life had been a lie, but knowing the truth made sense of the life I had lived."

She arches a brow. "What do you mean by that?"

"I mean that it allowed me to give myself grace. I didn't excuse myself. But I forgave myself for all the things I'd done wrong, just like I forgave my parents and my brother."

"Wait, you're not angry with them?" She peers out at the live audience seated behind the cameras. "I know I would be."

"Anger is easy, Rebecca. It's the most rudimentary of human feelings. Babies experience anger. Psychopaths experience anger. People with little to no brain activity experience anger. But compassion and forgiveness are challenging. They're the most complex of all the emotions. So, no . . . I'm not angry with them."

She tucks her chin in and flips through her cue cards quickly. "If your mom and dad were sitting across from you right now, what would you say to them?"

I smile the smallest smile at Rebecca. She's probably thinking I'll break down in tears, and she'll have this incredible moment for television, cementing her as a top journalist, maybe even getting her a Daytime Emmy nomination. But I won't shed any tears today.

"I would tell them I love them," I say.

"That's it?" She furrows her brow. "There's nothing else you would say to them?"

I pause for a moment, considering my answer and the one she wants to hear. "I'd also reassure them that they were good parents and that they did the best they could."

Rebecca moves her mouth side to side and flips through her cue cards again. "What about your brother, Michael, who might be watching?" She looks at the camera. "For those that don't know the story of the Thomas family, Michael Thomas is currently in prison for the next fifty years for the murder of his father, Brian Thomas; assault with a deadly weapon; kidnapping; and desecration of a human corpse, among a number of other charges." Rebecca looks back to me with her most serious face. "What would you say to your brother, Michael, if he was sitting right here, Nicole?"

"I'd tell him I love him. I'd remind him of the times he used to sleep on my bedroom floor when we were kids because I was terrified of the monsters that lived under my bed. I'd thank him for keeping me safe and keeping the monsters at bay. But I'd also tell Michael I'm sorry for not protecting him from them too." A single tear rolls down my cheek.

Rebecca's smile widens, and I hear the hum of one of the cameras zooming in to capture it. I don't wipe it away. Because it's not for them.

"You're going to read a little for us today from your book, right?" She lifts her hands to get the audience to cheer, and they do. Because this is show business and you do what the show tells you.

"Yes," I say. "But just the prologue."

"Perfect, let's hear it."

I pick my book up from the table beside me and open it to page one. Before I start, I clear my throat and exhale through my nose. Breathing in the present, breathing out the past.

"'The best stories come from those that are flawed, broken, really. Those who have endured trials and tribulations. Those who have faced the world and come out on the bottom. Only they can tell stories worth listening to, for they have had more than one beginning, more than one middle they've dragged themselves through, and more than one ending . . . and despite it all, their story continues. My name is Nicole Thomas. I'm a lot of things—a former drug addict, an older sister to a murderer, a younger sister to one of the bravest women I know, a daughter to flawed parents who loved their children to a fault, an aunt to a niece who has seen me at my lowest points but loves me anyway, an aunt to a nephew I hope never sees that side of me, a good friend and a bad friend, a liar and a straight shooter, but most importantly, I'm a storyteller. This is my story. And it starts at home . . . because home is where the bodies are.'"

ACKNOWLEDGMENTS

Recently, I read that most people don't even read the acknowledgments at the end of a book. I considered testing that theory and confessing all my deepest, darkest secrets in this text. But then I realized my secrets aren't all that deep or dark, so I figured I'd use this space as it was intended and thank the people that made this book possible. But maybe there will be a dark secret in here, so keep reading . . . just to be sure.

Allen's Grove is a real place. It's a small unincorporated community in southeastern Wisconsin, nothing special, but it's special to me because it was my home for sixteen years. I stuck my tongue to the frozen swing set in the park (I didn't think it would stick—it did). I fell off the back of a horse riding on the nature trail. I caught bass and carp in the creek with a fishing pole and caught leeches with my body. I helped build a house, because my parents decided that would be a fun childhood activity for me and my siblings. Spoiler alert: it wasn't. But I learned the value of a hard day's work and that if you want something life's not willing or able to give you, you have to go after it yourself. The Grove shaped me in more ways than one. I'm grateful for the time I lived there, and I'm glad I was able to incorporate my unincorporated community into this book.

Thank you to Patsy Ryan for not turning me away or thinking I was unhinged when I showed up at your home, telling you I used to live in it and that I was setting my next book there. Being able to revisit my childhood home, walk the property (which I describe in detail in this story), and take photos of it all was a surreal and wonderful experience.

It had a positive impact on both this novel and me, and I very much appreciate your hospitality. I'd also like to thank my aunt Flo for facilitating my return to Allen's Grove and for organizing a special little gathering with friends and family at the Boar's Nest.

Thank you to my agent, Sandy Lu, for continuing to champion me and my work. When you reviewed this book and highlighted all the quotes you loved, it was exactly what I needed to boost my confidence and keep me going.

Thank you to the entire team at Blackstone Publishing for being on this journey with me for the long haul. This is my third book with you, and I'm so appreciative to have the opportunity to work alongside a group of such talented individuals. Thank you to my editors, Josie Woodbridge, Celia Johnson, and Kathryn Zentgraf for improving this book tenfold. Thank you to Stephanie Stanton and Sarah Riedlinger for creating another gorgeous cover, which I'm beyond proud to have as the face of my work. Thank you to Rachel Sanders for being the best marketing director an author could ask for. You're an MVP (Marketing Vice President) to me. Thank you to Sarah Bonamino for your stellar publicity efforts and for keeping me organized and sane on the last book tour (which is not an easy task). Thank you to the sales team for hawking my wares all across the United States, especially John Lawton, Brad Simpson, and Bryan Green. Thank you to Stephanie Koven for getting my books into the hands of readers around the world. Thank you to the social media team for all your online support, especially Bella Bedoya. Thank you to Sean Thomas for creating the most stunning book trailers that I think could easily rival Hollywood. This is not an endorsement for Sean to join Hollywood because I would like more book trailers created by him. Thank you to Anthony Goff—a.k.a. "A" but not from *Pretty Little Liars*, I asked—for always being there to listen and provide advice or comedic relief. Thank you to Josh Stanton for CEOing like no other CEO has ever CEO'd before. I'm honored to be a Blackstone author because you've assembled a team more impressive than the Avengers themselves.

Thank you to my film agents Debbie Deuble Hill and Alec Frankel for championing my work off the page.

After I finish writing a book, I always have a select group of people read it before I turn it in to my agent or editor. Their job is to provide me with a delicate balance of criticism and compliments, and they do it well. Thank you to Bri Becker, Cristina Montero, James Nerge, Andrea Willetts, and Kent Willetts.

Huge shout-out to my beta reader **APRIL GOODING**. I am capitalizing and bolding your name to make up for the fact that Microsoft Word autocorrected it in the last acknowledgments, causing me to thank a person I do not know and may not even exist. April, this is the fourth book of mine you've touched . . . and once again, you made it so much better.

Thank you to my mom for capturing so much of my childhood with that hefty camcorder you lugged around on your shoulder. It was me watching those home videos when I was missing you that led to this story. I like to think it was you that brought the idea to me.

Shout-out to the extremely talented and equally kind authors who took the time to read and blurb my novel. I appreciate it so much. Thank you to: Ashley Flowers, Mary Kubica, Hannah Mary McKinnon, Karen Dionne, Stacy Willingham, Ashley Winstead, Lisa Gardner, Peter Swanson, and Lisa Jewell.

If I don't say thank you to my husband, Drew, I'll never hear the end of it. So, thank you, Drew. But seriously, I couldn't do any of this without you by my side.

Thank you to the people who make the book world a better place just by facilitating and sharing their love for reading. I'm looking at you: librarians, booksellers, booktokers, book reviewers, bloggers, teachers, and bookstagrammers.

Finally, thank you to my readers. Without you, my books would just be diaries as I'd be the only one reading them. You're the reason I get to do what I love, and I'm eternally grateful. Special shout-out to my gaggle of silly geese a.k.a. the members of my Facebook group, Jeneva Rose's Convention of Readers. The internet isn't always a kind place to be, but thanks to you, I've got a slice of paradise I can visit online.

Now, for my deepest, darkest secret . . . it'll be shared in the acknowledgments of my next book. Stay tuned! ;)